THE PLOT

A Kentucky Civil War Novel

Ed Ford

A/E Press
Richmond, Kentucky

A/E

PUBLISHED BY A/E PRESS
A division of Ford Public Relations
305 Wisteria Court
Richmond, Ky. 40475-6834
E-Mail: fordpr@mis.net

Library of Congress Cataloging-in-Publication Data

ISBN 978-0-9906086-0-8

ALSO BY ED FORD:

CIVIL WAR

The Draw

Silent Witness

YOUNG PEOPLE

Shelby and the Deer,
        with Shelby Ann Ford

RELIGION

The Centennial of First Christian Church
        Berea, Ky., 1895-1995

The Sesquicentennial History
        of Mt. Zion Christian Church
        Madison County, Ky., 1852-2002

Acknowledgements

No book is possible without the aid and encouragement of friends and associates behind the scene.

Robert Moody, Richmond, Ky., attorney and history buff, is a Madison County Civil War authority whose knowledge and research contributed much to the basis of this story. Retired Madison Circuit Judge James Chenault is a Kentucky legal mind and history authority par excellence. His perusal of an early draft of this book was of tremendous value.

Then, there's Roy Varney and Melvin Cooper. Roy is top-notch at putting websites together and making publications look good. And, Melvin has forgotten more about developing products into print than fellow associates ever knew.

Table of Contents

Dedication

To the men and women of the U.S. Marshals Service,
the nation's oldest and most versatile federal law
enforcement agency, serving America since 1789
in unseen, but critical ways.

Chapter I

The Dream

U.S. Marshal Clay McDowell sat up with a start, instantly awake.

He had been flailing his arms against an imaginary foe. His fight-or-flight thrashing left the bed covers on the floor, but his pounding heart and heavy breathing gave witness to something else. The Civil War Dream had returned ... and with a vengeance.

Mac had been dreaming the same dream for weeks now, and, each time it picked up where it previously had ended. It was like a serial, a continuing story, which initially he chalked off as a figment of his intensive interest in the War Between the States. But, it was so real. He could see the places, the people, the settings and even feel the tension encompassing Central Kentucky of the mid-1860s.

Clay swung his feet to the floor, turned on the light and entered the bathroom. He poured himself a glass of water, gulped half of it down and rinsed his face in cold water. He then followed Jon's suggestion and picked up the pad and pencil from his night table and began to write down everything he could remember. He wrote furiously for several minutes, then threw down the writing instruments, mentally exhausted. He sat on the edge of the bed, elbows on his knees, rubbing his face and eyes with his hands.

'I'm not going crazy,' he thought. 'I know who and where I am. It has to be something wild, something in my subconscious.'

Mac, age forty-two, had had a long-time fascination with the Civil War, particularly those battles and incidents that occurred in Kentucky. At 6-foot-2 and 195 pounds, he was a rugged physical specimen and an active participant in Civil War re-enactments. And, in recent years, he had immersed himself in research and reading about the political, economic and social issues of the period. In passing, he had mentioned his continuing dream to a friend, who happened to be a psychologist teaching at one of the local universities. Dr. Jon Porter became interested immediately.

"I'm doing a segment on Freud and dreams in one of my classes and I have a student doing research on Edgar Cayce for a term project," he had explained. "What you're experiencing is fascinating. Why don't you fill me in and keep me informed?"

Mac scoffed at the suggestion.

"You want me to be a guinea pig? Forget it, Doc. I don't have time to play mind games. If the service found out they'd retire me to the psycho ward."

Clay and Jon had attended college together and had shared several sociology classes dealing with criminology. Mac's law enforcement approach, however, differed from Jon's academic emphasis, which was that of a future psychologist. After graduation, Clay had become a police officer while Jon, who loved research, continued his studies and had entered the teaching field. Mac eventually had earned a post with the U.S. Marshals Service and now was headquartered in Lexington where he served as marshal for Kentucky's Eastern District. Ironically, Jon was located just several blocks away as an assistant professor at Transylvania University.

Their friendship, although interrupted at times by their occupations, had picked up when they both had settled in Lexington. They had married local women and had socialized as couples, but Mac's wife had died several years ago following the birth of their third child. That incident, however, had brought Clay, Jon and Lisa – Jon's wife – closer together. Since then, the Marshal and the Porters tried to get together periodically for dinner, just to keep in touch.

"The Dream," which Mac wished he never had mentioned, now was a topic on the front burner.

"Look, Clay, I am interested in it, but, other than Lisa, no one else will hear about it – I promise," Jon declared. "But, you have to admit, what you've been experiencing is fascinating. If we can work on it together, maybe we can make some sense out of it."

Jon suggested that Clay start writing down everything he could remember after the dream occurred. If the dream continued to build upon itself, this could be a way to document why it was happening and following this particular course.

"Dreams are imaginary," Jon explained, "but it's not unusual that they relate to true events that happened in the past. This could be because you're such a student of the Civil War. Also, you've been instrumental as a re-enactor in period battles and events. This is something you really know, something you have in common with those who experienced the situation first hand."

Jon asked Clay to call him if and when the dream continued. Mac agreed, but he pointed out that some things he was reading about the Confederacy's invasion of Kentucky were "laying some sort of foundation."

"You're talking about 1862, right?" Jon asked.

"Right," Mac replied. "And it seems that things are building from that point. I feel like my thoughts are influenced by some books about that period."

"What are you reading?"

"Some things written by Mary Margaret Thatcher."

"Yeah, I've heard of her. She's a Civil War authority and heads a new program at a college in east Tennessee.

"Yeah, she's director of a Civil War Studies program at East Tennessee State. Her books on the war's Western Theater have received great reviews and she's considered one of the better up-and-coming historians on the Civil War. Dr. Thatcher's done her homework and I'm really impressed with her knowledge and conclusions."

"What else has she done?"

"I saw that's she's now working on something about Mary Surratt and the plot to kidnap or assassinate Lincoln. She did an interview on TV recently and said that Surratt really was an innocent scapegoat in the assassination. Also, she claims to have some evidence that the plot to kidnap Lincoln extended throughout several southern states in addition to Washington.

"And, on top of that, there was a counterfeiting scheme connected with it."

Clay continued his narrative about Thatcher's research, her book and a more-than-cursory review of the author's background.

Lisa, who had been listening intently, looked at Mac and smiled.

"You seemed to be obsessed with this woman."

Clay sat upright in surprise.

"No, it's just that she's really good. She has quite a following."

"If you say so," Lisa grinned.

"Let's get back to the dream," Jon interrupted. "There is a theory that when you dream about historical periods, places and people, what you're really doing is tapping into a past life."

"Come on, Jon!" Clay scoffed. "You don't believe in this past life stuff do you?"

"Not necessarily," Porter replied. "There's no scientific proof that dreams are glimpses into previous lives, but I'm not going to just summarily discount it either. In past-life dreams, replays of events remain in the same sequence in which they actually happened. This may be why your dream is following a sequential pattern."

"You mean it could continue right on through the end of the war?"

"Well, that's possible, but don't count on it happening. Something or someone may bring the dream to a conclusion way before that. The theory is that past-life dreams provide an insight as to who you were in a previous life and may explain why certain skills come easy.

"A study was done once on a movie actor who made a lot of Westerns. He seemed to have an inborn skill where riding and handling horses was concerned. Also, he was especially adept at handling weapons. In a hypnotic trance, it was reported that he recalled in a past life of being a Russian Cossack who had been killed by a lance that was thrust through his chest. He apparently had a scar above his heart that he couldn't explain."

"That's a bunch of bull!" Mac exclaimed.

"You're probably right, but it is interesting," Jon acknowledged.

Lisa shook her head.

"Aren't we getting a little 'far out' here?"

"Okay, then let's concentrate on something a little more concrete," Jon said. "It's been found that characters in dreams may very well be individuals with whom we have some unfinished business. And, they may continue to be present in the dream until that situation or conflict is resolved. They also can help focus attention on a situation. Also, why and how do you know those particular persons who are in your dreams? It's also important to remember that all characters in your dreams are important; there's a reason why they're there.

"Dreams are the language of the unconscious mind. They represent our emotional issues and can even bring solutions to problems. That's another reason why I want you to make a notation of everything you can remember from your dream."

Clay pushed away from the table and frowned.

"All this is getting a little far-fetched, Jon. I'm beginning to believe that one of us is a nut case."

Porter laughed.

"Science is filled with problem solvers who were called 'nuts.' Just remember, from five to seven times each night we dream. That adds up to six years of dreaming per human life. It could be that our subconscious is really trying to tell us something."

Mac leaned over, kissed Lisa's cheek and disgustedly waved farewell to Jon.

"Good night, Shrink," he said, walking away. "Don't call me. I'll call you."

Jon laughed and waved back.

"Sweet dreams, Mac. And, keep that record."

Mac glanced at his watch, deciding it was too late to drive to the farm. He determined the cot at his office would suffice for this evening, and he quickly walked the three blocks to the courthouse.

The McDowell farm where he resided was a bit more than 300 acres, nestled in the rolling hills of Southern Fayette County. Clay had inherited the bluegrass acreage from his ancestors, who had been given the land by Henry Clay for favors provided the famed Kentucky senator and statesman. Mason McDowell, Mac's father, had named him Henry Clay McDowell in honor of the man known as the nation's Great Compromiser.

Like his forefathers, Mason McDowell had raised fine saddle horses, trotters and pacers on the farm. Together, he and Clay had renewed the farm's prominence as a mecca of fine horseflesh. Clay had brought his eldest son, Thomas, into the business and had turned operation of the farm over to Tom when he assumed the U.S. Marshal position. Clay's wife and Tom's mother, Sarah, had died twelve years ago giving birth to their youngest son, Claude. Tom, now 22, ran the farm with the help of his wife, Madlyn, and George McAdams, a horse trainer and blacksmith who'd been with the McDowells for more than twenty years. Clay's only daughter, 17-year-old Sarah Anne, also lived on the farm while her fiancé was serving overseas with the military.

Mac waved to the janitor as he entered the courthouse and yawned deeply as he unlocked the door to his office. It had been a long, yet uneventful day. He had enjoyed dinner with the Porters despite all of Jon's hogwash about the significance of dreams. Tonight, he'd fall asleep quickly, reasoning that he was too tired to dream.

Language of the unconscious mind? Where did Jon get that nonsense? And people with whom there was unfinished business?

'I'm getting too involved with the Civil War,' the Marshal thought. 'I need to get my mind around something else.'

For Clay, sleep did come quickly. But, then, so did The Dream.

Chapter II

The Fast Draw

For the Marshal, the suppressed remembrances of the subconscious and the thoughts of another time begin again. This time, it's late August 1862 and the Civil War is about to intensify in Kentucky.

"What in the hell are you doing?"

Clay stood transfixed in the doorway of his office as he watched his deputy, Logan Perry, repeatedly draw his revolver from an odd-looking holster.

"Watch!" Perry instructed.

The tall, lean deputy marshal lifted his hand above and to the side of his holstered pistol, then suddenly dropped his hand and cocked and drew the weapon in one rapid motion. He then eased the hammer down, spun the pistol toward him and dropped it back into the holster.

"What do you think?" Logan asked, smiling at his sleight of hand.

Mac was perplexed.

"Think about what?"

"What do you think about my fast draw?" the deputy asked.

"Fast draw? What's a fast draw for and why do you need it? And why are you wasting time doing something that's a waste of time?"

Perry shook his head in disgust.

"Don't you get it, Clay? I'm practicing to draw my pistol first before an outlaw or some other bad guy can draw his. Being the fastest can be the difference between life and death."

"All you're going to do is shoot yourself in the foot," McDowell allowed. "When was the last time we even had to draw a weapon?"

"That's not the point, Clay!" Logan persisted. "We're in a shooting war and we're going to be in situations where someone will be shooting at us or we'll be shooting at them. Being able to draw a pistol first means you'll get the first shot and have the advantage."

"Look, Logan, we're not in the Army and it's not like we'll come face-to-face with someone and be in a competition to get off the first shot. What's important – if we have to shoot – is to make that shot count. Just be sure to hit the target."

"I don't argue that," Perry continued. "But these are desperate times and we're going to be in situations that we've never faced before. We **DO** need to make that first shot count, but we also **DO** need to make sure we get that first shot. Mark my words, the day is coming that you'll see I'm right!"

Clay sat and noticed that Logan had modified his holster.

"Where's the flap?" he asked.

"What flap?" Perry demanded.

"The flap on your holster. It's gone."

"Oh, that. This is a new holster that I had made down at the saddle shop. I designed this without a flap so I could make a fast draw."

"But your pistol won't be protected and it could fall out of the holster!"

"Let me explain it to you, Clay," Perry said, stripping off his gun belt and handing it to the Marshal.

"That holster is cut, of course, to fit the pistol. The leather then was soaked in water and I greased the weapon and placed it in the holster. I left it there until the leather dried and molded itself to fit the weapon. Then, I greased and polished the leather so the pistol would slide out in one easy motion. But, it won't slide out on its own. Also, you'll notice a thin strap that can be placed across the pistol behind the hammer and connected to a button on the holster. That strap will help keep it in place if I'm doing any hard and fast riding. But, I can tuck the strap away behind my belt when I don't need it."

Perry took the gun belt from Mac and strapped it around his waist. He also tied a leather thong at the base of the holster around his leg.

"Now, by tying the holster to my leg, it won't work up when I pull the pistol. And, when I draw, I cock the weapon as I remove it and I'm ready to shoot as soon as I point at the target. Now, I don't aim the pistol – I just point and shoot."

McDowell watched in amazement as Perry executed his fast draw.

"But, can you hit anything?"

"Come outside and I'll show you," Logan said.

They walked to the end of the street and into a deserted alleyway. Perry picked up two empty bottles and placed them at the base of a mound of dirt and debris. He backed off, adjusted the gun belt and looked at Mac.

"Watch this!" he said.

Logan placed his hand in position and, in one sudden motion, drew the revolver and fired twice. He shattered the two bottles, gave the weapon a half spin and returned it to the holster.

"That's amazing!" McDowell exclaimed. "I don't know how or when you'll ever use it, but it is amazing!"

Although he doubted the value of his "Fast Draw," Clay had no doubts about Logan himself. He was tough, hard-working, a good horseman and an excellent marksman with either a handgun or rifle. He was fearless to a fault, had a good sense of humor and was a good and loyal friend. Perry's one hang up was with his weapons. He cleaned and oiled his firearms and practiced using them constantly. Clay doubted if any of Logan's weapons would ever fail to pass the most zealous inspection.

McDowell had been the U.S. Marshal for the Eastern District of Kentucky for several years. He'd been recommended for the position by Gen. Cassius Clay, the famed Kentuckian who'd been a state legislator, newspaper editor and publisher, soldier, politician and a former ambassador to Russia. A long-time friend of President Lincoln, Clay had helped his fellow Kentuckian get elected president and, when Confederate troops fired on Fort Sumter, he'd formed the "Clay Battalion," which kept Washington secure until Federal troops could arrive to protect the city.

The General had visited Mac along with Ward Hill Lamon, Washington's U.S. Marshal, to convince him that he should take the position. Like Cassius, Hill Lamon was a long-time friend of Lincoln and was the Illinois lawyer's partner in Springfield. He went with Lincoln to Washington after he was elected president and voluntarily became his bodyguard after accepting the President's appointment as U.S. Marshal for the district.

Lamon saw the need for sufficient lawmen to serve the national interest and the chief executive, as there was no other agency to do so. And, in McDowell, he found a man he wanted.

Mac and Logan entered the Marshal's office through the rear entrance. It was accessed from a walkway that led from a small barn to the frame structure, which was located next to the city post office and federal building. The barn could stable six horses and was fitted with a loft that ran the length of the building.

The office was a one-story affair containing three jail cells, a desk, several chairs, an iron stove and a sleeping area near the rear door. The bed was used by McDowell or Perry, depending on whomever might be on night duty. A boardwalk passed across the building's front porch where two hitching posts were available.

Clay's immediate supervisor was U.S. District Attorney Thomas Bramlette, a prominent attorney who many expected to be a future governor of the Commonwealth. On the national level, Mac ultimately reported to Lamon.

Bramlette's office, located in the Federal Building, was near a telegraph cubicle several doors down the main hallway. He was nearby and available, an excellent arrangement for McDowell.

Mac sat in the office going over some paperwork while Perry went next door to check with the telegrapher for any messages. That's when Mason Sanderson entered.

"Marshal McDowell?" he asked.

"That's me," Clay announced, rising to greet the visitor.

"Marshal, my name is Sanderson, Deputy U.S. Marshal from Washington. I need some help from you and your deputy concerning the First Lady."

"You, of course, mean Mrs. Lincoln," Mac stated. "Is she here?"

"No, not yet," Sanderson commented, "but that's what we need to discuss."

The family of Mary Ann Todd Lincoln lived on Lexington's Main Street and the Todds were among the more prominent aristocratic families in the Bluegrass area. Mary, like her husband, Abraham, was a Kentucky native. While living in Kentucky and before her marriage, she was rumored to be infatuated with Cassius Clay, and the feeling was that she would have married the Lion of White Hall had she not become enamored of the tall, gangly Lincoln.

Since her marriage and the election of Lincoln to the presidency, Mrs. Lincoln had little time to visit her Lexington family or other relatives in the vicinity. But a visit to her former home ranked high on her wish list of things to do.

The lawman placed his hat on the desk and pulled his chair closer to McDowell.

"I'll get right to the point, Marshal," he said. "Mrs. Lincoln wants to travel here to see her family and, perhaps, continue on to Richmond, where she has an aunt and some cousins. The only continuing protection for Mr. and Mrs. Lincoln and their sons is what Hill Lamon and our staff can provide. Hill has advised the President that with a war going on, this is no time for the First Lady to make a visit. But Mrs. Lincoln is adamant and the President, as you know, fails to believe that anyone or any group would wish his family harm.

"We know, of course, of the threat of a battle here in the Bluegrass. We understand that Union and Confederate troops could be in confrontation just about anytime now in Madison or Fayette Counties, so that's delayed the immediate plans of Mrs. Lincoln. However, she wants to make the visit as soon as it's practical, perhaps sometime this fall. We'll keep trying to discourage her, but she is a very determined lady and we think it best that we plan for her protection if and when the time comes."

Perry returned to the office and Mac and Sanderson quickly filled him in on the conversation.

"Do you have a plan at this point?" Clay asked.

'We do," Sanderson replied. "Our thought is to call as little attention to Mrs. Lincoln as we can. We'll ask her to travel by train from Washington to Lexington dressed in mourning clothing and wearing a heavy veil. We'll dispatch two other deputies and me with her and ask the two of you to join us when we arrive at the Lexington depot.

"We'll ask Mrs. Lincoln to speak as little as possible or not to speak at all.

"We'll need you to hire a rig and some horses and help transport her to the family home on Main Street. One of my men will drive the carriage and the four of us will be riding alongside. If Mrs. Lincoln is determined to visit Richmond, we'll need you and Deputy Perry to continue with us on a route that you feel is the most safe. And, of course, we'll need your help to get Mrs. Lincoln back on the train to Washington."

"You don't want us to hire additional deputies?" Clay asked.

"No," Sanderson acknowledged. "We can attract too much attention with more protection. Even five of us may be too much, but we need enough firepower to discourage anyone from attacking her."

"You're not anticipating an attack are you?" Mac inquired.

"No, not at all. And, we hope that no one will recognize Mrs. Lincoln or even know that she's visiting Kentucky. But, if such information leaks out, we could be up to our necks in a kidnapping or something worse."

"If she goes to Richmond, where are her relatives located?" Clay asked.

Sanderson pulled a packet of papers from a coat pocket and rifled through them,

"Here it is. It's a family named Breck on Lancaster Avenue."

Perry glanced at McDowell and nodded his head in the affirmative.

"We could go by your farm and cross on the Valley View Ferry," Logan said.

"Right, and that's a straight shot up to Lancaster Avenue," McDowell added.

"That sounds like as direct a route as we could follow," Sanderson commented.

"It is," Clay agreed, "and it's not a bad road. We should be able to make good time.

"But, there are several areas to beware of, places where riders could ride out of deep woods and hit us suddenly with a lot of firepower.

"Also, I'm assuming we'd want a carriage with some sort of roof or coverage for Mrs. Lincoln. If we hired a Phaeton, she could be partly hidden in the rear seat and only the driver would be visible."

"Good idea," Sanderson acknowledged. "And, let's get a two-horse rig. I'd like to have some extra horsepower in the event we need it."

"What about firearms?" Perry asked. "Some extra weapons would be good."

"I agree," Sanderson said.

"Let's each carry at least two additional revolvers," Mac suggested. "Logan, here, also has a carbine and shotgun that can be carried on his saddle and it might be a good idea to have some shotguns in the Phaeton."

"Can you get the extra weapons?" Sanderson inquired.

"We can and we'll be sure to have some good mounts," Mac said.

Sanderson stood and picked up his hat.

"I think we've got a basic plan here and we'll update and revise it as necessary. At this point, it's up to Hill and me to discourage Mrs. Lincoln from even making the trip. Failing that, we need to delay it as long as possible."

"What really is the possibility that someone might want to kidnap or harm Mrs. Lincoln?" Clay asked.

Sanderson rubbed his chin and momentarily stared at the floor.

"We believe it's a very genuine possibility," he stated, gazing at McDowell. "Hill is nearly paranoid about the situation, because the President will not take potential threats seriously."

Conversation was interrupted as the door opened suddenly and Bramlette stuck his head inside.

"We just received word the Battle of Richmond has begun! No one knows where 'Bull' Nelson is and Mahlon Manson has taken a stand near Kingston against Kirby Smith's army."

Brig. Gen. Manson commanded the First Infantry Brigade of the Union's Provisional Army of Kentucky and Major Gen. William "Bull" Nelson, although frequently absent, was the Union's commanding officer. Major Gen. Edmund Kirby Smith was in charge of the Confederate troops.

"This could be a real bloodbath," the U.S. attorney continued. "Don't be surprised if we have the Rebel army in our laps before the week is out."

Chapter III

Invasion

It was a hot and humid Tuesday morning as the Confederate Provisional Army of Kentucky rumbled unchallenged into Lexington. The Battle of Richmond had lasted two days as a lean and mean group of battle-savvy Confederates ran roughshod over an assemblage of green and inexperienced Federal troops.

Fed and rested, the Southerners paraded through Main Street looking for a fight that never was to come. Instead, an ample number of Lexingtonians sympathetic to the Southern cause cheered and welcomed General Kirby Smith and his rag-tag army.

Officers found lodging in the Phoenix Hotel and the Confederate forces washed over Lexington like a tide. Business establishments were converted into military quarters of every size and description and campgrounds were established in available open spaces. Many merchants were not open for business, but threadbare soldiers burst their way in, taking clothing, shoes and foodstuffs. Weapons and ammunition, however, were distributed willingly by Southern patriots.

McDowell retired to his office and he and Perry watched the groundswell of gray, realizing that their services depended upon the disposition of the Southern high command. Martial law was the order of the day.

Logan walked to the window as the sound of pounding hooves neared the office. A mule laden with the hardware of war ran onto the boardwalk and front porch, shaking the building and the "Marshal's Office" sign as it changed direction and rebounded against the front wall. Soldiers sprinted after the animal, spreading out to trap it within the confines of the porch. Logan stepped out as a corporal caught the mule's lead rope and began calming the jenny.

"Sorry, Marshal," the soldier apologized. "She got spooked over at the courthouse and got away."

"What's she carrying?" Perry asked, viewing the items strapped to her back and sides.

"We've got most of a mountain howitzer on her. The other pieces are on another animal."

As the corporal spoke, another mule was led toward them.

Other members of the cavalry troop rode up, led by a distinguished colonel. Mac joined Perry on the porch.

"My compliments, gentlemen, and my apologies for such a rude entrance," the officer said, tipping his hat. "I'm Col. John Scott, First Louisiana Cavalry."

"Good morning, Colonel," McDowell responded. "I'm U.S. Marshal Clay McDowell and this is Deputy Marshal Logan Perry. Can we be of any assistance?"

Scott swung down from his horse and wiped his face with a bandana.

"Well, we could do with a cool drink of water," he said. "Would that be possible?"

"Certainly," Mac said. "We've a well out back and a stable. Feel free to rest your horses and yourselves. Why don't you join me inside?"

"You're very kind, Marshal," the Colonel said. He motioned to a sergeant and a stocky corporal.

"John, why don't you and Werth take the horses out back and relax a while. I'll be inside with the Marshal.

"Just one more thing, Mr. McDowell. If you and Deputy Perry would be so kind as to relinquish your weapons, I would appreciate it. I'm sure there's something in the Articles of War requiring it."

Clay and Logan reluctantly pulled their revolvers and handed them to the Colonel.

"Again, my apologies, but I'm required also to ask for any backup weapons," Scott informed.

McDowell retrieved a derringer from his coat pocket and Perry delivered a Colt from his waistband.

"Please, gentlemen, is there anything else?" Scott inquired.

Logan glanced at Clay and got a nod in return. Perry freed a knife from his boot and McDowell handed over another derringer secured in his boot.

"On your honor as gentlemen, I assume there is nothing else you would need to contribute?" Scott intoned.

Mac held the door for Scott, offered him a chair and asked if he could be of any other service.

"Thank you, Marshal," he replied. "We just need to rest a bit."

Clay reached down and opened a bottom drawer, sitting a bottle of sour mash on the desk along with two glasses.

"I hope our reputation for fine bourbon whiskey is known in Louisiana, Colonel. If it is or if it isn't, may I invite you to join me in a glass of Kentucky's finest?"

Scott smiled and moved a glass toward the Marshal.

"Indeed, sir. Your reputation for smooth sipping whiskey is well known. Your invitation is readily accepted."

"To your health, Colonel," Clay offered in toast.

"To you, sir," Scott responded.

They drank and Mac topped off their glasses.

"If I may say so, Marshal, your hospitality is most appreciated," Scott related. "I've been in Kentucky for several weeks and this is a moment of relaxation that has been long missing."

"War doesn't leave much time for the good things in life," McDowell stated.

"Duty before pleasure," Scott remarked.

McDowell again topped off their glasses.

"It's good to see you again, Colonel."

Scott raised his brow in surprise.

"My apologies, sir. I was not aware that we previously had met."

"Not officially, Colonel," Mac explained. "I was on the outskirts of Richmond when you and your men were rounding up a stampede of Union soldiers. You were very effective."

Scott tossed his head back and smiled in recollection.

"I hope you weren't spying on me."

"I guess you'd have to hang me if I were," Mac replied.

The door banged open and a ragged Confederate soldier staggered in, a bottle in one hand and a pistol in the other.

"I ain't killed me a Yankee today," he slurred. "Any Yankees in here?"

"There's one!" he snarled, snapping a shot at McDowell.

Scott backhanded his glass into the gunman's face and charged him in the next motion. He grabbed the pistol in his left hand and wrenched it from the soldier's grasp. Snatching his own pistol from its holster, he smashed the weapon into the drunk's face.

The Colonel kicked the intruder's pistol away and, satisfied that he was unconscious, walked to the back door and called for the sergeant.

"John, are you out there? John, answer me!"

A barn door opened and the sergeant sprinted toward Scott when he saw him with pistol in hand. He drew his own weapon as he neared the office door.

"Take this man prisoner!" Scott ordered, motioning toward the fallen soldier. "Tie him up and keep him in the barn for now. We'll turn him over to the provost marshal."

"Anybody hurt?" the sergeant asked.

"No," Scott replied. "Just a case of drunk and disorderly."

McDowell fingered the hole in the table.

"Glad that wasn't you, Marshal," Scott stated. "Do you have another glass?"

The afternoon was growing late as the two men finished the bourbon and started on a second bottle. By now, they were using first names, swapping stories and enjoying one another's company as the drink was having its effect.

"You're a long way from Louisiana, John," Mac commented. "What have they had you doing in Madison County besides rounding up strays and preying on druggists?"

Scott was surprised.

"Preying on … ???"

He laughed and pointed his glass at McDowell.

"Oh, you must mean my good friend J.B. Hart? I guess you know him!"

James Bowman "Bowie" Hart, a prominent Lexington druggist, was one of McDowell's closest friends. He'd run into

Mac yesterday, telling him about his visit to witness the Battle of Richmond. Bowie had been "shot at, arrested as a suspected spy and spent an interesting day and night" with the Confederate command, including John Scott.

"We've been friends for a long time," Clay declared. "He told me all about the arrest and the threat to hang him. And, he had nothing but good things to say about you and the army brass."

"Hang him!" Scott exclaimed. "Hell, the generals loved him! Kirby Smith and Pat Cleburne would have given him a Confederate commission if he'd stayed another day.

"It's the first time I've ever seen two generals take to a Yankee civilian."

Scott leaned his arms on the table and stared at McDowell.

"Tell me, Clay?" he asked bleary-eyed. "Is J.B. Irish? Cleburne says Bowie must have kissed the Blarney Stone a thousand times."

Mac refilled their glasses.

"Bowie's quite a person," he began. "He knows more, can talk faster, and can out-con any confidence man. Oh, and don't ever play poker with him. He'll out-fumble you until you're bankrupt."

They both laughed and Clay poured them another drink.

"Go easy, Marshal," Scott said. "You may get me drunk, but you're not going to loosen up my tongue so much that I'll reveal all our Confederate secrets."

"You know some secrets?"

"Of course," John confessed. "I'm also trained to recognize and arrest spies."

"Like Bowie?" Clay chuckled.

Scott pushed away from the table and wiped his hand across his mouth.

"No, not like Bowie," he replied. "I mean real spies. The kind that carry secrets that get men killed."

"That's serious business," Clay noted. "You know a lot about that?"

Scott nodded affirmatively.

"You'd be surprised at the spy network – both Confederate and Yankee – that's active in your state alone," John said.

"How about Madison and Fayette counties?"

"Certainly. Does that surprise you?"

"Somewhat," the Marshal admitted. "I just wouldn't think we'd be important enough to warrant a spy system."

The Colonel tilted back his chair and hooked his thumbs in his belt.

"We each have a president who's a Kentucky native, Lincoln's wife is from Lexington and both sides have wanted to control this state since the war began. Your president said it himself – 'I think to lose Kentucky is nearly the same as to lose the whole game.'

"And, it's no secret that we hope our offensive will give us control of a good portion of the state."

"Maybe even control across the Ohio River?" Mac inquired.

Scott raised his eyes and studied McDowell intently.

"Don't try to pump me, Clay. I like you and I want to keep our association on a friendly basis. But, I will tell you this. Take care of your non-combatant citizens and keep them from harm's way. But don't stick your nose into military affairs. Things can get unhealthy for you in a hurry."

McDowell raised his hands in surrender.

"Easy, John, no offense intended."

Scott eased his chair back to the floor.

"We're getting too serious, Clay. I'll make you a bet!

"If we weren't in a war on opposite sides and were meeting for the first time, I think we could be really good friends. I wouldn't be surprised if you invited me to your farm and let me ride some of your finest horseflesh."

"We might do that anyway," Mac suggested.

"I wish we could, but I have to win a war and you have to guard the entire Eastern District of Kentucky," Scott laughed.

Both looked up as the odor wafted past.

"That smells like ham and beans," Clay said.

"The boys must be cooking out back," John noted. "We picked up some things this afternoon and Henry Werth must be putting them together. Henry not only is the best artillery man in our regiment, he's also the best cook. Why don't you and your deputy join us, Marshal?"

"Well, seeing as how it's our place, we'll take you up on that."

Scott slapped McDowell on the back and they walked toward the barn.

Werth was frying ham while beans simmered in a pot. Someone even was preparing cornbread.

"Got enough for us?" Scott asked.

"Pull up a stump and join us," Werth grinned. "We'll be ready in just a minute."

Everyone ate his fill and they stretched out on the straw-covered lot to let the food digest.

"Are you going to spend the night with us, John?' Mac asked.

"Is that an invitation?"

"Just thought I'd check to make it official. Did I read your mind?"

"You had me worried, Marshal. I was beginning to think you'd never ask," Scott smiled.

The cavalry troop bedded down in the barn after tending to their stock. Mac, Perry and Scott entered the office and the Colonel asked for the keys to the cells.

"You going to lock us up?" Clay inquired.

"Now, Clay, don't you start," Scott warned. "The Articles of War state that all opposition must be secured in a confined area or placed in cuffs, leg irons and chains. I'll place you and Logan in one of those cells with two bunks and I'll let you out in the morning."

"Where are you going to sleep?"

"If you don't mind, I thought I might use your personal sleeping area."

"Is that also in your Articles of War?"

"Oh, absolutely," Scott confirmed. "It's a thick manual and we have to take an oath to abide by it under penalty of death."

"Could you leave a copy?" McDowell asked. "I don't think I've read it."

"Sorry, Marshal, I don't have one with me," the Colonel winked. "But, don't worry, I have it memorized. And, I'll be glad to answer any questions."

"Some friend you are," Mac snorted. "But, maybe I can return the favor. That is, if we meet again."

Scott locked them in the cell and smiled.

"That could be sooner than you think, Clay."

Chapter IV

The Visit

McDowell walked next door to the telegraph office. He or Logan routinely visited the Federal Building cubbyhole, although any urgent messages would be delivered directly to them.

Fred Thompson was responding to a wire and waved at Clay as he entered. Mac waited until Thompson was finished and Fred stood quickly as he signed off with a "thirty."

"I just received a cable for you from Washington," he said. "I thought it might be important as it was from your contact, Ward Hill Lamon."

Fred had been the Federal Building telegrapher for some time and always was alert to any messages pertaining to law enforcement or the war effort.

Clay read the coded dispatch with no visible reaction. But, there was nothing routine about it.

SANDERSON EN ROUTE TO LEXINGTON. WILL ARRIVE WITH PASSENGER MIDWEEK. ASSIST AS DISCUSSED. EXTENDED TRIP ANTICIPATED.

Mac scribbled a three-word response.

"Fred, send this for me when you can," he requested.

Thompson took the slip of paper and glanced questioningly at the Marshal.

"Is that it?"

"That's it," Clay said.

It read:

UNDERSTOOD. WILL DO.

"You must be worried about the cost," the telegrapher suggested. "Thanks for limiting my workload."

"Just trying to stay within budget," McDowell smiled.

Mac walked down the front steps, mentally calculating what he had to do next.

Mary Todd Lincoln was on her way.

* * *

McDowell and Perry had been lounging at the Depot for about an hour. The train connection from Washington was late and no one knew why.

"Could be anything," Darryl Harper, the station agent, shrugged. "If it were anything major, we would have heard something."

Minutes later, the engine chugged into the station and Logan drove the carriage near the boardwalk where the passengers would be deposited. Mason Sanderson and his deputies would be the last to disembark, providing ample time for Mrs. Lincoln's departure, minus potential prying eyes.

The diminutive First Lady stepped down and took the waiting arm of Sanderson. She was dressed as planned in black mourning attire wearing a heavy dark veil. Mason led her directly to the carriage and helped her get seated as Perry turned the reins over to Clarke Bookman, the deputy who would drive.

"No serious problems," Mason stated, answering the Marshal's question before it could be asked. "We were delayed when some Pinkerton men searched the cars for fugitives suspected of train robbery. I was able to intercept one of the detectives before he questioned Mrs. Lincoln. Fortunately, she played the role of bereaved widow to the hilt, saying nothing and dabbing her eyes with a handkerchief.

"Are we ready to roll?" he asked.

"Logan is distributing extra weapons to your men as we speak," Mac informed him. "We've got two fast horses for the carriage and we'll take the back roads to Main Street and the Todd house. There's a carriage entrance at a side door and a stable in back. I'll take the point and you and Logan will ride alongside the Phaeton. We'll let one of your deputies drive and the other will bring up the rear.

"Does that sound okay?"

"Sounds good," Sanderson replied. "Let's ɪ

The First Lady's stay at her family home

Sanderson kept watch inside the house and Bookman anɑ Arnold Hastings, the other deputy, provided outside protection from the stable. Mrs. Lincoln remained at the Todd house for several days, then announced her intention to visit her relatives in Richmond. Although not unexpected, the travel provision of the protection plan was back in prominence.

Seeing no reason to change their plan, Sanderson and McDowell followed the same procedure. Bookman would drive, Clay took the point, Mason and Logan were the outriders and Hastings brought up the rear.

Also as planned, the party took the Valley View Ferry to Madison County and would return by the same route. Things were progressing smoothly, but Sanderson wasn't going to feel safe until they were back in Washington. He checked and double-checked with McDowell concerning the return trip arrangements.

Another two days passed and Mrs. Lincoln announced she was ready to leave Richmond. An early morning departure was planned and everything went well until they neared the ferry. That's when the raiders struck.

They came out of the deep woods as two riders opened up on McDowell and two from each side rode down on Perry and Sanderson. A seventh man fired at Hastings who was hit hard and only kept from falling by grabbing his mount's mane.

Mac rode low over his horse's withers and one of his shots took out the raider on his right while the other charged past and leveled his revolver at Perry. Logan, who had emptied his shotgun and taken out the raiders on his side, charged the rider racing at him. Perry's horse ran headlong into the man's mount and both horses and men hit the ground hard. Mac saw them fall as he signaled Bookman to whip the carriage horses into a full gallop.

The invaders were clothed in a variety of garments. One wore a Confederate kepi and another sported a Rebel cavalry slouch hat. Only one was in full uniform and he was trying to stop the team on the side opposite McDowell. Clay snapped a glance at one of the most-vile looking men he'd ever seen. He had a long scar down one side of his face and his filthy shoulder boards bore the rank of an officer. He glared at Mac as he reached for the reins, intending to pull the horses and carriage to a halt.

Mac and the "officer" were riding neck-and-neck on opposite sides of the team. Clay snapped a shot at him, but the raider ducked as he fired and drifted back to the carriage. Bookman was using his whip and the horses were in an all-out sprint that threatened to wreck the Phaeton. The "officer" leveled his pistol at Bookman, but the deputy kicked instinctively and, luckily, knocked the weapon from his hand.

Sanderson fired point-blank at the attacker, but the hammer clicked on an empty cylinder. Using the revolver as a club, Mason charged alongside the raider and swung at his head. The "officer" ducked the blow and dived at Mason. The lunge knocked the marshal's horse off stride and it skidded to the ground, throwing the two men into the brush. The raider rolled to his feet and, drawing his Arkansas Toothpick*, ran the long dagger-like blade through Sanderson's arm.

The team was running out of control and the carriage teetered on two wheels as it rounded a curve. The horses broke away and the Phaeton, almost as if in slow motion, fell onto its side and slid to a stop, supported at a precarious angle by some broken saplings. Bookman was thrown from the vehicle, but the First Lady was caught inside.

Sanderson, Bookman and Hastings were down and Perry was nowhere in sight as McDowell slowed his mount and turned back to check on Mrs. Lincoln. He dismounted at the carriage and found the First Lady to be bruised and battered, but, miraculously, in one piece. A rebel yell sent a chill up his spine as he turned to see a rider wielding a sabre. It was the man who had shot Hastings. Clay felt for his pistol, but found it missing. He jumped away and fell on the unconscious body of Bookman, whose head was twisted at an odd angle. A revolver was in the driver's waistband and Mac jerked it out as the sabre swished past his head. He rose to his feet, straightened his arm and took aim at the man on horseback, who was turning back.

The sabre-wielder was riding low and McDowell had, at best, a risky shot. He waited until the sabre was raised in a death blow and squeezed off his round. Struck in the shoulder, the man lost his blade and dropped to the ground as he passed the Marshal.

Logan was on foot, running toward him and the damaged carriage. He crawled over the driver's seat and helped Mac lift out the First Lady. She was shaken, but mouthed her thanks as they helped her to her feet.

"Are you okay?" Clay panted.

She nodded that she was, then stumbled back with alarm.

"Look out!" she cried.

The wounded sabre-wielder was on his feet, reaching across his body to draw his pistol. The revolver was halfway out of the holster when Clay saw a sudden movement to his right. Perry's hand dropped and the deputy whipped up his weapon and fired in one motion. The raider jolted backward as if struck by a battering ram.

The Phaeton had overturned some one-hundred yards from the final approach to the ferry. Logan swung his pistol as someone lumbered up the road. It was Moses McCubbin, the ferryboat captain, running with shotgun in hand. Moses had heard the shooting and knew it was the Lincoln party, recognizing the runaway team that had been separated from the carriage and was thundering toward him. Mose, as he usually was called, had been on the lookout for the group's return, although he was not sure when the trip would occur.

"Drop your weapons, NOW!"

The order, made with the click of a cocked weapon, came from behind the three survivors and Mac and Logan reluctantly did as they were told. The two lawmen, although surprised, kept their cool.

"Can we turn around?" Clay asked after several seconds passed.

"Slowly, Marshal. Do it slow and easy."

They did and stared in shock at the man standing before them, pistol in hand.

"What is this?" Mac cried. "Are you insane?"

Mason Sanderson had stuffed a bandana under his shirt to slow the bleeding around his wounded shoulder. He held the revolver in his left hand, his right tucked into his shirt that was serving as a makeshift sling.

"No, Marshal," he said. "I'm very much sane and just doing my duty as a loyal Southerner. I'm really sorry, Mrs. Lincoln, as we had hoped to kidnap you. But now, that's impossible. And, I'm in no shape to take you with me."

Mason leveled the pistol and Mac stepped in front of Mrs. Lincoln.

"Get out of the way, Marshal … and you too, Deputy," he motioned. "There's no need for you to be shot first."

"I don't understand, Mason," Clay interrupted. "You killed one man and were wounded by others who were trying to do the kidnapping. Whose side are you on?"

Sanderson smiled and shook his head.

"Any of us are dispensable in this war," he said. "I'm on the side of the Confederacy and have been since we were forced into this madness. I didn't know any of the men on this raid and they didn't know me. That was the beauty of the plan. If they got away with Mrs. Lincoln, that was fine. If they didn't, I'd handle the kidnapping, or, failing that, do what I have to do now.

"I'm not going to make it, Clay. I'm bleeding too bad. That SOB who stabbed me got away, but I managed to make it through the woods and was just fortunate enough to fall into this ideal situation.

"Now, let's get it over with. My time's running out. I have no reservations about killing you and Logan, but I prefer to take out Mrs. Lincoln first. I have to be sure she doesn't survive."

The First Lady pushed past Clay and stood defiantly in front of Sanderson.

"Before you shoot, sir, just remember this. The Union will survive in spite of you and all our deaths. I have brothers in the Confederate army and a husband who is charged with keeping this country together. We fight for what we believe in and I'm as opposed to the stance of my native South as I am to slavery. May God forgive us all."

Mason was growing weaker.

"It's not all about slavery, Mrs. Lincoln, and you know it," he stated. "I don't own slaves and my family in Virginia freed all those it had years ago. No man should be forced to serve another. And, the North should not force the South to serve it unfairly through high taxation and ungodly tariffs. This war is about states rights.

"I agree that we should all pray that God will forgive us. But, I hope God will understand that some of us must be sacrificed to right the wrongs of those who have nothing but the devil in their hearts."

The double-barreled blast cut Sanderson in half. McCubbin had run into the woods when he saw Mason coming and had worked his way above him, then silently tread onto the road unseen.

The three survivors and the grizzled Valley View mariner stood quietly, but breathing heavily as minds and bodies fought to regain a sense of normalcy. Mose lowered his shotgun and spat.

"Let's get Mrs. Lincoln home," he said softly.

* The Arkansas Toothpick is sometimes confused with the Bowie knife, but is a totally different weapon. Similar to a long dagger, the toothpick blade is twelve-to-twenty inches long and is straight and pointed. Well-balanced and weighted for throwing, it also can be used for thrusting and slashing. The Bowie Knife, named for Kentuckian Jim Bowie, is eight or more inches long and about an inch and a quarter wide with a curved point. The curved area also is sharpened so the weapon can be used for "back slashing." It also has a cross-guard to protect the hand.*

Chapter V

Middle Creek

The two men strode into the office with a no-nonsense attitude. They were very tall, lean and rugged and carried new Henry repeating rifles.

"My name's Joe Layne," the older of the two said, placing a wanted flyer on Mac's desk. "Understand there's a bounty on this man."

McDowell was familiar with it. It read:

WANTED
$500 Reward
Zachary Holston

Zachary (Zach) (Zak) Holston, also known as "The Major," is wanted in Kentucky and Tennessee for murder and distribution of counterfeit money. Subject is 5-feet-11 inches tall and weighs approximately 160 pounds. Is of slender build and fair complexion, dark brown or black hair and eyes. Has distinguishing scar on left side of face, extending from forehead to lower neck. Is armed and dangerous. A reward of $500 will be provided for information leading to arrest and conviction. Contact the U.S. District Attorney or U.S. Marshal in your area.

"You have information about this man?" McDowell asked.

"You bet I do!" Layne stated. "He raided my farm, attacked my wife, slaughtered my livestock and stole two of my best horses."

"Do you know where he is now?"

"Hell, no! But he wuz at my farm in Betsy Layne – that's in Floyd County. Me and my boy, Bill," he motioned to the tall youngster, "have been lookin' for him since January."

"You haven't seen him since January?"

"Nary hide nor hair, but we know he's in these parts."

"How do you know that?"

"Hell! It's just common sense, man! Folks have seen him in one thing after another all winter! Fella up at left Beaver said he even tried to kill Mrs. Lincoln!"

Word had traveled fast, Mac realized. But did folks know about the plot behind the attempt on Mrs. Lincoln?

"That's true, Mr. Layne, but we need information as to his exact location in order to arrest him."

"Can't do that," Layne shook his head. "He's harder to find than a polar bear in a snowstorm."

"Well, Mr. Layne, I can't authorize a reward unless you can give me exact information that will lead to his arrest. Believe me ... we want him in the worst way, but we've got to find him first."

The younger Layne motioned toward the Marshal.

"Then, he won't give us the money, Pap?"

"Reckon not, son,"

Layne pulled a dirty bandana from his pocket and placed it on the desk. He undid the knots and dumped the contents atop the poster.

"Then, how about these?" he asked.

Dried and ill shaped, the leathered objects appeared to have been taken from an animal.

"What are they?" Clay asked.

"They're ears, six sets to be exact," Layne explained. "We took 'em off that gang of Rebels that raided my farm. How much for these?"

McDowell squinted at the tall man, shook his head, then flicked through the objects with a forefinger.

"Looks like you did them in, but, I can't help you with this either," he said. "We don't know who they belonged to and we don't pay bounties for ears anyway. Even if we did, this is a military matter that should be taken up with an appropriate Union or Confederate officer."

"Already tried that," Layne explained. "I showed these to Col. James Garfield before the Battle of Middle Creek and he finally agreed they looked like Rebel ears. But, he said the Union army wasn't payin' anything for ears, whether they were

Union or Confederate. He suggested I see you or the U.S. District Attorney."

"I'm guessing you've already seen Mr. Bramlette, the district attorney."

"He's the one who sent me here," Layne explained.

Logan Perry sat on the corner of the desk and examined a set of the ears. Two ears each were connected by fishing line that had been run through holes punched into the objects.

"You'll notice there's a right and left ear for each Rebel," Layne pointed out. "It's wuz hard keepin' them straight, but I guarantee that each set matches up with a specific soldier. And, another thing. You'll notice that each ear in each set matches up with its mate, but each set of ears is different from the others."

"Well, I'll be!" Logan declared. "He's right, Clay. Look at these! Each left ear goes with a right ear even though they're opposites, but each set is different from the other sets."

Mac rested his forehead against the fingers of a hand. He shook his head.

"I know, Logan, I know. But, that's not the point! We don't do ears! That is, we don't give rewards for ears!"

"You don't?" young Bill Layne asked with surprise. "Pap said you must give rewards for taking care of thieves and scoundrels!"

"Sorry, son," Clay allowed. "But you don't qualify for a reward."

Logan still was excited about the ears.

"There's got to be an interesting story about this, Mr. Layne? What is it?"

Layne motioned to his son and they pulled up chairs.

"Well, Bill and me and two neighbors had gone to Prestonsburg to do some tradin'," Layne began. "These Rebel soldiers were hangin' around waitin' to fight this Col. Garfield and his Federal boys. In the meantime, they were raidin' every farm they could and takin' things they could eat, use or trade. They hit my farm while we were gone and just the missus and my other six younguns were there.

Hannah saw them comin' and told the kids to hide in the barn loft and keep quiet. Eight Rebels rode in and began shootin' at anything they saw. They killed our milk cow and all our pigs and chickens and raided our smoke house and made off with all the hams we had curin'.

"Then, they jumped Hannah. Two of them held her down while this skinny black-headed fellow had his way with her. Well, Hannah was able to get to this long dagger he had on his side and she tried to stab him. He caught her hand and they wrestled a spell before Hannah was able to stab him in the side of his head. He tried to pull her away, but she ripped that knife all the way down his face and tried to run it through his heart.

"She must have gotten him pretty good, because, when we got home, there was blood all over the floor and all over Hannah. They'd beaten her and knocked her cold and were gone when she came to.

"Hannah was sittin' on the door stoop when we rode in. She didn't even look up at me. She just said, 'Go kill that son-of-a-bitch who raped me.'

"We grabbed all the weapons we had, includin' these Henry rifles we traded for in Prestonsburg. We gathered up some extra ammunition and took off.

"Jeb Parker, who was with us, can track a ghost over a hard rock trail. Jeb picked up their sign right off and we followed 'em for about five miles and found 'em in a clearin' just below a hill. They had built a fire and were fryin' slices of ham. My two horses they stole were picketed off to the right.

"Well, we split up and circled around until we had good position. Me and Bill opened up and the others joined in. We killed three right off and wounded two others. Jeb caught one who was tryin' to escape, but the man with the cut face and another one got away.

"The fella that Hannah cut up wuz a mess. He had bandages all over his face and head and the blood had soaked through something fierce. When we opened up, he lit out like his pants wuz on fire. After we rounded up the others, I decided it was gettin' too dark to trail him.

"The three who were still alive asked us what we were goin' to do with 'em. One begged us to take 'em to the Confederate camp over at Paintsville, but we told 'em we'd already wasted too much time on a bunch of thievin' varmits. The same man asked us if we'd take 'em in for a trial and, of course, we had a good laugh at that.

"One of the men we'd wounded said he guessed that we'd just shoot 'em. I looked at Jeb and he grinned at me. So, I turned to this soldier and said, 'No, we're not goin' to shoot you. We're goin' to hang you.'

"Well, this one fellow commenced to scream and cry and said to hang 'em was inhumane treatment. He claimed that all they wanted was some food to keep from starvin' to death. That hit me wrong and I just walked up and busted him one in the mouth.

"'You scared my children half to death and you raped my wife,'" I told him. "'Now, you're goin' to get what you deserve.'"

"We didn't have enough rope, so Bill rode back to Jeb's place and brought back a considerable coil of new hemp and we made loops and placed them around their necks.

"The one who complained so much wanted us to make a hangman's noose so that their necks would break when they fell. Jeb told 'em to forget it, they'd be pulled off their horses and would choke to death. And, that's what we did.

"Then, we placed all the bodies together and cut off their ears. We figured this would be the easiest way to identify their bodies and get the rewards.

"After we got turned down by Col. Garfield, we got together the next day and rode over to Paintsville. We figured we'd look up Humphrey Marshall who was the general in charge of the Confederate troops. Jeb's daddy had a job over at Frankfort at one time and knew Mr. Marshall when he was a state representative. Mr. Marshall was born and raised in Frankfort and Jeb said his daddy claimed there was no finer man than Humphrey Marshall.

"Well, we got to Johnson County and this Rebel picket stopped us and Jeb told him who we were and we wanted to see the General. At first, he didn't believe us, but after Jeb talked for a while, he told us where the General was and how to get there.

"We ran into all kinds of military protocol problems at the camp before we finally got to see the General. Now, he and Jeb had never met, but he sure did remember Jeb's daddy. He took us into his tent and asked us what he could do for us. Jeb told him the whole story and how we'd caught most of the men, but how this one man who'd raped my wife had got away. He didn't tell the General that we'd hanged three of 'em.

"Gen. Marshall said he wuz sorry to hear what we'd been through, but said it was out of his hands. He said this Holston fellow – he's the one who raped my wife – was not officially a member of his staff, but wuz with a 'Special Forces' group out of Richmond, Virginia. He described Holston as 'a loose cannon' and had warned him he had no official capacity with the Eastern Kentucky forces and he wuz not to be involved in any battles in which Confederates were engaged.

"The General said he didn't know anything about the men Holston had with him or what their orders might be. He said if Holston were servin' under him and had committed such acts against civilians, he would court martial him and his men. If convicted, they'd be shot."

Layne stood and stared at McDowell.

"Well, I guess this trip was for nothin'," he said. "We're not goin' to get a reward and probably nobody is goin' to catch this Holston fellow."

Mac also stood.

"If it's any satisfaction, Mr. Layne, I've had a run-in with this Holston myself and if we can capture him, I guarantee you that either the army or the U.S. Marshals Service will prosecute him to the full extent of the law."

"You mean you'll kill him?"

"If convicted of war crimes, yes. If he resists arrest by our office, we won't ask any questions or take any prisoners. Let's just say that he'll get his."

"Let's go, Bill," Layne said.

They walked to the door and Layne offered a parting thought.

"We probably won't meet again, Marshal. But if you get another set of ears, you'll know which army they're from."

Layne paused, then added,

"And who sent 'em."

Chapter VI

The Lincoln Plot

"It's real, it exists, it's extensive," Philip Miles emphasized. "Now, we've got to stop it."

The U.S. Marshal from Virginia had asked McDowell to meet him in his room at the Phoenix Hotel. His coded telegram of two days ago underscored the importance of this clandestine encounter. Ward Hill Lamon and his association of marshals in the extended Washington district (City of Washington) area had been investigating a possible plot against the President for nearly two years. Now, they had confirmation.

Jacob Thompson, director of the Confederate Secret Service organization, had put together a strategic plan that potentially could disrupt the U.S. Government and the Union Army and bring decisive victory to the Confederate States of America. If successful, the war could be over within days.

"Clay, you know how paranoid Hill Lamon has been about the safety of the President and his family. Hill asked me and the marshals from Maryland to work with him and his Washington staff and investigate all the leads he had about a plot to kidnap Mr. or Mrs. Lincoln and hold them for ransom. He claimed that Jake Thompson had an intricate plan that could bring the nation to its knees.

"Now, I think the world of Hill and would do just about anything for him. But, between you and me, I thought he was off his rocker about this so-called Confederate plot. I humored him, as did Roy Barnes and Jack Lewis up in Maryland, and we followed up on all the allegations of kidnapping and even murder.

"Well, we have enough evidence at this point to indicate that Lamon knows what he's talking about. It appears there is a plot, and it's well conceived. And, frankly, we need to get on top of it and we're going to need your help, because this situation extends from Tennessee and Kentucky to Virginia, Maryland and Washington City.

"And, that's why I'm here."

"You must know about the kidnapping attempt where Mrs. Lincoln was concerned?" Clay asked.

"That's what really cinched this for us," Miles explained. "We really could not confirm how involved this plot was until we heard about the attempt here on the First Lady. Now, we can connect a lot of things and, frankly, it's really scary when we see the detail that's involved in the scheme."

McDowell held up his hand, signaling that Miles should halt his commentary. Clay opened the door and checked the hallway, then closed and locked the opening.

"I hope I'm not as paranoid as Lamon, but let's assume this conversation would be of interest and value to our opposition. Let's at least limit their opportunities. Now, please continue."

"Let's start at the beginning," Miles suggested. "Because of our proximity to Washington, Hill asked Barnes, Lewis and me to begin meeting with him and his district staff. This was about a year ago. His idea was to follow up on any leads relating to infiltration of the U.S. Government or plots against the government by Confederate spies.

"As you know, Lamon is adamant that a plot to abduct or kill the President was initiated right after the election. Hill claims that Lincoln is less than popular with a good many groups, particularly, of course, with those sympathetic to the Southern cause. He cites, as a case in point, the supposed threats against Lincoln by individuals who wished to do him harm while he was en route to the White House and the inauguration. As you know, the Pinkertons reported the threat and urged Hill to get the President directly to the White House instead of letting him parade through Maryland as he had planned. Hill always has been of the opinion that this was a plot by a Washington group that has organizational ties with Tennessee, Kentucky, Maryland and Virginia. And, we've found that the group has an organizational safe house headquartered in Canada.

"The group's plan, apparently, is two-fold. First, devalue the U.S. currency by issuing fake bills and coins. In other words, counterfeiting. Second, kidnap the President and/or members of his family and hold them for ransom. The goal here is to either exchange them for Confederate prisoners of war or force the Union to surrender.

"We have reason to believe your area of Kentucky harbors several individuals involved in both counterfeiting and kidnapping. The incident with Mrs. Lincoln tends to confirm the kidnapping aspect."

"But, Phil, Mason Sanderson was ready to kill Mrs. Lincoln when the kidnapping scheme failed," McDowell pointed out.

Miles nodded in agreement.

"That's right! If the kidnapping fails, then they'll kill the parties involved. But, that's a second choice, as they can't have witnesses. But, all their bargaining chips are with the kidnapping. And, frankly, they don't care where the incident occurs, as long it does.

"I know you were surprised about Sanderson, but no more so than we were. He'd been with the Marshals service for some time and we had no idea that he wasn't loyal. But that underscores what we're up against. There may be other traitors and other things that we don't know. We've got to derail this as soon as possible."

"So, you think a Kentucky connection is part of the overall plan?" Clay asked.

"Definitely," Miles stated. "I'm speaking now as a member of Lamon's Washington group. Number one, we think some of the counterfeit bills are being printed in your district and transported to Virginia and Washington. Number two, we know that the first kidnapping attempt took place in Madison County. So, here's what we want you to do.

"First, find out where the counterfeiting is being done, seize the printing paraphernalia and arrest those involved. Next, try to identify others who may have been involved in Mrs. Lincoln's kidnapping and see if there are any leads to conspirators in Virginia, Maryland or the Washington district. And, report any findings directly to Lamon."

"Who am I looking for?" Mac inquired.

Miles removed a list secured in his wallet.

"I'll leave this with you," he said, "but listen to these suspects. An actor, John Wilkes Booth, is a ringleader. Lewis Weichmann, his college friend, is a close associate, as is John Surratt, Junior. Mary Surratt, who runs a boarding house in Washington, is John's mother and also is involved. Then, there's George Atzerodt, David Herold and Lewis Powell. This Powell is an odd one. He may be some sort of mental case.

"We've uncovered a Confederate spy in Washington, Rose Greenhow, who's being 'extradited' to Virginia, and we're closing in on another Virginia spy suspect, Antonia Ford. And, through 'Bull' Nelson, we've learned about a spy in your area, Mary Beth Robinson. She and her husband are well-to-do and have a home in Richmond and a farm in Madison County."

"She's the one with ties to John Hunt Morgan?" Mac questioned.

"Right," Miles continued. "Her husband, John Robinson, is a strong Southern supporter and he and Morgan are cousins.

"Then, another crazy one is a Zachary Holston, also known as 'The Major.' I believe you've already had a run-in with him."

Clay smiled.

"We became acquainted at the Mary Todd Lincoln affair."

"Make no mistake, Clay, these folks are very much involved and are extremely dangerous," Miles affirmed. "Don't be surprised by anything they do."

"I won't be, particularly after what happened with Mason Sanderson," McDowell said. "I never would have believed he was a double agent."

"As I said, we were as surprised as anyone," Miles stated. "I guess I knew him better than anyone else in the Marshals service, and I would have testified he was as loyal to the Union as the President."

"What are we doing to combat this spy ring?" McDowell asked. "I assume we have some spies of our own?"

Miles nodded.

"We do and we're running a check on a young lady who happens to be in Lexington right now. It's very likely she'll be our next recruit. Her occupation and access to those involved on the other side could make her extremely helpful."

"If you bring her in, will I meet her?" Clay asked

"Not necessarily. If you need to know, the answer is yes."

"Tell me more about this counterfeiting ring," Mac requested. "Isn't this awfully new to be so extensive?"

"Well, you know that the Northern banking community was in a crisis mode two years ago because of a gold shortage. The Union losses at Bull Run and Ball's Bluff, plus the possible support for the Confederacy by England, caused a lot of people to have doubts about the Union's ability to win the war. As a result, the purchase and hoarding of precious metals depleted gold reserves of the banks and the Federal Treasury. We had a meeting with the Treasury secretary and attorney general and they said we just about lost it all at that point.

"All this led to the bill making paper currency legal tender, despite the fact that it was not backed by gold or silver. At this point, we have 'greenbacks' totaling more than $400 million.

"What's complicating all this is the fact that more than 1,000 different state banks are designing their own bills, which makes counterfeiting detection nearly impossible. One of the few ways to identify counterfeit bills is by the paper that's used. Basically, official U.S. currency is printed on stock that has a cotton base with some linen included. If you wad up that bill, you can still straighten out most of the wrinkles. But that's more difficult with other paper. Also, counterfeit bills often are printed on thicker paper stock.

"Now, Clay, this isn't foolproof. But unless there's an obvious printing mistake, examining the paper stock is one of the better methods of identifying counterfeit bills. Also, the $20 bill is one of the most often to be counterfeited. The $10 and $5 bills also are popular choices. Some may even try to make fake $1,000, $5,000, $10,000 or even larger denominations, but, it's my guess, that the more common bills will be the ones they'll want to print."

McDowell cast a disparaging eye at Miles.

"You sure you don't want me to look for a needle in a

haystack?" he asked. "I could do that while I'm looking for fake money."

Miles sighed and gave Mac a grim look.

"Maybe we are grasping at straws here," he said. "But, dammit, Marshal, this is a major problem! I really have my doubts about printing money when there's nothing of value to back it, but that's happened and we have to live with it! When we start making the rules, I'll be in touch! But, for now, we're the ones in the trenches trying to make bureaucratic theories function! Don't make light of it!"

McDowell threw up his hands in surrender.

"Sorry, Phil, don't forget that I'm on your side. I know you and Hill and everybody else in Washington are frustrated about the effect this could have on the economy. I know this is important. But you and I also know how impossible a task this is. If I really have no way of identifying a bogus bill, how can I do it?"

Miles opened a satchel and withdrew several greenbacks. He laid them on a table, one after the other.

"Okay, Marshal," he demanded. "Tell me which bill is legitimate and which ones are counterfeit?"

"You're joking?" Clay responded.

"**NO!** I'm not!" Miles retorted. "Now, make a choice. And, make it as if your life depended upon it."

Mac looked at the bills, picked them up, examined them closely, felt the texture of the paper, and placed them back on the table.

"Choose!" Miles ordered.

Clay smiled at his comrade.

"That one!" he said. "It's legit."

"Congratulations!" Phil responded. "You've chosen a counterfeit bill from your own state and you've just devalued the U.S. dollar another thousandth of a percent. In terms of inflation, monetary value and who knows what else, you've probably killed another soldier and cut the supply of ammunition for another."

Mac jumped to his feet.

"That's enough, Phil!" he shouted. "Don't play games with me! How in Hell can I identify a counterfeiter and break up a fake money scheme when I don't even know what I'm looking for!"

Miles leaped to his feet and swatted the bills from the table.

"Now, do you get the point!" he cried. "It's a guessing game! I only know because I've been working at it so long! Just go out there and stop anyone from printing money! Arrest them, beat hell out of them, shoot them – I don't care! Just stop them!"

They glared at each other from across the table. Finally, Miles held up his hands and sat.

"None of us have the answers," he groaned. "That's the problem. All we can do is the best we can. Just do it, Clay. That's all any of us can do. Let's face it, we're in uncharted waters."

Mac sat and nodded at Miles.

"It's one helluva war," he said.

"That," Phil responded, "We can agree on."

Chapter VII

The Counterfeiters

"Where do we start?"

McDowell and Perry were nearing Richmond, and Logan, since they'd left Lexington, had voiced a steady stream of questions and complaints about their mission. Mac had explained about the suspected counterfeit ring and how they needed to get a lead as to where the fake money was being produced and distributed.

"We don't know who's doing it, how to recognize it, or where or how they're printing it," Logan repeated. "Where do we begin?"

"How many times are you going to ask that?"

"Look, Clay, you know I'm willing to take on just about anything. But, I just don't know where we're headed with this. This is the craziest assignment we've ever had."

"Let's start at the sheriff's office," Mac announced.

"Do you think Hiram Wagers will tell us anything, even if he knows?" Logan asked.

Clay shook his head.

"We have to try and we at least need to give him a chance. But, you're right. Chances are he won't cooperate even if he could."

"Well," Logan commented, "as my granddaddy used to say, 'Life is simpler when you plow around the stump.'"

Mac glanced at Perry and grimaced.

"And to think your grandfather didn't even know Hiram Wagers."

As a border state, Kentucky refused to take sides where the Civil War was concerned. But, the Commonwealth was pretty much divided between Union and Confederate supporters. And, Hiram Wagers, despite the fact he was the Madison County sheriff, was a strong Southern patriot and had not the least bit of interest in assisting the U.S. government in any shape or form.

As U.S. Marshal for the Eastern District of Kentucky, McDowell felt he was duty bound to include local law enforcement in any criminal investigation in which he was engaged. That's why he always kept in touch with Wagers on Madison County matters, although he was certain that Hiram wouldn't throw him a line if he were drowning.

One of Wagers' deputies was leaving as Clay and Logan dismounted.

"Marshals," he acknowledged. Although it wasn't friendly, at least it was a greeting.

Wagers was seated at a desk, one leg propped up on a corner. He offered no more acknowledgement or greeting as they entered. His steely stare went from one to the other.

Finally, he spoke.

"What's up, Gentlemen?"

"We'd like to talk with you, Hiram," Mac began. "It's about an investigation into counterfeiting here in Madison County."

Wagers burst out laughing.

"You've got to be kidding!" he stated. "Counterfeiting in Madison County? That's ridiculous!"

Although not invited to do so, Mac and Perry pulled up chairs and sat.

"I wish we were kidding," Clay replied. "But, we're very serious. We have reason to believe that someone or some individuals here in Madison are printing U.S. paper money and distributing it in the Northern states and, perhaps, even in the South.

"I'd appreciate it if you could give us any leads or had any thoughts about who, where or how this is being done."

Wagers made a big point of wiping his eyes as he was laughing so hard.

"Sounds to me like the Feds are attacking another windmill," he grinned. "But, I guess it helps keep their minds off the fact that they're losing the war. Tell me what you know about this snipe hunt."

Mac kept his cool.

"Don't know a whole lot myself, Hiram. But our folks in

Washington have found that quite a bit of fake money is showing up these days and they've traced it back to several Southern states and Kentucky. We think it's being printed somewhere near Richmond and transported to Virginia for distribution. As you know, printing and distributing counterfeit money is illegal and those responsible could be facing prison time or worse."

"I see, I see," Wagers reflected. He stood and stroked his chin.

"Now, when you say this alleged counterfeiting is against the law, I guess you must be saying that it's against Yankee law. I don't believe Kentucky, as a border state, is subject to Yankee law, so, if these counterfeiting allegations are true, that law doesn't apply in the Commonwealth.

"Now, I'm just a humble country sheriff, but I don't believe these charges will hold water in this state."

Perry straightened in his chair and glared at Wagers.

"To the best of your knowledge, Sheriff, has Kentucky seceded from the Union?" he asked.

"No, deputy, no, I don't believe it has. But, as a neutral state in this war, is Kentucky any more subject to the laws of the North than it is of the laws of the South? How would you describe neutral?"

"Kentucky is still part of the Union," Perry emphasized.

"Is it now?" the Sheriff asked. "Seems I read somewhere that Kentucky was trying to establish a Confederate government down at Bowling Green. And, just the other day, Kirby Smith and his boys from Dixie took over the Capital and set up a good old Southern sympathizer in the governor's office."

"And how long did that last?" Logan demanded. "Don Carlos Buell and his men attacked Frankfort and ran him out before he even finished his acceptance speech."

Wagers gave the deputy a patronizing nod.

"That's just my point, son," he said. "Everybody wants to govern Kentucky and people are so divided as to who should be in power that there's a genuine question about whose laws we should be following – the North or the South.

"Now, my advice is to leave well enough alone," he gestured to both lawmen. "If you were to push your point and end up in a court of law, well, I think you'd end up embarrassed. We've got some good lawyers in Kentucky, and I think they'd tell you the same thing I am. Just relax and don't rock the boat."

Perry was on his feet and red in the face with anger. He stomped to the door, but stopped as Clay held up his hand.

"Let's get back to the subject, Hiram," Mac suggested. "There's an organization that wants to hamstring the nation financially by flooding the market with fake bills. Also, that same group would like to kidnap President Lincoln or members of his family and use them as barter to end the war. Now, we're not going to let that happen. And, we're asking for your help."

Wagers stuffed his hands in his rear waistband and paced the floor.

"You know, Marshal, I'd really like to help you. I really would. But, I'm just not sure that your facts are accurate.

"Why, I even heard that whopper about you trying to protect Mrs. Lincoln. The story I heard was that you and your deputy got a lot of men killed because you thought somebody was trying to kidnap her. But, I also heard the real story was that her carriage horses got spooked, wrecked the buggy and injured Mrs. Lincoln. A fellow told me that the tale about a bunch of raiders trying to kill her was just that – a tall tale to cover up what really happened.

"You see, Marshal, I'm the law in this county and sworn to protect all its residents. I just can't go against some fine and honest people – and excuse me for having to say it this way – because of some harebrained story about counterfeiters and kidnappers."

Clay rose from his chair.

"So, we can't count on your help?"

"I'm afraid not, Marshal. I'd sure like to help you, because you're a nice fellow. But, you can't expect me to drop everything just because you're on some wild goose chase."

"Well, Sheriff, thanks for hearing us out. We'll continue the investigation on our own, and I trust you won't interfere with that."

Wagers jumped as if he were struck.

"Interfere? Why, Marshal, I'd shoot anyone who'd say I'd interfere with another lawman!"

Hiram drew his weapon for emphasis as he spoke and pointed it in Clay's general direction.

Perry's hand suddenly fell and the sound of his pistol being cocked drew the Sheriff's attention.

"Drop it, Sheriff!" he called.

Wagers' eyes narrowed in anger, but he gently bent down and laid his revolver on the floor.

"You're awfully touchy, son," he said. "A sudden move like that could get you killed."

"Me or you?" Logan asked.

Wagers straightened and stared at Perry.

"Pick up the weapon with your left hand and put it back in the holster," Logan ordered.

He motioned with his revolver as he spoke and the Sheriff stooped slowly and returned the pistol to his gun belt. Perry also returned his weapon to its holster.

"Now, Sheriff, anytime you want to fill your hand…"

"What do you mean?" Wagers asked.

"I mean, draw!"

Logan's hand hovered over his pistol and his eyes bored into those of the Sheriff. Wagers swallowed and he raised his palms toward the deputy.

"Let's just calm down," the Sheriff's voice cracked. "I meant no harm."

Clay jerked his head toward the door.

"We'll be going now, Hiram," he announced. "Let us know if you can help."

They backed through the threshold, watching the door as they mounted their horses and slowly rode away.

"You're awfully touchy, son," Clay grinned at Logan, mocking the Sheriff. "I believe you would have shot him."

Perry's expression was grim.

"It was his call, " the deputy said. "And, yes, I would have."

* * *

McDowell and Perry walked their mounts down Richmond's Main Street and slowed when Mac pointed to a barbershop.

"Let's see if the town barber knows anything," he said.

There was only one customer inside, and he was getting a shave.

"Have a seat, Gentlemen," the barber smiled. "I'll be right with you."

He finished and turned to the lawmen.

"Who's next?" he asked.

Clay rubbed the stubble on his chin and stepped into the chair.

"I'd like a shave and some information," he said, producing his wallet and showing his badge.

"I can do one and maybe even the other," the barber smiled.

"I imagine you know most of the men here and something about their occupations," Mac began. "Do you have any customers who are printers?"

The barber wrinkled his brow in thought.

"You mean folks who print handbills, newspapers, that sort of thing?"

"Exactly," Mac replied. "Most of them would have ink stains on their hands or under their fingernails."

"Well, I have some regular customers from *The Richmond Daily Dispatch* – that's our newspaper here."

"Anybody else?"

The barber paused and sharpened his razor.

"Come to think of it, I do have several others that I don't know very well. There's a stocky-built man who seems to wear the same clothes a lot. I tried to brush him off after a haircut and he said not to worry with his vest.

"'Those are ink stains,'" he said. "'You can't brush them off.'"

"Does he work at the *Dispatch*?" McDowell asked.

"No, he said he's involved in a project down at Rogersville. That's all he said and I didn't ask him anything else."

They talked in generalities until the shave was finished.

"Where are we going now," Perry asked as they walked outside.

"Let's go up to the *Dispatch*," Mac directed.

After talking with the editor and touring the composing room, McDowell met the printer and left convinced that nothing but job printing and a newspaper were being produced at that location.

The editor called to the lawmen as they left.

"Marshal, that man you mentioned down at Rogersville … well, you'll think this is silly," Herb Wiggins began. "A house down there on the Terrill farm burned down several years ago and the only thing left standing was an outhouse. It was a big one – a four-holer – and I heard it was being used as some sort of work shed since the fire. I've heard a lot of jokes about it and, I know this sounds crazy, but you might check it out."

Clay suppressed a smile.

"An outhouse?"

"That's right," the editor replied. "Come to think of it, it is kind of funny. You'll find it by just following your nose."

Mac tipped his hat.

"Thanks, Mr. Wiggins, I'll do just that," he grinned.

Wiggins began to laugh.

"I hope this won't raise a stink," he chortled. "But, you must follow up leads that don't always smell right."

Wiggins continued to laugh as he returned to the building.

"What a headline!" he snorted. "Odor leads marshal to messy discovery."

Perry pulled his horse from the hitching rail and mounted.

"This is the craziest thing we've ever done," he declared.

Chapter VIII

The Outhouse

The remnants of war still littered the Old State Road.

McDowell and Perry worked their way slowly down the macadamized roadway, the path used by Kirby Smith's army as they encountered Union forces in the late August Battle of Richmond. The wrecked and left-behind items mostly were Federal, evidence that the green Union troops were overwhelmed by the veterans from the South.

Bodies of men and animals had been removed, but parts of uniforms, knapsacks and wagons still littered adjacent fields. Broken weapons and discarded bayonets lay beside the road and the canvas covering for a Union ambulance remained where it had caught in a tree.

It was a sobering sight and the lawmen rode quietly.

Rogersville was a small farming community in an area that boasted some of the best agricultural land in Madison County. The Terrill farm, Clay recalled, was off to the right, less than a mile away. They turned onto a dirt road and spotted what remained of a house several hundred yards in the distance. The fire had totally consumed what had been a sizeable structure. Only a rock foundation remained.

A barn, untouched by the blaze, was off to the left, but already was showing signs of disuse. One of the double doors was hanging by a single hinge and a weather vane was listing to the left.

They dismounted and walked around the ruins, finding nothing of significance. A path led from the back of the house to a nearby wooded area. The horses were ground-reined and Clay and Logan followed the walkway into a clearing, amazed at what they discovered.

The building was constructed in a Victorian style with a cupola on the roof and fancy wood trim. Mulberry bushes were planted around the structure. Clay pushed open the door and, as described, saw that it was a four-hole unit. Partitions that had been placed between the openings had been removed and what remained was a long seating area approximately three-by-nine feet.

There was no odor and, as Clay looked into the pit, he saw that it had been thickly covered with lime. A bucket of the white powder and a scoop were in the corner, appearing to have been recently placed there.

Logan tapped the bucket with his toe.

"Somebody's been keeping the place odor free," he announced.

Clay nodded.

"Let's get out of sight and see what happens," he ordered.

They retrieved the horses and hid in a covering of brush and trees. They sat quietly and, after about an hour, Perry touched McDowell's arm.

"Clay?" he whispered.

"Yeah?" Mac responded.

"Forget what I said earlier about the craziest things we've ever done. **THIS** has to be the craziest thing we've ever done."

"Do you wonder what your granddaddy might say?" Clay questioned.

"Yeah," Logan reflected. "'Good judgment comes from experience and a lotta that comes from bad judgment.' You ready to leave?"

Before he could answer, they heard a vehicle being driven up the road. They watched as a horse and wagon were maneuvered to the clearing where the outhouse stood. Two men were seated and one braked the wagon while the other tied off the reins. They removed a tarpaulin and began unloading the contents. A heavy wooden crate was carried inside, followed by several smaller ones. They waited as they heard items being set in place, supplemented by sounds of a systematic process. They waited another fifteen minutes before McDowell motioned to Perry for them to approach the door.

He and Perry stood a safe distance from the opening before Mac called.

"This is U.S. Marshal Clay McDowell. We have you covered and I'm ordering you to throw out any weapons and come outside with your hands raised. You'll not be harmed if you do as I say."

All activity stopped and total quiet prevailed. Finally, someone inside spoke.

"Who did you say it is?"

"U.S. Marshal Clay McDowell. Come out slowly with your hands raised."

It was quiet again. Then, the two inside were heard exchanging comments.

"We're coming out, Marshal! We're not armed! Don't shoot!"

The door opened slowly and a stocky-built man and a taller, thinner individual walked out, hands raised and wide-eyed.

"Keep your hands up and walk toward us!" Mac demanded.

They walked closer and were ordered to halt some six feet away.

"Keep your hands up and don't move," Clay stated. "Search them, Logan."

Other than pocketknives, neither had a weapon. No identification was evident.

"Now tell us who you are and what you're doing here," the Marshal directed.

The stocky one appeared to be in charge.

"I'm Jackson Sturgill and this here is Oscar Burdette. We're not criminals, Marshal, just out-of-work printers doing a job. I'm from Louisville and Oscar here is from Clay County. I used to work for *The Louisville Daily Journal* and Oscar was with a commercial printer in Manchester. We've both been out of work since the war started and just pick up odd jobs whenever we can find them."

"What are you doing here?" Mac asked.

"It's a long story, Marshal," Sturgill suggested.

"Just go ahead and tell us," Mac replied, then waved his weapon toward Burdette. "And, if you've got anything to add, feel free to speak."

Burdette swallowed hard and nodded that he would.

Clay told them to lower their hands, but not to move. He holstered his pistol, but Logan kept his in his hand as he folded his arms.

"Are we in trouble, Marshal?" Sturgill asked. "We're not doing anything illegal, just producing some bills for a bank here in Madison County."

Mac and Logan glanced at one another, both reflecting looks of disbelief.

"Let me put it this way, Mr. Sturgill," McDowell stated. "We're arresting you on suspicion of printing and distributing counterfeit money. If you're convicted, you could go to prison for a long time. But, if you cooperate and tell us what you know, it may go easier for you in court. I'd urge you to cooperate."

Sturgill looked at his companion, who nodded that they should do so. Sturgill cleared his throat and began to speak.

"Well, after I lost my job in Louisville, I came to Lexington and ran into Oscar here."

Burdette nodded that was correct.

"We sort of joined up and started making the rounds, looking for work. Everybody was worried about the Confederates invading Kentucky and just weren't hiring. A commercial printer told us there wouldn't be any work until the battles in Kentucky were over.

"Well, we traveled on down to Richmond and a nice fellow offered to buy us a drink over at the saloon. We took him up on it and got some beers, and he even got us something to eat. To be honest, Marshal, we hadn't been eating regular and this was really something for us.

"We ate our fill and he kept buying us beers and we got real comfortable like. We'd told him that we were looking for work and were printers. He said he could tell that by looking at our hands. If you know anything about the printing business, Marshal, you know it's the very devil to get your hands clean. That ink gets under your fingernails and just soaks through your skin. The worst, though, is when you have to clean those presses. That stuff gets all over you and ..."

"I know, Mr. Sturgill, just get on with your story," Clay interrupted. "Did he offer you a job?"

"Well, yessir, he did. He said he represented a bank in Madison County that was printing scrip that could be redeemed at any of their locations. He said this was a big bank that had holdings even in Jackson and Rockcastle Counties. Business was booming, he told us, and the bank needed some extra money – scrip that is – to take care of its hundreds of customers.

"He said the banking business was highly competitive because of the war, and his bank didn't want any competitors to know the amount of scrip it was providing. Because of this, they were using this farm building to print 'greenbacks,' as he called them, and he wanted us to do the printing, but keep quiet about it. He asked us if we could do that, and we said, 'yes.' Right, Oscar?"

Burdette nodded in agreement.

"So, he set you up here?"

"That's right," Sturgill agreed. He brought us a horse and wagon and a cast-iron chase and printing press and put us in business."

"Weren't you suspicious about being located in an outhouse?"

Sturgill and Burdette both nodded.

"But this fellow said, 'That's the beauty of it! Who would ever think that somebody was printing scrip in an outhouse?' Well, Oscar and me agreed."

Oscar again nodded in agreement.

"What were you printing?" the Marshal asked.

"Well, this fellow gave us wood cuts of $5-, $10- and $20-dollar bills, plenty of green ink and paper and told us to print as much scrip as we could."

"Did he give you an amount he wanted?"

"No, I told him that we worked real fast and he was happy with what we produced."

"What did you do with it after you printed the bills?"

"We hung up the sheets of paper to dry just like you'd do with clothes," Sturgill explained. "The next day, we'd come back and cut the bills, sort them into stacks, and place them in cloth bags he gave us. At the end of the week, we'd load everything into the wagon and deliver the bills to a location in the eastern end of the county.

"We'd transfer them to another wagon," he continued, "to a man who had a long scar on the side of his face. Sometimes, a woman would be with him – and she was a real looker. They didn't want to talk, just wanted us to load them up right away so they could leave. I never did know their names."

"What about the man who hired you?" Mac asked. "What was his name?"

"He never told us," the printer said. "He'd meet us back here the next week and give us a $10 dollar bill each.

"Didn't you ever wonder if you were doing something illegal?"

"Never did, Marshal. The fellow who hired us was real friendly and explained that bills were being used as scrip by all sorts of banks and businesses. And, all of them were making their own bills.

"He told us he represented a number of banks in Kentucky, Virginia and Washington City and he was obtaining scrip for all of them."

Mac asked when their next delivery was scheduled.

"Tomorrow – Friday – we'll deliver a load then," Sturgill said.

"Okay, here's what we're going to do," Clay explained. "You and your friend will go to the meeting place as usual and Perry and I will be trailing at a safe distance. You unload and make the transfer and we'll do the rest."

"Will there be any shooting?"

"I hope not, but keep your heads down," Mac instructed. "No one will know you've told us anything if you just act naturally."

"What do you think, Oscar?" Sturgill asked.

Burdette nodded in agreement.

"Hey, mister!" Logan cried. "Don't you ever speak?"

Burdette shook his head.

"Don't need to. He talks pretty good."

* * *

McDowell and Perry cuffed the printers, unhitched their wagon and had them ride double as they left for the county lockup. A surprised Hiram Wagers deposited them in a cell and prepared to leave.

"Why don't you stay here with us?" Clay asked. "You can help us stand guard tonight."

"Sorry, Marshal, but I have some other business to tend to."

Logan stood in the doorway, his hand resting on his revolver.

"Are you refusing to honor the request of a U.S. Marshal?" he asked.

Wagers glared at Perry and swallowed.

"Don't you interfere with me!" he warned. "Stop me from leaving and I'll report you to the district attorney and have your badges!"

Logan shook his head.

"Now, just which district attorney are you referring to? You say the Federal government has no jurisdiction and we're not affiliated with the Confederates, so there's really no one for you to contact, is there?"

Wagers was red in the face, but could think of no rebuttal.

"Just sit down and join us, Hiram," Mac invited. "We'll ask the hotel to send us over some food, then we'll get some rest and leave in the morning."

Hiram sat.

* * *

Sturgill and Burdette turned off the Old State Road at Rogersville and made their way east. They continued at a pace they usually followed on delivery day and stopped at the assigned meeting place. The lawmen stayed behind, but close enough to keep the printers in sight.

Clay motioned to a rocky shelf that would provide adequate

cover while they waited for the contacts to show. The dirt trail continued easterly into a forested area where Zak Holston and Mary Beth Robinson sat in a wagon. Mary Beth trained field glasses on Sturgill and Burdette and scanned the area before giving the Major an "okay" to proceed.

Holston drove alongside the other wagon and motioned for the printers to transfer their load. Meanwhile, Mac and Logan waited in hiding. They wanted some of the bills transferred before springing the trap.

Perry's horse was getting edgy and finally he reared and whinnied when the snake began to rattle. He bucked like a wild bronc and the noise attracted attention from the other wagon.

Holston immediately sensed a trap and drew his pistol. Sturgill and Burdette began to protest their innocence, but never received a chance to plead their cases. The Major shot both in the chest, then whipped his wagon toward a grove of trees.

Perry brought his mount under control, but, by then, Holston and Mary Beth had disappeared and the printers lay dead beside their wagon. Most of the fake money still was there as the transfer had just begun when the turmoil occurred.

"We going after them?" Perry asked.

"No, they're too far ahead and I'm sure they'd have a welcoming committee waiting for us," Mac said.

The lawmen dismounted and checked the bodies, and, as expected, both men had died instantly from the close-range shots. The marshals transferred the bills to their horses and loaded the bodies into the wagon. Logan tied his mount to the back and climbed into the seat. He glanced at McDowell who nodded.

"Let's go home," he said.

Chapter IX

Mary Beth

"Bull" Nelson had described Mary Beth Robinson as beautiful, cunning, intelligent, resourceful, dedicated and a cold-blooded killer.

Clay McDowell read the report from Washington and shared it with his deputy. Logan Perry reviewed it and looked inquisitively at the Marshal.

"Are you thinking the same thing I am?" he asked. "Was Mrs. Robinson the woman in the wagon?"

Logan was referring to the recent incident east of Rogersville. Two itinerant printers had been killed when a transfer of counterfeit money had taken place. They'd been shot by a man driving a second wagon, but he was accompanied by a woman, who, even at long distance, was so stunning in appearance that she demanded a second look.

"She's a Confederate spy, Logan, and I think she's associated with this whole network of counterfeiting and kidnapping," Mac commented. "I don't know if she was the woman we saw in the wagon, but who else could it have been? Nelson says she killed the captain he sent to arrest her and suspects she disrupted much of his plans for the Battle of Richmond.

"He feels she supplied information to Kirby Smith through John Scott and that she and her husband, John, were dedicated Confederate spies."

Clay gave the report a second look.

"She's apparently a real charmer. According to Nelson, she's originally from Alabama, has a brother in the Confederate army and her husband is a cousin of John Hunt Morgan.

"We need to make another visit to Richmond."

Perry raised his brow in question and disbelief.

"I'm with you, Clay. But, if we have to go through Hiram Wagers, just for the record, I'm against it."

Logan had no more taste for the Madison County sheriff than he did for the venomous snake that startled his horse at Rogersville. As a faithful Southern supporter, Wagers was not likely to take a stand against any Confederate sympathizer.

"This time, Logan, I think we'll bypass the sheriff," Clay said. "I know where the Robinsons live, in town and on their county farm. Let's start in Richmond and go from there. I have a federal warrant from Hill Lamon for the Robinsons' arrest on suspicion of conspiracy to overthrow the government. Let's serve that and tell Hiram later."

Perry smiled and slapped the desktop.

"Now, you're talking, Clay! Let's do it!"

The trip to Richmond was uneventful. Even Mose McCubbin offered nothing new about activities involving the war or its participants. He waxed philosophical, however, as he ferried the lawmen to the Madison shore.

"Things have become downright boring since Kirby Smith returned to Tennessee," he said. "You know, Clay, I really liked that man. He crossed the river several times with me, the last being when he and his men retreated from the loss at Perryville. I think if he'd linked up with anybody besides Braxton Bragg he would have whipped the Union and taken those Southern boys all the way to Cincinnati."

"You've been around Bowie Hart too much," Mac said. "He thinks Smith and his men hung the moon."

"No, I talked with Bowie about the General and he and I agree. Gen. Smith is a first-class individual. He really likes this area and said he'd like to visit after the war's over."

Perry leaned his back against the rail and surveyed the ferry.

"You know, Mose, what you really need to do is install a promenade deck on this barge. That way, Gen. Smith, Bowie and you could walk around telling lies and drinking mint juleps."

McCubbin spat into the river and glared at the lawmen.

"You two have no souls," he declared. "Why don't you swim across on your way back."

Clay and Logan rode to Main Street and turned north. Some of Richmond's finest homes were located on the road to

Lexington, including the townhouse of John and Mary Beth Robinson. Clay opened the gate and they stopped at the carriage entrance. They made their way to the front door where they were greeted by a well-dressed servant.

Mac showed his credentials and asked to see the Robinsons. He was informed that Mrs. Robinson was in and the servant would see if she was available.

They stood in the entryway and took in the lavish structure and its furnishings. A highly polished and winding stairway led to the second floor, and, shortly, Mary Beth Robinson appeared, and slowly made her way down. She was dressed in a royal blue gown that highlighted her light brown hair and dazzling blue eyes that were almost violet in color.

A wide-eyed Perry was mesmerized.

"Easy, son," Clay whispered. "She's just a woman."

"She is that!" Logan murmured.

Mary Beth smiled and extended her hand. Clay took it and bowed slightly.

"Welcome, gentlemen," she said. "I understand you'd like to see me. Let's step into the parlor where we can be more comfortable."

They were directed to comfortable chairs and asked if they would like something to eat or drink. They politely declined and Mary Beth folded her hands in her lap and smiled again.

"I must apologize, gentlemen. I was preparing to go out, but felt I needed to speak with you, as I'm sure you're here on business and not making a social call. Unfortunately, my husband is away on business."

"It is about business, Mrs. Robinson," Clay acknowledged. "We're doing an investigation in Madison County concerning activities involving counterfeiting and possible plots against the U.S. government."

Mary Beth blinked in surprise.

"My heavens! That is serious! And, you believe that's happening here in Madison County?"

"I believe you and your husband know Gen. William Nelson," Clay stated.

"Oh, yes, we certainly do. The General was a guest in our home several times."

"To get to the point, Mrs. Robinson, the General has reason to believe that you and your husband are involved in espionage activities on behalf of the Confederacy. He has implicated you in the murder of a Capt. Norris and, possibly, a Sgt. Collins. Also, we believe you may be involved in counterfeiting and transporting Federal bills across state lines and in the attempted abduction recently of Mary Todd Lincoln."

Mary Beth sat quietly and had no reaction.

Finally, she said, "These **ARE** serious charges, Marshal."

"Yes, they are," Mac agreed. "We have a Federal warrant for your arrest and for your husband. Would you like to tell us where he is?"

"So, you're going to arrest us? Well, Marshal, I hope you know what you're doing. I'm very disappointed in Gen. Nelson. I don't believe I've had anyone react so negatively toward the hospitality that Mr. Robinson and I extended to him and his officers.

"And, as for Mr. Robinson, he's in Louisville, Marshal, and I really don't know when he'll be returning. He's involved in a very pressing business situation."

Clay stood and removed the warrant from his coat pocket.

"This is the warrant, Mrs. Robinson, and, if you will, please read it then place your hands behind you."

Mary Beth examined the document, returned it to Mac and, with a nod of surprise, placed her hands behind her. Clay handcuffed her and asked if she had any weapons on her person.

"Would you like to search me, Marshal?" she smiled.

She turned toward Logan.

"How about you, Deputy? Would you like to do the honors?"

"Do you have a maid, Mrs. Robinson?" Clay asked.

"Why, yes, I do."

"Would you call her please?"

Mary Beth did and Mac instructed the servant to inspect her mistress's clothing.

"Would you like to watch, Marshal," Mrs. Robinson said seductively.

"I'm afraid we must," he said, "including your footwear. I understand you have the habit of placing a derringer inside a boot."

The servant produced the derringer, but no other weapons.

Clay instructed the manservant to bring around a carriage. He told Mary Beth that he would ride with her as she was transported to a county holding facility, and, ultimately, to the Federal prison in Lexington.

"Mac, we're not going to put a fine lady like this in the county jail are we?" Perry asked.

"She's a criminal, Logan. But, no, we'll put her up in the Zimmer Hotel. We'll find a secure room and keep a matron with her and a guard on the door. We'll need to get some transportation from Lexington tomorrow and place her in Federal security."

Clay grinned at his deputy.

"You like her don't you?"

Logan shook his head.

"I can't believe a beautiful woman like that could be a criminal."

"Well, they come in all sizes and shapes," the Marshal offered.

"Yeah," Perry drawled. "And, what a shape!"

* * *

Mary Beth was shackled and handcuffed to a bed. The corner hotel room was on the second floor and overlooked Main Street. Clay made sure the room next door and those across the hall were not occupied and would not be made available. The matron sat inside next to the door and Logan sat in the hallway guarding the entrance.

Mac walked to Wagers' office and informed the Sheriff that Mary Beth was in custody. Hiram had a fit.

"What in hell do you think you're doing!" he shouted.

"The Robinsons are one of the finest families in Madison County and folks around here won't stand for this! Do you want to incite a riot! They'll storm the hotel to rescue Mary Beth!"

"I'm depending on you to see that doesn't happen," Clay replied.

"I'm just one man!" Hiram declared. "I won't be responsible if things get out of hand!"

Clay grabbed a fistful of Hiram's shirt and slammed him against the wall.

"You damn well better be responsible!" he said. "If anything happens while I'm gone to Lexington, I'll hang you out to dry! You may be a pitiful excuse for a lawman, but you better act like a real sheriff or you're going to wish they'd never pinned that badge on you!"

Wagers swallowed hard.

"You're out of line, Marshal!"

"No, Hiram, I'm not. But I will be if you let me down. Logan Perry hates your guts and would love to adjust your attitude. But, mess with me, and he'll never get the chance."

Mac pulled Wagers from the wall and slammed him against it again.

"I mean it, Hiram!"

Wagers stared into the Marshal's cold eyes. They were like the eyes of an assassin. He could think of nothing to say.

Clay released his hold and walked to the door. He turned and glared at the Sheriff.

"Remember this discussion," he said. "I'll see you tomorrow."

* * *

McDowell doubted that Mary Beth's incarceration would produce a Madison County version of the Storming of the Bastille. However, in a community deeply divided between Union and Confederate supporters, it was possible that someone might attempt to free her. He wondered if her husband really was out of town. If not, John Robinson might make a move.

Or, if word got out – and he had to assume it would – Zak Holston could consider a rescue.

The weak link was Wagers. Clay felt he'd scared him sufficiently to discourage his liberation of Mary Beth. But, he was certain Hiram would not prevent someone else from doing so.

Clay identified himself as he took the stairway. This was the only route to the second floor and Mary Beth's room was as secure as he could make it. Logan sat beside the door holding a shotgun. He smiled as Mac drew near.

"Getting ready to leave?" he asked.

"Just want to be sure you're all set," he replied. "I'll be back early with a prison wagon and I'll try to scare up some extra help to bring back with me."

"Who's the lady guarding Mary Beth?" Logan asked, gesturing toward the room.

"Daisy Hanson. She used to work in Lexington at the Federal lockup. She quit several years ago when her husband bought a place in Madison County. And, don't let the name fool you. She's as tough as a pine knot. She can handle any weapon and may be a better shot than you."

Perry grinned his approval.

"What about feeding the prisoner?"

"I've already made arrangements downstairs. They'll be bringing something up for Mary Beth around six o'clock. After she eats, they have something for you and Daisy."

Perry shook his head.

"I can't get over a guard named Daisy," he laughed.

"Better not let her hear you say that. I saw her once break up a riot at the county jail single handed. She unlocked a holding cell and busted heads until everybody understood she was in charge."

Logan chuckled, still not convinced.

"Let me put it this way, Deputy," he added, "If you have trouble, you'll be glad she's on your side."

Chapter X

Jailbreak

Logan Perry struggled to stay awake.

The prisoner had been fed, he and Daisy had eaten and all was quiet. What remained was a night of vigilance, waiting for McDowell to return with a penal wagon and guards so that Mary Beth Robinson could be placed in maximum security.

The oil lamps on the hallway walls provided a yellowish cast of light. Not enough to give details to subjects, but sufficient to determine objects and their movements. Logan sat away from the light in a straight-back chair that was against the doorway wall. He had an unobstructed view of the area, including the top third of the stairway.

A creaking sound on the stairwell jolted Perry fully awake and alert. He leveled the shotgun toward the walkway and listened. It came again, the sound of carefully placed boots as someone made his way to the second floor. The crown of a hat came into view and Logan called to its wearer.

"Hold it! Stop and identify yourself!"

"Is that you, Deputy?" a voice was heard.

Perry cocked the weapon, a double click that immediately halted movement.

"It's me, Deputy! Sheriff Wagers!"

"I've got both barrels trained on you. Get out of here!"

The hat disappeared.

"Listen, Deputy! I know we're not friends, but I'm here to help. Really!"

Logan recognized the low-volume voice. It was, as announced, that of Hiram Wagers.

"I don't need your help. Leave!"

There was movement on the stairway, as if someone was sitting.

"I'm serious, Logan. We've got trouble! Zak Holston is outside with some men and they aim to rush you and take

Mary Beth! I'm here with two deputies. Let us come up and we'll back your play."

Perry was out of his chair and crouched near the floor.

"Stay where you are, Sheriff! If you want to help, make a stand in the lobby."

"It won't work, Logan, there's too many of them. If we're with you, we can concentrate our fire at the head of the stairs. We can pick them off as they try to come up.

"I'm tossing up my shotgun and pistol. I'll come up unarmed."

"Don't do it, Sheriff! Try it and you're a dead man!"

"I don't believe you, Logan. You're not a killer. I'm honestly here to help. Here are my weapons."

The shotgun slid up against the wall, followed by a pistol.

"Here I come, Logan, with my hands up. Don't be foolish. Don't shoot."

Wagers never had called him by his first name, Logan thought. In his heart, he knew this was a scheme, a ruse. But, he'd never shot an unarmed man. He hesitated as the figure slowly walked up the stairs and turned, with his hands raised, to face Perry.

"Kick your weapons to me, then walk over here slowly," Logan ordered. "Slow! Take it very slowly!"

Wagers did as he was told.

The Deputy used his foot to scoot the weapons beneath his chair. He then called Hiram to him, shoved his pistol into the Sheriff's midsection and felt for other sidearms. There were none.

"Okay, Sheriff. What's this about?"

"It's just as I said. Zak Holston's bunch are going to rush you! I don't know when, but I've seen them on the street and heard the talk! You can't hold them off by yourself and I promised Marshal McDowell to help you."

"What?"

"Okay! The Marshal threatened me. Before he left, he said I'd better help you if you needed it, or else!"

Perry was between a rock and a hard place. He didn't trust the sheriff, but he didn't like the way things were developing.

"Look, Logan! Let me call up my deputies! We're running out of time! They're on the stairway!"

"Okay, call them," Perry said. "But I'll have my pistol in your back."

Perry wrapped his left arm around the Sheriff's neck and shoved his revolver against the man's backbone."

"Okay, boys! Come on up ... but slowly! Logan's got a gun in my back!"

They did as they were told and, as they came nearer, Perry recognized them as Wagers' men.

"Can I have my guns back?" Hiram asked.

Logan pulled Wagers back a step, used his foot to shove the chair away, then kicked the shotgun and pistol toward the stairwell.

"Tell your men to get them, but move carefully," Perry instructed. "If I don't like anything I see, you get it first."

Their attention was drawn to the sound on the stairway and weapons were trained on the walkway.

"Who's there?" Perry called.

The sound of movement continued.

"Watch it, Logan!" Wagers whispered. "It's Holston!"

All of a sudden, there was just quiet. Tense, on edge, they waited.

"Logan, it's me. I'm coming up," the familiar voice announced.

Puzzled, Perry strained to see. In that split second, with the Deputy's attention drawn to the voice, Wagers smashed his elbow into Logan's stomach. With surprising speed, Hiram spun, wrapped an arm around Perry's gun hand and grabbed the Deputy's throat. The weapon fired as Perry struggled to break free.

Logan staggered as Hiram's two deputies slammed into him, then fell to the floor as he was struck repeatedly with their pistols.

"What's going on out there?" Daisy called from behind the door.

Wagers dropped to his knees and knelt over Perry.

"Daisy! Come here quick! The Deputy's been hurt?"

"I can't leave this room," she yelled. "Who's there?"

"It's me, Sheriff Wagers! Perry's hurt bad and he'll bleed to death! Mary Beth's not going anyplace! Help me, now?"

Daisy unlocked the door and partly opened it, enough to see Wagers bending over the injured Perry.

"Help me stop the bleeding!" Wagers called over his shoulder. "We're about to lose him!"

Daisy looked both ways down the hallway, and, seeing no one, lowered her shotgun and stepped outside. Suddenly, her weapon was snatched away and she was grabbed by the hair and thrown to the floor. A crushing blow to the back of her head followed.

"It's okay, Colonel," Wagers called. "Come on up."

Hiram pushed open the door and smiled at Mary Beth who was shackled to the bed. He was followed by his deputies and another individual, well known by the beautiful spy.

"John!" she called. "I was counting on you!"

"Hello, Darlin'," he said. "I couldn't let an old friend down."

John Scott bent down and kissed Mary Beth on the lips.

"Get me the keys, Sheriff, and let's get her out of these chains," the Colonel ordered.

Wagers found the keys on Daisy and tossed them to Scott. He unlocked the cuffs and leg restraints and rubbed Mary Beth's wrists.

"We'll get you out of here, girl, but we'll have to stay at the Caves tonight," he smiled, kissing her on the forehead. "We'll stop by the farm and get some things first."

"How long will we be at the Caves," she asked.

"Long enough to make arrangements for getting you back to Huntsville."

"Can we get through?" Mary Beth asked. "I hear the fighting is pretty bad in Tennessee."

"Don't worry about it," Scott assured her. "I'll always take care of you."

She threw her arms around Scott's neck and kissed him passionately.

"Will you go with me?"

"Can't do it, Darlin', I've got some things to do for The Group. They need some funds in Virginia and I've got to see to some other arrangements that Powell and John Junior are up to.

"It may take a while, but I'll be down to see you. You can count on it."

They embraced and Wagers placed a hand on Scott's shoulder.

"You better not let John Robinson see you like this," he warned.

"John's gone for good," Scott replied. "Things got too hot for him and he grabbed all his money and left town.

"But, he foolishly left this treasure behind," he added, kissing Mary Beth's hand.

"Now," he said, clasping her hands in his, "we need to wrap you in a blanket and get you out of here. I'm going to carry you downstairs and you need to appear as injured and unconscious."

Scott turned to Wagers.

"You and your boys need to remove Logan and the woman before they come to."

One of Wagers' deputies interrupted.

"No need to worry about them, Colonel. Daisy's dead and I'm not sure Perry's going to make it."

Scott jumped to his feet.

"My, God, Hiram! What have you done? You were just supposed to knock them unconscious!"

He walked quickly into the hallway and inspected the bodies. Daisy had no pulse and Perry had one, but it was very faint. Scott examined the head wound, forced back the eyelids and looked at Logan's eyes.

"Dammit, Hiram, you've fractured his skull! I like that boy and you better see that he pulls through! Get him to a doctor right now!"

The Colonel wrapped Mary Beth in the blanket and carried her to the lobby.

"Get up there and give us some help!" he called to the clerk as he walked outside. "We've got two more injured! Help the Sheriff get them to a doctor!

"Move it!" he shouted and the clerk sprinted up the staircase.

"What happened, Sheriff?" the clerk asked.

They had covered the other two bodies with blankets.

"Someone broke into the room," Wagers replied. "I'm afraid he killed them all. Help us take them over to Doc Chase's office."

* * *

It was just after dawn when McDowell and two security guards arrived at the hotel. The guards were driving the penal wagon and Mac was riding alongside.

Clay walked into the lobby and was hailed by the desk clerk.

"I've got to talk with you, Marshal," he said. "We had a real mess here last night and three people were killed."

"What!" Clay shouted.

"I don't know all the details, but the Sheriff did everything he could."

"The Sheriff! What was he doing here? What about my deputy and prisoner? Who was killed?"

"Well, I was on duty all night, and..."

Mac grabbed the clerk by the collar and dragged him up to the room. Blood still remained on the hallway floor. The room door was open and things inside were in a shambles. Cover had been ripped from the bed, but the shackles that confined Mary Beth remained – minus Mary Beth.

"They took Mary Beth, your deputy and Daisy over to Doc Chase's several hours ago," the clerk explained. "The Sheriff said they were all dead, that somebody broke into the room through the window and killed them."

"That's impossible!" Clay snarled. "We're on the second floor and there's no way to get to a window from outside. And, besides, all of these windows still are locked. Didn't you question Sheriff Wagers?"

"No," the clerk responded nervously. "I just assumed the Sheriff knew what had happened."

Clay ran down the stairs and on outside, sprinting to the physician's office. A light was on in Dr. William Chase's building and Mac raced inside. Logan Perry was on an examining table and Dr. Chase was checking his vital signs.

McDowell flashed his credentials and asked the physician his deputy's condition.

Bandages covered the front and back of Logan's head and ran under his chin. A minimal amount of blood was around his nose and mouth.

"He has a severe concussion, Marshal, and, possibly, a fractured skull," Chase explained. "He was struck on the forehead and side of the head by a heavy blunt object. I treated a patient once who'd been pistol-whipped and these blows are very similar. I'm guessing he was struck with a handgun."

"Has he been conscious?"

"No, and I don't expect it. There's bleeding inside the skull along with a lot of trauma. He may regain consciousness, but he may go into a coma, or he could die. There's not much else I can do for him. We'll just have to wait and see."

"What about the two women?"

Chase looked surprised.

"Two women? I only saw one and she's dead," he replied.

"Who was the woman?"

"Daisy Hanson. Do you know her?"

Clay nodded.

"Yes, very well. How did she die?"

"Same thing," Chase stated. "She was struck with a blunt object, again, probably a handgun, and died with a severe skull fracture."

"Do you know Mary Beth Robinson?"

Chase rubbed his chin.

"Well, I've seen her, but don't really know her. Beautiful woman, but know her husband better."

"She wasn't brought in with the others?"

"No."

Clay thanked Chase and said he'd keep in touch. He asked to be informed if there was any change in Perry's condition. He saw Logan's gun belt hanging on the back of a chair, and, as an afterthought, drew the pistol from the custom holster and stuffed it in his waistband.

He had a good use for it.

Chapter XI

The Plan

Mac returned to the hotel and caught the desk clerk as he was going off duty.

"Let's go somewhere and talk," he said.

They took a table in the dining room and Mac, apologetically, asked, "I'm sorry, but I don't know your name?"

"It's Parsons, Boston Parsons. Most people call me 'Boss.'"

Clay explained the reason for their meeting.

"I need you to give me all the details you can recall about last night," he said.

"I'll do the best I can, Marshal, but I really don't know too much."

"Let's start right after I left," Mac suggested. "You know how we were set up and what our plans were. Did anyone go to the second floor after I left?"

Parsons reflected for a moment.

"I didn't see anyone until much later when the Sheriff and his deputies came in. He told me they would be assisting in guarding the prisoner – Mrs. Robinson – as he had heard that an attempt might be made to kidnap her."

"He used the word 'kidnap?'"

Boss nodded "yes."

"I explained that you'd given orders for no one to get near Mrs. Robinson or her room, but he said this was a new development and that you'd asked him to provide any assistance that Deputy Perry might need.

"I said I wasn't sure about this, but Sheriff Wagers told me he'd take full responsibility. He suggested I stay out of sight, as there could be a gunfight.

"I was plenty nervous, but I kept an eye out just in case.

"The Sheriff had drawn his pistol and began walking up the stairs as quietly as he could. At first, I was afraid he was going to shoot Deputy Perry, but he called out to him and asked if he could come up. He said he and his deputies were there to

-70-

'provide backup.' Deputy Perry told him to leave, but they kept talking and, finally, the Sheriff threw his weapons to the top of the staircase and walked on up.

"They talked some more and I could tell that Deputy Perry was not pleased. After a while, the Sheriff called down to his deputies. They holstered their pistols and went up slowly with their hands in the air.

"They all talked some more and then a third man came in. He asked me if the Sheriff was upstairs and I told him 'yes.' This third man had a hat pulled down over his eyes and a big bandana that covered his chin. I couldn't get a good look at him, but there was something familiar about him. I felt like I'd seen him somewhere before.

"He also told me he was here to help with the prisoner and that he'd identify himself to Sheriff Wagers. I heard some more talking, what sounded like a scuffle and then a shot was fired. It sounded as if the Sheriff called out to the room for some help. I started to go up, but remembered that the Sheriff had told me to stay out of sight. I heard a door open and a loud sound like something hitting the floor. I thought I'd better take a look, but the man on the stairs signaled for me to be quiet. Then, I heard the Sheriff call down to him.

"'Come on up, Colonel,'" he said. "And this other man went on up the stairs.

"Funny thing is, Sheriff Wagers called him 'Colonel,' but the man wasn't wearing a uniform."

Parsons paused and took a sip of water.

"Then what happened?" Clay asked.

"I heard what sounded like the room door being banged open and people running in and out. I decided I'd better see what was going on, when this man the Sheriff called 'Colonel' came down the stairs carrying what appeared to be a woman in a blanket."

"How do you know it was a woman?"

"I don't know for sure, but I assumed it was a woman because it wasn't a very big person."

"Go on," Clay urged.

"This man called the 'Colonel' told me to get up the stairs because there were two more people who were injured."

"Where was the Colonel going?" Mac asked.

"I assumed he was taking the injured person to Doc Chase," Parsons explained. "So, I went on upstairs and the Sheriff had covered two bodies with blankets. I asked what had happened and he said someone had broken into the room and killed everybody and the Deputy. He said I should help get everyone over to Doc Chase's and I did."

"Was anyone else there when you arrived? Like the Colonel or the person he was carrying?" Mac inquired.

"No. I went ahead and I was the only one there until the deputies brought in the other two bodies. Doc Chase uncovered them and said Daisy was dead and Deputy Perry was in bad shape."

Parsons shook his head, "Mike Hanson, Daisy's husband, is going to take this really bad."

"Did you see Mary Beth Robinson?"

"Never did. I guess that's who the Colonel must have had in the blanket, but I don't know where he took her."

Clay had been scribbling some notes as they talked.

"Is there anything else you can remember?"

"No, that's about it, Marshal. I sure hope the Deputy's going to be okay."

Mac stuffed the papers into a pocket and stood.

"So do I, Mr. Parsons."

Boss remained seated with a puzzled look.

"I can't figure out who might have attacked Mary Beth, Daisy and the Deputy," he stated. "And, after talking with you, how they got access through a window. And, you say all the windows were locked. It sure is a mystery."

Clay put on his hat.

"And how could someone get through a window on the second floor unless they had a ladder? Did you see a ladder?"

"No," the clerk said.

"It makes you wonder if someone weren't telling the truth," Mac suggested.

"Good point!" Parsons acknowledged.

* * *

McDowell left the hotel, crossed the street and walked quickly toward the Sheriff's office. He was furious and spoiling for a fight.

"Keep calm," he kept telling himself.

By the time he reached the building, McDowell was boiling mad. He drew his pistol and smashed the door open with his foot, shattering the latch and lock. Wagers and a deputy looked up in surprise.

"Get out of here!" Mac ordered the deputy, gesturing toward the open door with his pistol. "Get on your horse, don't look back and ride. And keep going! Don't come back unless you want some of what the Sheriff will be getting!"

The deputy never hesitated. He was out the door and on his horse in an instant. Clay backed up and slammed the door shut with his heel. He began walking toward Wagers, who had jumped to his feet and was backing away with hands outstretched.

"Now, look, Marshal!" he pleaded. "I don't know what you've heard, but it's not true. I was forced up there by John Scott. He had a gun in my back and was threatening to kill me if I didn't free Mary Beth. He killed Daisy Hanson and maybe your deputy and said he'd kill me if I didn't cooperate.

"That man's a maniac! He would have done anything to free Mary Beth!"

Wagers had backed against the wall. He licked his dry lips and kept his hands raised. McDowell just stood and cocked his revolver.

"Why don't we talk about this, Clay?" the Sheriff asked nervously. "I'll tell you the straight of it! You warned me to stay out of it and I would have if that crazy cavalry colonel hadn't threatened to kill me!"

Mac lowered his weapon. He had his emotions under control, a deadly control.

"You're right, Hiram. Let's sit down and talk. Why don't you tell me what happened?"

"It's just like I said, Clay. This crazy John Scott stormed into my office waving a gun at me and saying he'd kill me if I didn't get Mary Beth free. You see, this Scott is sweet on Mary Beth, has been ever since the big battle here.

"Well, he forced me over to the hotel with a gun in my back and made me walk up the stairs to Mary Beth's room. He pistol whipped your Deputy and clubbed Daisy on the back of her head. He got Mary Beth loose and got her on a horse. But, before he left, he told me he'd kill me if I tried to come after him.

"Now, that's the truth of it. I just hope your Deputy is going to be okay."

Mac stared steadily at Wagers. The Sheriff licked his dry lips and looked away, unable to maintain eye contact.

"Is that the whole truth, Hiram?"

The Sheriff shook his head in the affirmative.

"Look me in the eye and say it!" McDowell demanded.

"It's the truth, Marshal! I swear it!" he cried, glancing at Clay, then bounding nervously to the far side of the room. He then began pacing.

Clay stood quickly and kicked his chair aside. It skidded across the room and banged against the wall, making Wagers jump back in alarm. Mac pulled Logan's pistol from his waistband and spun the cylinder. He then began unloading each chamber.

"What are you doing?" the Sheriff asked, his voice cracking.

Mac didn't respond, but continued to unload until he reached the sixth chamber. He clicked the cylinder back in place and spun it again.

"There's one live round in here, Hiram," the Marshal announced. "I'm going to spin the cylinder and ask you a question. When you answer, I'm going to pull the trigger if I think you're lying. If I believe you, I'll spin it again and ask another question. We'll keep going like that until I'm satisfied that you've told me the entire story – and told it correctly.

"I'm giving you a real opportunity here. You have one-sixth of a chance each time to tell the truth. All you have to do is make me believe you."

Hiram paled in fear.

"Good God, Marshal! Don't do this! You know I wouldn't lie to you!"

"I hope not, Hiram. Let's begin."

Clay spun the cylinder and pointed the pistol at Wagers.

"First question. Did John Scott force you to rescue Mary Beth?"

Wagers gulped and breathed in short breaths.

"Yes, I mean no! I mean he threatened me!"

McDowell cocked the pistol.

"No, no!" Wagers shouted. "I misunderstood him! He didn't really force me to do anything!"

Mac released the hammer and spun the cylinder again.

"So, this was your idea?"

"The Colonel really suggested it and…"

The Marshal cocked the weapon and trained it on Wagers' forehead.

"No!" he cried. "It was my idea!"

Mac spun the cylinder again.

"Were you the one who pistol whipped Logan and killed Daisy Hanson?"

"I didn't mean to, Clay! I just wanted to knock them out so we could rescue Mary Beth! Honest!"

Another spin of the cylinder.

"Where did Scott take Mary Beth?"

"I don't know. Believe me, I don't know!"

Mac cocked the pistol.

"I don't know!" Wagers bellowed.

The revolver clicked on an empty cylinder and the Marshal stepped closer to the Sheriff and again gave the cylinder a spin.

Wagers was perspiring and could move no further.

"I don't know, Clay!"

McDowell pulled the trigger, and again it hit on empty.

"You got to believe me! I don't know!"

He took another step toward Hiram and squeezed. Another blank.

By now, Mac was just a few feet away. He pulled back the hammer and placed the barrel directly between Wagers' eyes.

"For God's sake, stop it!" the Sheriff clamored. "They went to the Cave! They'll hide out there until Scott can get her to Alabama!"

Another spin.

"And, where's the Cave?"

"It's east of Old Cane Springs! It's in a big rock ledge near the county line! The Confederates use it as a hideout and a post office. Messages and people go through there all the time and get delivered to God knows where! I swear, that's the truth!"

"One final question, Hiram. Are you a member of this secessionist group?"

Wagers was now on his knees, arms and hands flattened back against the wall.

"**NO!** I don't need to be! All they want from me is to look the other way, and sometimes I'll do them a favor!"

"Did they ask you to free Mary Beth?"

"No, that was my idea! John and Mary Beth Robinson are friends of mine and I knew the Yankees would hang her as a spy. I thought I could get away with it if I blamed everything on John Scott and said that he forced me to do it. I planned the whole escape myself and just got word to Scott that he should take Mary Beth after we got her out of the room. He showed up earlier than I expected, but we didn't plan to kill anybody. It just happened."

McDowell grabbed a handful of Wagers' shirt and lifted him back on his feet. Logan's revolver remained in his other hand.

"Are you going to shoot me?" Wagers yelped.

"No, Hiram, I'm not going to shoot you, I'm just going to do **THIS!**"

Using the pistol as a club, he slammed it into Wagers' face, bloodying his mouth and nose. He swung it again and knocked out the Sheriff's front teeth. Hiram slid to the floor, holding his face in his hands.

"Oh, God, you broke my nose!" he screamed.

For good measure, Clay kicked him in the ribs.

"The difference now between you and Logan is that you'll live," he said.

"But, if he dies, I'll be back."

Chapter XII

The Post Office

The Old Cane Springs Area of Eastern Madison County was like a piece of the Old South. It's appearance and culture were similar to that of Mississippi and Georgia with huge farms tending to be more like plantations and the way of life strictly southern and its politics undeniably Confederate.

McDowell had heard more about the area than he had seen. Its "Confederate Post Office" was legendary, a network of messengers and dispatchers who delivered letters, notes and cards throughout the South to civilians and soldiers alike and who transported Southern Sympathizers safely to home ports and fields of battle in a timely and efficient manner.

Folks in Madison simply called it "The Post Office." But the new network of spies, raiders and demolition experts described it as "The Caves." The new name accurately described the rocky outcropping, which was pocketed by chambers of various sizes and descriptions. Many were equipped with provisions, water and sleeping facilities. It was a great hideout for overnight marauders and even those who required an extended stay.

No one ever said who serviced the area, but it was suspected that a dedicated team of Old Cane Springs residents maintained the caves with food, drink and blankets. Thick woods hid the area and it was possible to ride past without ever knowing it existed. But, pity the poor soul who might ride in unannounced. It was a one-way trip for strangers and those who had no official business being there.

Clay knew he was taking a chance. But he suspected it was the primary hiding place for the Southerners who called themselves "The Group." And, if he were to get a lead on any of their activities, he needed to make a visit. A man alone would have greater success than a posse. He could always claim he was lost and had wandered in by mistake, and hope for the best.

Mac was in no hurry. A relaxed and casual rider would

attract less attention. He thought that until he heard the shot that killed his horse.

The missile hit his mount in the head, and the gelding fell to its knees and rolled onto its side, pinning McDowell's leg. Two more shots just missed as Clay lay on his back, partly protected by the body of the horse.

The shots were coming from a hill, and, after a while, he determined it was a lone shooter with a repeating rifle. 'Probably has one of those new Henrys,' Clay guessed.

After some acrobatic twisting and turning, Mac got his single-shot carbine from its saddle sling. To use it, however, he'd have to expose himself to the fire from the hill. He was pinned under and pinned down with nowhere to go.

Mac kept maneuvering his leg and finally pulled it loose, minus his boot. He reversed his position, pulling himself behind the horse's haunches where he had more cover. He fired two blind shots with his pistol, then sprinted toward the base of the hill where there were trees and other cover.

The shooter levered one shot after another as Clay slid behind a pile of rocks. He felt one round jerk at his shirt sleeve, but his luck continued as he'd not been hit. They exchanged fire for a time and Clay realized he was wasting ammunition at a target he could not see. However, his location was such that it was a difficult angle for the shooter to get a good bead on him.

Mac began to work his way up the hill. He wasn't drawing as much fire as earlier and wondered if his opponent might be running low on ammunition himself. It was tough going with one unshod foot, but Clay kept at it and was nearing the top.

"That's far enough! Drop it and turn around!"

McDowell had been concentrating on his climbing and had not heard his assailant moving down and behind him. He had paid the price for his lack of attention.

"Now move over toward that ditch!"

There was a deep crevice in the rock, a good place to dump a body. Unless he thought of something quick, he'd be residing here soon, Mac thought.

The lookout with the gun motioned for Clay to move

quickly, which he tried to do, but the sharp rocks made for rough going. Mac stumbled and grabbed for his bootless foot, rolling onto his side in pain. He pushed himself into a sitting position, gritting his teeth as he pulled sharp fragments from his foot. He used his left hand while he dropped his right toward the top of his remaining boot. His hand found the derringer and he removed and cocked it in one motion as he slid it down to his side.

"Damn! This really hurts!" he exclaimed, removing shards from his sock. "Give me some help!"

"Get up! Or, I'll shoot you where you sit."

McDowell struggled to his feet and leaned against the rock wall, raising his left foot off the ground.

"Now, move to that gully!"

"You've got to be joking!" Mac replied. "I can't put any weight on this foot!"

The gunman gave Clay the opening he was seeking. He shoved the Marshal toward the crevice with one hand, placing himself slightly off balance. Mac jerked the derringer toward the gunman's midsection and the .44 slug ripped through his would-be assassin.

McDowell watched as the body rolled downhill, stopping when it struck a boulder. He "borrowed" the lookout's boot and slipped it on, and, although it was too small, it enabled the Marshal to reach his dead mount and retrieve his own footwear.

Mac ran his hands though the dead man's pockets, and extracted a note.

A.

'Next shipment will be in Culpeper in two days. Have lost our printers, will be delayed until new ones found. Major will handle details. Use him for upcoming.'
M.B.

Who was 'A?' Someone, obviously, in Virginia. Another spy? Probably. Only M.B. was certain. It had to be Mary Beth. The lookout was charged with handing off the note to the next messenger. Zak Holston? That was likely.

Clay took the man's Henry and remaining ammunition and covered the body with rocks. The repeating rifle was new and extra ammunition was available. It was a real find. Mac found the lookout's horse in the woods behind the hill, switched saddles and again headed toward the caves.

No one approached or followed him on the open trail, but when Mac turned off and entered the woods, he knew he was being watched. He couldn't see it, but could feel it. Picking his way through the heavy woods, he knew he must be closing in on his destination. And, suddenly, there it was. A limestone barrier nearly three-stories tall, and there was no way up.

Clay walked the horse along the base of the cliff, stopping when he reached a clearing where someone recently had camped. A rough walking trail led up the side of the precipice. He tied the horse to a tree limb, checked his pistol loads, and shoved one weapon into his waistband. He then began to climb.

It was rough going, but a plus in that it's rugged course would discourage someone from discovering a hideout.

Clay continued his climb until reaching a ledge that leveled off toward a cave. He hauled himself up and paused to catch his breath. He was drenched with perspiration and out of breath. He sat and recovered before continuing.

He drew his revolver and cautiously moved toward the entrance. No one was at the mouth, so he entered and saw a light further down the corridor. Cloth bags were stored along one side, quickly identified by the Marshal as containers for the counterfeit money. This load, he guessed, was on its way to Virginia and, probably, Washington, where it would be used to further deplete the value of the U.S. dollar.

The cave was huge and had been made larger by some man-made tools. Clay eased past a corner and froze. A man was bending over and stuffing something into a sack, but the Marshal knew him, although his face was not visible.

Mac must have made a sound, as the Major drew his pistol and fell to the ground. Caught off-guard, Clay drew back against the wall, but Holston chambered two rounds and, by chance, one struck the Marshal's weapon, knocking it from his hand.

The shot so numbed Clay's hand and arm that he could not draw the other pistol. He ducked as Holston continued to fire, then crouched and ran for the mouth of the cave.

Holston was right on his heels and Mac ran for the ledge, but slipped and fell. He rolled off the walkway, but caught himself before he fell to the ground, some forty feet below. He, literally, was hanging by his fingers.

His feet caught an outcropping, but the Marshal was suspended in a vulnerable position as the Major ran up before him. Holston stared down at Clay and paused, obviously enjoying the lawman's situation. The Major cocked his weapon and aimed between Mac's eyes.

"Hold it, Major!"

John Scott walked onto the ledge, his pistol aimed at Holston's head.

"Ease up, Zak," he said. "I don't want you to shoot my friend."

Holston snarled and kept his pistol aimed at McDowell.

"How many damn Yankee friends do you have?"

"Just a few," the Colonel responded. "But I don't need you to clean out the few I have. Now, **BACK OFF!**"

Reluctantly, Holston stepped back and re-entered the cave. Scott gave Mac a hand up and stared at him with his arms akimbo.

"What in the hell are you doing here, Clay! That stupid SOB would have killed you!"

The Marshal sat and leaned against the wall.

"I guess I owe you one, Scott," he said. "Just doing my job."

The Colonel turned toward the cave and kicked some loose stones.

"Don't give me that!" he complained. "You shouldn't even be here!"

"You know better than that, John," Clay said. "You know I had to follow up on Mary Beth and the money affair."

"Look, you damn hardhead! I can't be available every time you poke your nose into places it's not wanted! Just go home and mind your own business! Aren't there enough civilian crimes to keep you busy?"

Clay was exhausted and wiped his brow with his sleeve.

"Why don't you and Kirby Smith appeal to Jeff Davis to give up? We can get along a lot better if we're not on opposite sides!"

"Go home, Clay, and don't come back! You're going to get yourself killed if you keep being so nosy."

Mac wiped his face and reflected.

"John, I'd like to think you didn't pistol-whip my deputy," he said.

"Dammit, Clay, you know better than that! I like Logan and I wouldn't do anything to hurt him! That stupid sheriff of yours is another matter. Have you questioned him?"

Clay smiled and looked at Scott.

"Your betcha! I just wanted to ask ... for the record."

"How's he doing?" the Colonel asked.

"Logan? I'm not sure. He still hadn't regained consciousness when I left."

Scott shook his head.

"I'll sure be glad when this war's over and Gen. Lee takes over the White House."

"Lee? Even if you win, don't you think Jeff Davis would assume the presidency?"

The Colonel shook his head.

"Naw, Jeff has no interest in running the country. He didn't even want the Confederate presidency. Marse Lee would be the one to do it and he'd do a great job.

"That man is the best leader this country has produced in a hundred years."

Clay rested his back against the rock wall.

"I guess you won't hand over Mary Beth or give me the counterfeit money in those bags?"

"You know better than that, Clay!" Scott smiled, shaking his head. "Forget that you ever saw anything and just go home. You've got a real enemy in Zak Holston and the next time you see him may be your last."

"You know I'll have to come back," Mac said.

"You do and I may have to shoot you myself. This operation

is bigger than anything you can imagine and the less you know the better."

Clay looked down, then back up at his adversary.

"I know a lot more than you think, John. I know this operation extends all the way to Washington and is part of a plot to end the war. It involves the President and his family and we can't let this happen. I'm just sorry that you're involved. I wish you could get out now before you come to any harm."

"For God's sake, shut up, Clay! You're in no position to dictate terms and you know it. Get your sorry ass on that horse and get out of here … NOW! This conversation can only lead to one of us getting killed, and I've got the upper hand. LEAVE … NOW!!"

Mac rose to his feet and announced his departure.

"Thanks, John," he said, "I owe you more than I can say. Let's get together and swap lies when all this is over."

Scott shook his head as he shook hands with Clay.

"Just keep your head down and stay out of things that don't concern you. And, take care of that deputy. I think a lot of that boy."

As Mac began his descent, Scott saw his mount down below.

"Say, that looks like one of our horses."

"It is," Clay responded.

"Either you're a horse thief or you had a disagreement with our lookout and he lost."

"He shot my horse," Mac explained, "then he started picking on me. And, you're right, he lost."

"I guess you're going to keep that horse," the Colonel declared.

Mac took another step down, then paused.

"Chalk it up to the spoils of war."

Scott sighed and placed his hands on his hips.

"As God is my witness, I don't know why I put up with you."

Clay looked up and grinned.

"See you soon, John."

Chapter XIII

The Opera House

The playbill caught his eye as he passed the Opera House.

McDowell turned his mount to take another look. "Julius Caesar" the poster read in twelve-inch letters. "Starring the Renowned Edwin Booth." Then, in smaller letters, "featuring Junius Booth and J. Wilkes Booth."

Further down, it was noted the play would begin a seven-day run next week.

Mac tied his horse to the hitching post and entered the theatre. He passed the ticket window and walked directly to the manager's office. Arvil Haskins was going over some paperwork as he called for the Marshal to enter.

"I see you've got the Booth brothers here in another week," Mac said after introducing himself.

"I didn't know you were one of their fans," Arvil smiled.

"Well, I've only seen Edwin perform, but this could be something really special. I don't imagine the brothers work together very often."

Haskins nodded, "You're right. I had to work hard to pull this off, but this is going to be a huge event for Lexington. I hope to have a sellout every night."

"How much do you know about the Booths?" Mac asked.

"Only that they're great actors," Haskins replied. "Edwin, with that deep booming voice, is in a class by himself. Junius is top-notch and, I understand that young Wilkes is beginning to make a name for himself."

"Let me rephrase that," the Marshal explained. "I meant, what do you know about them other than their acting ability. What kind of people are they? What are their political leanings? Who are their friends?"

"I have no idea, Marshal. I see that you're interested in something other than their talents as thespians. I'm more concerned that they know their lines and show up on time.

John Ford has booked them at his theatres up East and is really high on them. Why do you ask? Is there a problem?"

McDowell shook his head.

"Not necessarily. I just hear that John Wilkes is some kind of political zealot when it comes to the war. He's a dyed-in-the-wool advocate for the Confederacy, and I don't want him creating any problems around here. You don't mind if I talk with the Booths do you?"

"Help yourself," Arvil offered. "Edwin will be here within the next few days and the brothers won't be far behind."

"Is it okay if I look around?" Mac asked.

"Just don't fall over any props. It's pretty dark back there."

Clay walked backstage and found himself in an area marked "Dressing Rooms." He opened one door and peeked in. It was cold, gray and bare except for a few tables and chairs. The next room was surprisingly better. The floor was carpeted, the lighting was substantially improved and the walls were in pastel colors. 'Must be a women's dressing room,' he mused. He opened another door and was startled to see a woman in her undergarments pulling up a skirt.

"Whoa!" she exclaimed, covering herself with hands and arms.

Clay blushed, muttering a hasty apology as he backed out of the room and closed the door.

"Just a minute!" he heard the feminine voice say. "Give me a chance to cover up!"

McDowell hesitated, not certain if he should leave or stay. Then, the voice was heard again.

"Come on in," she called. "It's okay."

Mac removed his hat, took a deep breath and stepped inside. No one was there.

"Over here," he heard the voice from behind a dressing screen. "I'll be out directly."

He heard footwear being dropped and the dragging of a chair.

"I need to see the man I'm to marry," the voice announced. With that, a beautiful woman stepped out, fluffing her hair into place. She smiled at Clay.

"In New Orleans, a gentleman is required to marry a lady if he sees her ankle, and you've seen much more than that. Tell me your name so I can inform my daddy, who, incidentally, owns the biggest shotgun in Louisiana."

"My sincere apologies, ma'am. My name is Clay McDowell and I'm looking through the theatre as part of an official investigation. I'm a U.S. Marshal," he related, extracting his wallet and credentials from an inside coat pocket.

"I'm Pauline Cushman," she replied, "not a ma'am, but a miss ... unfortunately. I'm also an aspiring female lead who intends to perform before kings and queens, heads of state, chieftains and potentates. But first, I need to finish my run here.

"Let me see your credentials."

Clay passed his wallet across and Pauline grinned as she viewed his badge and identification.

"Pauline Cushman McDowell," she intoned, adding his name to hers. "Has a nice sound to it. Let's see, there's a church just down the street. Why, we can have everything nice and legal by this time tomorrow. May I call you Clay, Marshal or just 'husband'?"

Clay purposely had no reaction. He stared at her for several seconds, reached for his wallet and stuffed it inside his coat.

"Hm-m-m," she observed, "a reluctant bridegroom. What could be the reason?"

Pauline folded her arms, walked back and forth in front of McDowell, her lips pursed as if in deep thought. Suddenly, she stopped.

"Oh, no! Are you married?"

"No, I'm a widower," he said.

"Ah, that's good ... I mean, that's not good your wife is dead ... I just mean it's good that you're single ... available ... unattached ... you are available, aren't you?"

Clay couldn't contain himself. He burst out laughing and shook his head.

"Lady, you do have a one-track mind. Since you're determined we're to be married, may I call you 'Pauline'?"

"Please do, Marshal," she chuckled. "And, I can't tell you how relieved I am that you're eligible and available. Especially, when I'm so close to the altar. Now, let's get down to basics.

"Other than matrimony, to what do I owe this visit? Am I being investigated?"

"Not at all. I'm doing some routine investigation, some preventive maintenance, actually, where war activities are concerned."

Pauline shook her head.

"Well, you do sound like a government man. Are you saying there's a deep, dark plot against President Lincoln and you're trying to stop it? And it's going to take place in a theatre, for goodness sake? This could make a great play!"

"No," Clay laughed. "Just routine. Why would you think there's a plot against the President?"

"Well, there is a war going on and this part of the country is not all pro-Union."

"Is that a political observation?"

"No, just the observations of a traveling thespian."

Clay smiled and nodded that he understood.

Pauline, however, changed her demeanor, suddenly becoming serious.

"I hear a lot of things traveling from town to town," she said. "If there is a plot against the President and if you're investigating it, I'd like to help."

"Hmmm, is that right?"

"Absolutely," Pauline replied.

Clay was surprised at the sudden change in attitude. Pauline reached for a dressing table chair.

"I'm really serious, Marshal," she declared as she seated herself. "I can be useful as a Union spy. I've offered my services to the Louisville Federal provost marshal and I've already been involved in some activities. In fact, I was fired at the Woods Theatre in Louisville because I offered a toast to Jeff Davis and the Confederacy. But, in the process, I earned the trust of Southern sympathizers and, unfortunately, the indignation of Union supporters. However, I did all this with official Federal approval."

McDowell frowned, then smiled in recollection.

"So, that was you!" he exclaimed. "I read about that in *The Louisville Journal.*"

'And,' he thought, 'you must be the one Philip Miles has mentioned.'

"How about it, Marshal? I really want to help," Pauline appealed.

Clay pulled his chair closer.

"I'm not saying there's any kind of plot against Mr. Lincoln or anyone else where the Union is concerned. But all of us hear rumors and idle talk. Most of it has no substance. However, if you'd really like to keep us informed about what you see and hear, there may be a way you can help. If you're really serious, let me do some checking. Give me some time and be patient. Let's see what develops."

Pauline's features softened. She blinked her eyes and her long lashes and smiled. 'Wow!' Mac thought.

He was quite taken with her beauty and personality. Which gave him an idea.

"Tell you what. Why don't we combine business with pleasure?" he suggested. "How about having supper with me tonight?"

"Good! You like me! However, I'll do it only if you attend tonight's performance," she replied. "I want you to see how good an actress your future wife really is."

McDowell rolled his eyes.

"That wife thing again," he snarled in mock indignation. "Okay, **MRS.** McDowell, I'll be here right after the performance, so be prepared to be swept off your feet. Incidentally, what's the play?"

"It's called 'A Rustle of Silk' – about a jilted Southern Belle and a reluctant bridegroom," she grinned, then paused for effect. "Sound familiar?"

"Don't get any ideas," he warned.

"More importantly, don't **YOU** get any ideas!"

Clay stood, preparing to leave.

"Your charm, grace and beauty are exceeded only by your dogged determination," he smiled as he kissed her hand. "See you tonight."

"Don't be late, lover," Pauline grinned.

McDowell made his way to the courthouse, wired Miles in Washington, and, an hour later, was informed that Fred Thompson had received a reply. Fred looked up as Mac entered the telegraph office and waved a long sheet.

"It's an answer to your inquiry," he reported.

Clay unfolded the sheet that contained detailed information. It was almost as if Phil were expecting his query.

Pauline Cushman, born in New Orleans as Harriet Wood, had moved to Michigan with her family and changed her name when she went to New York at age 18 to become an actress. There was other biographical material and additional information that supported her potential as a secret agent. She was appearing in "A Rustle of Silk" in Louisville when two paroled Confederate officers offered her $300 to toast Jeff Davis during her performance. The Union provost officer approved the endeavor, recognizing that the expression of secessionist loyalty would give her entrée into Confederate camps and could make her a valuable Union spy.

Miles suggested that McDowell take her into his confidence.

Clay pocketed the information and drew a long breath. 'This could be an interesting evening,' he reflected.

Mac hired a rig and tied up behind the theatre. His seat was near the stage and he watched the play with interest, impressed by the charm and personality Pauline brought to her role.

'Maybe I'm prejudiced,' he thought, 'but she really is good.'

The Marshal waited until most of the audience departed, then made his way toward the dressing rooms.

Clay stopped at Pauline's dressing area, gently knocked and announced himself. Pauline opened the door and smiled.

"Come in, Marshal, and tell me how great I was," she winked. "I'll change while we talk."

McDowell hesitated when he saw the other women. Pauline shared the room with four other actresses who were seated in front of mirrors removing makeup. They turned, smiled at Clay and invited him in as he reluctantly sat in a spare chair at the opposite side of the room. He returned their greeting with an embarrassed nod of his head.

"This is U.S. Marshal Clay McDowell, ladies," Pauline announced. "He and I will be dining at the hotel this evening."

"Oh-h-h," they exclaimed in unison.

"Can I come along, Marshal?" a pretty redhead grinned.

"Not a chance, Alice," Pauline replied in mock defiance, her hands on hips. "He's all mine."

She turned toward the dressing screen, then looked back at Clay.

"I'll change back here," she nodded at the screen. "If that's okay with you," she smiled.

Clay returned her smile and nodded. Alice grinned and nudged Claire, the girl seated next to her, who chuckled and whispered in the redhead's ear.

"Well, Marshal," Pauline began, tossing her costume on top of the screen. "Didn't you think I was great? I thought my speech in the second act was worthy of an award."

She stood on tiptoes and smiled at the lawman over the screen.

"You're the best, Miss Cushman," Clay grinned. "A beauty with your personality will go far."

"And maybe even in the theatre, too," Claire snickered.

Alice elbowed her and stifled a laugh.

"Please, remember, you're supposed to be a lady," she snorted, biting her lip.

Pauline, visible only to the other actresses, made a shushing sound, holding a finger to her lips.

"Alice, how about giving me a hand?" Pauline asked.

The redhead joined her behind the screen and, in a few moments, Pauline stepped out wearing a royal blue gown. Highlighted by a white sash, lacy collar and trim, it was dazzling. The scent of a suggestive perfume and her provocative hourglass figure were addictive bonuses.

"Well, what do you think, Marshal?" she asked, smoothing her skirts.

McDowell smiled his approval as she slowly twirled around.

"I think I'm a lucky man," he replied. "You're beautiful."

Clay offered his arm and Pauline waved as they walked to the door.

"Oh, Pauline," Alice sighed, clasping her hands to her chest. "I'm green with envy."

Pauline gave a theatrical smug as Clay closed the door. She stopped as they entered the hallway.

"I hope you're not offended by my friends," she said. "You just received a dose of theatre humor instead of proper etiquette. They're rather bawdy, but really nice people. It's just their way of unwinding."

Clay shook his head.

"No offense taken. They're a delight."

McDowell halted the carriage at the stage door and helped Pauline negotiate the stone steps that aided her entrance into the cab. She snuggled close to him as he drove toward the hotel. As they turned onto Main Street, the carriage unexpectedly struck something and Pauline was thrown against Clay. She took his arm and steadied herself.

"Are you alright?" the Marshal asked.

"I am now," she smiled. "You don't mind if I hang onto you for support do you?"

"Not at all," he grinned.

"This is so nice," Pauline cooed, resting her head on Clay's shoulder. Shortly, she began to hum.

"What's that tune?" he asked.

"It's a new song called 'Aura Lea.' A baritone sang it when I performed in Louisville. It's so beautiful I can't get it out of my mind. It's become one of my favorites."

Clay smiled, but kept his eyes on the road. She felt good curled up against him.

They dined by candlelight, the soft glow enhancing Pauline's striking features. She was very desirable.

Clay cleared his throat.

"I hate to destroy the mood, but I need to ask some questions," he said.

Pauline dropped her gaze to the table, then looked provocatively at Clay and smiled.

"Then ask away, Marshal."

"Do you know the Booth brothers?"

"I take it you mean Edwin, Junius and that good-looking younger brother, John Wilkes. I had an under-sixes role once with Edwin and a walk-on with Junius, but I've never met Wilkes. I'm sure you know they'll be doing 'Julius Caesar' here next week."

"Under-sixes? What's that?" Clay asked.

"That's a bit part where you have six lines or less. I'm sure Edwin and Junius don't even remember me, but they're fine actors – especially Edwin. He has a dominating presence and the voice of God."

"Would you know John Wilkes – or Wilkes as you call him – if you were to see him?"

"Oh, absolutely," Pauline replied. "I saw him once in Albany with his brothers and asked who he was. He's a handsome specimen, dark-headed, lean and moves like an athlete. He's almost as good-looking as you," she grinned.

"Right … uh, thanks, Pauline," Clay growled. "But, you could identify him?"

"Why do you ask? What's he done?"

McDowell, taking her into his confidence, explained how Wilkes might be involved in a plot against the Lincolns, mentioning the attempted kidnapping of Mary Todd, the counterfeiting ring and Confederate post office.

"I ultimately report to Hill Lamon who's with the Marshals service in Washington and is the President's self-appointed body guard," Clay continued. "Lamon's convinced there's a spy network that extends from Kentucky and Tennessee into Virginia and Washington. He's mentioned that Booth, a John Surratt, Junior, and a fellow named Lewis Powell, among others, are the key conspirators. I have fugitive warrants for the arrest of some of the Kentucky and Tennessee people and we need someone who can keep an eye on Wilkes. Could you do that?"

Pauline thought for a moment, then nodded.

"I'm scheduled to be in Virginia soon at the Richmond Theatre. One of the girls said Wilkes also was supposed to be there. Sure, I can keep my eyes and ears open."

"Good!" Clay smiled, squeezing Pauline's hand. "Send me a wire about anything you find. I'll show you how to code it so only you and I will know what it's about."

Pauline reached for Clay's other hand.

"Now I know how to get your attention," she replied, then sighed. "Although it's not of my choosing, I need to get some rest, Marshal. I've got a final performance tomorrow."

Clay accompanied Pauline upstairs to her room and waited as she unlocked the door.

She turned and smiled seductively.

"Sorry I can't invite you in, Marshal. How about another time?"

The hall was deserted. McDowell bowed and kissed her hand. Their eyes caught and held and Clay moved closer, then, instinctively, slowly pulled her to him. His kiss was strong and passionate and Pauline willingly returned it. She finally pulled away, blinked her eyes and caught her breath. She cocked her head slightly and caressed Clay's cheek.

"You're going to make a great husband," she said softly.

Clay smiled and again pulled her toward him, but Pauline put a finger across his lips.

"Let's save something for later, dear heart."

Pauline stepped inside, partly closed the door, pressed her face to the narrow opening and smiled.

"Good night, Marshal," she softly whispered, then mouthed a good night kiss.

Chapter XIV

Edwin Booth

Logan Perry still was recuperating in Richmond. With his talkative deputy missing, the office was quiet as a tomb, and Clay was in a hurry to get going. Edwin Booth had arrived and today was the day Mac planned to visit him at the Opera House.

The Marshal was halfway through the door when he paused, thinking he might need something to encourage their conversation. He returned to the desk and removed a small jug from the bottom drawer. He stuffed the vessel in a saddlebag and left for the theatre.

Clay entered the playhouse with the jug in hand and was delighted to learn the actor had arrived and was in his dressing room. His knock was answered immediately with a dramatic, "Please enter."

Edwin Booth's appearance was everything one might expect where a prominent thespian was concerned. He was handsome, distinguished looking, and – as advertised – possessed the deep, powerful voice of a god. He stood as Clay entered and clasped the Marshal's hand in a strong grip.

"You must be Marshal McDowell," he said. "I was told that you would be meeting with me concerning an urgent matter."

Mac was impressed. Booth had a commanding presence, not unlike that of the Roman politician he would be portraying.

"Perhaps urgent is not the proper word, Mr. Booth," the Marshal said. "However, it is an important matter that concerns your brother."

"Junius or Wilkes?" Booth asked.

"Wilkes," he replied.

The actor walked away, then returned to face Clay.

"Is this concerning a breech of contract or an offense that may be relevant to our engagement in New York?"

"Is there something you need to tell me?" Mac asked.

Booth took a step back and studied the Marshal, hands on hips.

"Perhaps you first need to tell me the reason for your visit."

"I need some information about Wilkes," Clay stated. "And, if there is any reason to believe he is in violation of an agreement or rule of law, you would be wise to provide that information."

Booth motioned for Mac to take a seat.

"It was my understanding that the breach of contract charge was dropped when Wilkes appeared with us as scheduled at the Winter Garden," Edwin said. "True, he did not show up for rehearsals, but he was there for our performance. And, I might add, our production of 'Julius Caesar' was well received and the performance was hailed as 'the greatest theatrical event in New York history.'

"I also understand that the proceeds from that engagement were more than sufficient to fund the statue of William Shakespeare in Central Park, as planned.

"In view of that, I had hoped that this breach of contract incident would not continue to haunt us. Believe me, there is no need to persist with this matter."

Mac's interest was aroused.

"Then, why was the breach of contract charge made?"

"The theatre management became alarmed when Wilkes did not appear for rehearsals," Booth explained. "He was three days late and just arrived in time for the performance. We did the show with no prior preparation, other than the fact that each of us had performed our roles previously. Wilkes played Mark Antony, Junius was Caesar and I had the larger role of Brutus. Wilkes not only remembered his lines, but performed with a spontaneity that won the hearts of the audience.

"It was a remarkable performance, if I must say, particularly since it was the first time that we had performed together."

Clay was surprised.

"So, your performance next week is only the second time that the Brothers Booth have appeared together?"

Edwin nodded.

Although he was totally surprised by the actor's misunderstanding of his visit, Mac saw the opportunity to use it to his advantage.

"Is Wilkes prone to go his own way, not honor a contract nor obligation?"

"Not necessarily," Edwin said. "He does tend to be a free spirit, but I have emphasized to him there is much to be gained by us performing together. And, he knows how important it is to honor the contract for this engagement."

"Obviously, you hope that Mr. Haskins will have no reason to consider breach of contract possibilities."

Booth leaned toward the Marshal as if to take him into his confidence.

"I very much doubt that Wilkes will create any problem. However, I have contacted another actor who is ready to step in should a difficulty occur."

"So, the show will go on?"

Edwin nodded.

"Trite, but true."

Clay had placed the jug on the floor when Booth invited him to be seated. The actor had glanced at it several times, and curiosity got the better of him.

"What is it that you have there?" Booth asked.

"This?" Mac responded, picking up the jug. "I have an appointment with a friend this afternoon who enjoys good bourbon whiskey. I promised to bring him a sample of a new recipe developed by an acquaintance."

Booth smiled.

"I don't believe I've ever sampled Kentucky bourbon, although I've been told that it is the best ... oh, what's the term? ... best sipping whiskey in the world."

"That it is, Mr. Booth," Mac replied. "Would you like to have a taste?"

"Do you think your friend would mind?"

"Not in the least! There's plenty here."

Clay lifted the jug, removed the cork and handed him the container. Booth jiggled it and sniffed.

"It has an unusual aroma," he said.

"It has an even better taste," Clay said. "Take a sip."

Edwin lifted the jug in both hands and took a swallow, some of the liquid spilling onto his shirt.

"Oh, sorry to be so messy!" he said, flicking at his shirt front.

"You didn't get a good taste," McDowell announced. "You need to hold a jug like this."

Clay ran his forefinger through the loop and rested the container on his forearm. He lowered it to his mouth and drank several mouthfuls.

"This is the way to enjoy good bourbon," he said. "Now, you try it."

Booth followed his lead and drank deeply.

"My!" he exclaimed. "That's delightful!"

"You're getting the hang of it," Mac said. "Try it again."

Edwin took another drink, paused, and drank again.

"I could get used to this!" he said.

"Oh, what was it we were discussing?"

"I was asking about your brother, Wilkes," Clay stated. "You don't mind if I ask a few more questions do you?"

He motioned for Booth to take another drink, which he did.

"What else do you need to know, Marshal?" the actor asked. "I sometimes get quite frustrated with him, which, I guess, older siblings tend to do. But, the lad really is talented and he should have a brilliant career if he would just focus on the theatre.

"John Ford, who is a friend of the family, owns the Holliday Street Theatre in Baltimore and gave Wilkes some of his early acting opportunities. He helped Wilkes get some roles in Philadelphia and continued to encourage him even after the lad performed so poorly in 'Lucrezia Borgia.'"

"What happened?" Clay asked.

Booth took several more drinks and continued.

"Well, the lad experienced stage fright and stumbled over his lines. Instead of introducing himself by saying, 'Madame, I am Petruchio Pandolfo,' he said, 'Madame, I am Pondolfio Pet – Pedolfio Pat – Pantuchio Ped – Who am I, dammit?'

"People roared with laughter and a reviewer said Wilkes played his parts with such enthusiasm that audiences were wild about him, even when he did forget his lines.

"Wilkes played 'Hamlet' with me in Virginia and did the role of Horatio so well, that I led him out for a special curtain call. The audience was absolutely thrilled with his performance."

Clay encouraged Booth to imbibe some more.

"In view of what you've said, why do you question his focus?"

Edwin was becoming very relaxed and enjoying his conversation with the lawman.

"Wilkes gets sidetracked too easily," he said. "Just like failing to show up for rehearsals and instigating issues of contract violation. Want to know why he missed those rehearsals?"

"He got involved in something else?" Clay inquired.

"Yes, he did!" Edwin slurred. "He's been running around with some people in Washington for some time that have no interest at all in the theatre. He was doing something with them and forgot all about our 'Julius Caesar' performance. Junius had a friend in Washington fetch him to a train and journey with him to New York. This friend delivered him to the Winter Garden just in time to get into costume.

"I ask you, Marshal. How could you forget a major benefit like that in New York? Would you forget to show up?"

"Good point, Mr. Booth. It would seem something major is distracting him."

Booth turned up the jug, then shook it.

"Marshal, I'm afraid there won't be much remaining for your friend."

"Don't worry, Mr. Booth," Clay assured him. "I've another jug at my office. Go ahead, enjoy yourself."

Edwin did, then smiled and exhaled.

"Where were we, Marshal?"

"We were discussing how good an actor Wilkes is, but how easily he becomes distracted," Mac summarized. "What's the source of this distraction? Is it politics?"

"Precisely!" Booth belched. "What a waste of time! Wilkes has become a staunch secessionist. You may have heard that he lost favor in Albany when he called the South's secession 'heroic.'

"Wilkes became interested in political science as a teenager, and has never lost his fascination for it. He has been outspoken in his love for the South and of his intense dislike for the

President. Although we are from Maryland, our family is not political by nature. We would never denunciate the North nor Mr. Lincoln."

By now, Edwin could be described as being "deep into his cup." He drained the remaining contents of the jug and sat it on the floor, looking at Clay through bleary eyes.

"You understand now, Marshal, why I get so frustrated with Wilkes? He may be the best in a family of dedicated thespians. So, what does he do? He tends to throw away his extraordinary talent for a political adventure.

"If he doesn't show up for next week's performances, I'm done with him!"

McDowell steered the conversation toward specifics.

"This political distraction of his ... do you know anyone who may have a negative influence on Wilkes?"

"There's a Surratt family and some others in the Washington district and Maryland," Booth replied. "Wilkes seems to be in league with them and some silly schemes that never come to fruition."

"What kinds of schemes?"

"They sometimes come to visit with Wilkes and I've heard them make such outlandish proposals as kidnapping Federal officials, disrupting the economy and playing havoc with logistical activities. It's all hogwash! Ideas that interfere with theatrical pragmatism!"

"When do you expect Wilkes to arrive?" Clay questioned.

"Oh, any day now. Although, I do wish it were soon. There were a few lapses in the New York engagement that require some attention and we do need to find solutions to a few scenery difficulties. Some items were damaged on a set for the Roman senate. Mark Antony is the key character in most of the scenes and we'll have to change the blocking to compensate."

"You must also be directing the play?"

"One must assume many roles in the theatre, Marshal," Edwin explained.

"I would like to speak with Wilkes when he arrives," Mac commented.

Booth did not appear favorable to such a meeting, but shrugged it off, saying, "I would hope this would conclude discussion of the alleged contract violations."

"Unless it occurs a second time," McDowell allowed.

Edwin recoiled at the suggestion, unaware that Mac again was using the incident as a ploy.

"I'm looking forward to seeing next week's performance," the Marshal said, rising to leave.

"I'm glad you'll be attending," Edwin smiled. "I think you'll find that the Booths know their Shakespeare."

"And, I hope Wilkes won't disappoint either of us," Mac added.

As it turned out, Wilkes did not show up and Edwin had to employ another actor for the part of Mark Antony, and, at his own expense. Edwin was furious and McDowell was simply curious.

He hoped Pauline would turn up something soon.

* * *

One of the ironies of the Booth family relationship with the President occurred later in 1865. Edwin was waiting on a train platform in Jersey City, New Jersey, late one evening as passengers were purchasing sleeping car passages from a conductor. There was a crush of individuals making purchases when the train began to move and a person fell into the opening between the platform and the entrance to the car.

Edwin Booth seized the individual by the coat collar and pulled him up onto the platform. The person, whose life had been saved by the actor, recognized Booth immediately and profusely thanked him. Months later, Edwin received a letter from Col. Adam Badeau, an officer on the staff of Gen. U.S. Grant, who informed him that he had saved the life of Abraham Lincoln's son, Robert, who then was a captain on Gen. Grant's staff.

Chapter XV

The Message

The man looked as if he were a fugitive from a Victorian opera. He wore a frock coat and a stovepipe hat, carried a cane and spoke in a clipped British accent.

"May I see the chief law enforcement official please?" he inquired. "I believe he's a chap known as Clay McDowell."

Logan Perry, back from his Richmond recuperation, turned from his desk and carefully studied the visitor.

"And whom shall I say is calling?" Logan asked in his best English prose.

"Donald J. Strathmore, sir, formerly of London and Stratford-on-Avon ... my card."

Perry took the card, which informed him that Strathmore was a "Thespian, Playwright, Author and Shakespearean Orator."

"Pardon me, Mr. Strathmore, what's a Shakespearean Orator?"

"I recite the Bard's most significant declamations," he replied.

"Such as 'To be, or not to be'?"

"Precisely. The Melancholy Dane ... his soliloquy is one of my specialties."

Perry tapped the card several times against a thumb and suppressed a smile.

"Just a moment, Mr. Strathmore, I'll see if Mr. McDowell is accepting visitors at this hour."

Logan opened the back door and met Clay who was returning from the stable. He handed over Strathmore's business card.

"A most proper gentleman who claims London as his hometown has asked to see you," the deputy explained. "But before you do, just remember that every path has a few puddles. Watch where you're stepping."

"You mean sometimes you get, and sometimes you get got?" McDowell asked.

"Hey, that's good! Hear that from your granddaddy?"

"No, from a bank robber in Pike County."

Clay pushed open the door and sauntered toward his visitor.

"I'm Marshal McDowell, Mr. Strathmore," he announced, extending his hand. "What can I do for you?"

"I have a private communiqué for you, sir," Strathmore said, handing Clay an envelope. "I believe you know a Miss Pauline Cushman?"

The container was sealed and "Clay McDowell" was written on the cover in feminine script.

Clay opened it and saw it was, indeed, a two-page document from Pauline. It was an extensive message, written on the front and back of both sheets. He scanned it hurriedly, then looked at the messenger.

"Pauline … Miss Cushman … gave you this?"

"She did indeed, sir, and asked me to deliver it to you personally. I recently completed my engagement at the Richmond Theatre in the Old Dominion and I'm on my way to another obligation in Louisville. I'm to play a major role in 'Richard the Third,' you see."

"How is Miss Cushman … is she well?"

"Most assuredly, but she seems a bit agitated. I had the sense that she penned the document in haste."

"Could she have been afraid, of something or someone?"

Strathmore straightened himself and peered about the room.

"Are we alone, sir?"

"Yes," Clay nodded.

Strathmore clutched McDowell's arm and stepped closer to the Marshal.

"Hell, yes, she was afraid!" he snapped. "I asked her what was wrong and she refused to answer, just wanted me to get this letter to you as fast as I could. She apologized for taking me out of my way, but said this was important and she desperately needed my help. She wanted someone she trusted to make the delivery.

"Pauline and I have known each other for several years, even performed together at various playhouses on the circuit. If the shoe were on the other foot, she would have done this for me.

I don't know what's in the letter, but I doubt it has anything to do with the theatre or her career. It must be something extracurricular.

"Now, I ask you … is she in trouble?"

"I hope not," Clay replied, "but, if she is, we'll take care of it. Thanks for delivering this. And, good luck in Louisville."

"Glad I could help," Strathmore said, tapping his hat with his cane. "Give Pauline my best and take care of her. She's what we call in the theatre 'a blithe spirit'."

He turned to leave, but stopped as Clay called to him.

"I take it you're not from London."

"Daviess County," Strathmore smiled. "I grew up in Owensboro."

Clay turned back to the letter and frowned as he read the contents in more detail.

Marshal –

I've run across more here in Richmond than I bargained for. Wilkes Booth showed up several days ago and I can't believe all the activity that's resulted. And, none of it is about the theatre. Please forgive my penmanship for I'm writing in haste as I have little privacy and am fearful of discovery. So far, I've avoided close scrutiny as I've played the role of a "Wilkes Girl" – these are the many female performers here who are so taken with Mr. Booth. As I've told you, he's quite handsome and attracts many admirers, who hope to engage him in conversation and be noticed.

Wilkes has a private dressing room here. He's very popular with Richmond audiences and was a stock company player for several years at this very theatre. He knows many people in Richmond and has received rave notices from a number of reviewers. Some of the theatre clippings I've seen refer to him as "the handsomest man in America" and a "natural genius" – whatever that means. He's noted for having "an astonishing memory" and his ability "to enthrall women."

One of the stagehands told me that Wilkes was thrown out of Albany some years ago because of his outspoken admiration for the South's secession. He was said to have called the action "heroic," which enraged local citizens who considered his remarks treasonable.

I've also been told that Wilkes has a lady friend in New Hampshire who's the daughter of Senator John Hale. I believe her name is Lucy. The Senator and his family evidently are unaware of Wilkes' Southern sympathies.

As the war has progressed, Wilkes seems to have appeared mostly in Union and border states. John Ford, who owns several theatres, is a friend of the Booth family and recently employed Wilkes at his new theatre in Washington. An actor friend told me that Wilkes was one of the first leading men to appear at the new theatre and starred in a play attended by President Lincoln. He said at one point in the performance, Wilkes shook his finger in the President's direction as he delivered a line of dialogue. The President apparently was amused at the incident, although several people thought it to be a threatening gesture.

I also heard that one of the President's sons saw Wilkes perform on another occasion and was so thrilled by his performance that Wilkes gave him a rose. The President invited Wilkes to visit with him and his family in the Presidential Box, but Wilkes ignored the invitation.

Mr. Ford apparently agrees with the critics who have described Wilkes as "the most promising young actor on the American stage." It's rumored that Wilkes can perform at Mr. Ford's new playhouse whenever he wants.

There are a number of individuals who seem to come in and out of the theater and speak with Wilkes briefly, either in his dressing room or in a secluded part of the building. One appears to be a "Mr. Powell" and another is a man who is

*called "John" or "John Junior." Mr. Powell is an odd sort
who sometimes displays a rather erratic behavior. He laughs
at things that aren't amusing and has a wild look about his
eyes. I sometimes believe him to be deranged.*

*Another is a man with a lengthy scar down one side of his
face who has met several times with John Junior. He never
says much, but I've seen him with a small valise that appears
to interest John Junior. The scar-faced man always leaves with
the valise. I don't know if he is delivering something or taking
something he has been given. It could be either one or both.*

*I have not been successful in engaging the visitors in
conversation and have not been near enough to overhear any
of their discourses. I will attempt to do so.*

*This document is quite lengthy and has been written during
a period of several days. I trust it is readable and helpful. I will
keep you informed.*

Pauline

Perry entered from the back door and saw McDowell
reading the letter.

"What's that?" he asked.

"A letter from Pauline Cushman that Donald Strathmore
delivered," Clay responded.

"Ah-h-h, so that's what he was about," Logan smiled. "Can
I read it?"

McDowell handed over the document without comment. He
sat at the desk and rested his chin in his hand as he considered
the letter's contents. If nothing else, Pauline had established a
connection between the Kentucky and Washington suspects.
But how deeply was the Major – Zak Holston – involved? Clay
guessed that the valise contained counterfeit notes and, possibly,
messages from the Confederate post office in Madison County.

John Scott and Mary Beth Robinson may no longer be involved since the Colonel "rescued" Mary Beth from the hotel. On the other hand, he wondered if Mary Beth was now in Virginia and still active in the Southern spy network.

The John Ford-Wilkes Booth relationship had some interesting possibilities. Booth now had a seemingly open invitation to performing at the new theatre, which President Lincoln liked to frequent. If Hill Lamon's suspicions about a plot to kidnap the President or members of the Lincoln family were correct, the theatre provided a genuine door of opportunity. And, Pauline, as well as Edwin Booth, had established that Wilkes was pro-Confederate and anti-Lincoln.

"Whew!" Perry exclaimed as he finished reading. "If Pauline's information is correct, we've got a rough road ahead. It's time to keep our fences horse-high, pig-tight and bull strong."

McDowell sighed and shook his head.

"As long as you're alive, your grandfather will never die," he groaned. "But, you're right about what's ahead. Lamon's conspiracy theory is beginning to make sense."

"Then, what's our next move?"

Clay reached for his hat and made his way to the door.

"I'm going to see if Tom Bramlette is in," he announced. "As district attorney, he'll see that the appropriate Washington folks are informed. Then, I'm going to telegraph Hill Lamon. This time, maybe he can convince the President that he needs to be cautious and on guard."

"Lincoln's too much a trusting sort, Clay," Logan offered. "I can't believe he'll listen to anyone, even Lamon. I'm surprised that Hill convinced him to be wary of a possible assassination plot when he was elected."

In that situation, the President reluctantly had followed the advice of Lamon and a Pinkerton detective and entered the nation's capital directly from Baltimore instead of riding publicly through the Maryland city. Since then, however, he had scoffed at Hill's pleas to be cautious. He refused to believe that anyone would cause him harm.

"How about Edwin Stanton?" Perry inquired. "Should he be informed?"

It was no secret that the Secretary of War was not particularly fond of Lincoln.

"The attorney general will do that," McDowell said. "Anything involving the President has to have an impact on the war effort. Ed Bates has the President's ear and I don't believe Stanton or anyone else in the cabinet would refuse to hear what the Top Lawyer has to say."

Logan shook his head in resignation.

"The President has his hands full," he remarked. "I don't envy him. Trying to work with that cabinet is like trying to herd a mess of wildcats. They can't get along with each other, much less the President."

They nodded in agreement, then fell quiet, each with his own thoughts.

"You must be proud of Pauline," Perry finally commented. "She's done a good job. I hope she's okay."

Logan must have read his thoughts, Clay reflected. If the Richmond group were on to Pauline, she was in big trouble. None of the conspirators would hesitate to dispose of the actress and dump her body in the James River. The dirty work would be done by Zak Holston. He'd love taking his "toothpick" to Pauline.

The thought sent a chill up McDowell's spine, so strong and cold that it made him flinch.

"You okay?" Perry asked.

"Yeah," the Marshal responded. "Just thinking about Pauline. I hope I wasn't too quick to get her involved."

Chapter XVI

Morgantown

Mac stood in a line of rail patrons waiting to "debark" their passenger car at Morgantown. They were halfway to Washington, but a layover was required as a new engine and cars had to be put in place for the final leg to the nation's capital. The gauge, or uniformity of track widths, varied as America struggled with its rail travel, a still young means of long-distance transportation. Until a standard gauge was effected, vehicle wheels had to be matched with rail widths as cars of one line often could not be used on that of another. This was the case at Morgantown. The substitution of engines and cars often was a long and cumbersome process, but passengers took it in stride, realizing it was better than travel in a wagon or stagecoach.

Clay, who had been called to Washington by Hill Lamon, was preparing to step onto the station platform when a waving motion caught his eye. It was a lady holding a white handkerchief. He watched the back-and-forth motion for a while before gesturing to himself and mouthing "Me?" She nodded enthusiastically.

As he drew near, his heart beat faster.

"Pauline!" he exclaimed. "What are you doing here?"

She was a vision in a blue plaid dress, complete with bonnet, parasol and reticule in white. A white shawl was draped loosely over her shoulders.

"You're looking good Marshal," she smiled, slipping an arm through his.

"And you especially!" he returned.

"Walk with me," she continued to smile, "and focus on the small talk. We're being watched."

Pauline steered their way into the depot waiting room.

"Find us a private place to talk," she whispered, sitting on one of the benches. "Do it quickly … now!"

Clay saw a buyer step away from the ticket window and promptly positioned himself in front of the screened opening. He removed his wallet and flashed his badge and credentials at the agent.

"I'm U.S. Marshal Clay McDowell," he said. "I need a secure area for an interrogation. Can you help me?"

"Are we in danger?" the startled agent inquired.

"No," Mac shook his head. "I just need some place private for a few minutes. I'll tell you all about it later. Is the station agent in?"

The ticket seller indicated he was out, but would return soon.

"Why don't you use his office? It's right over there," he motioned, "and it's unlocked."

Clay nodded his thanks and escorted Pauline into the rather spartan enclosure. He pulled shades at the door and a window facing the waiting room, then sat down before Pauline.

"Are you okay?" He clasped her hands in his as he spoke.

"I am now, but our Richmond friends are suspicious and I'm sure I'm being followed." Pauline explained. "A tall, attractive woman and a man in a gray suit seem to be everywhere I go," Pauline explained. "I wired your office yesterday and your deputy explained that you had left for Washington and had a layover today at Morgantown. I arrived here about an hour ago and a new train should be ready to leave soon. I'm on my way to Cincinnati and hope to find a theatre job there."

"You don't have a booking?" Clay asked.

"No, and I didn't have time to inquire about one. They're after me, Marshal. I'm certain of it."

She shivered and Clay pulled her to him and held her.

"Okay, Pauline. Tell me from the beginning."

She sat back, took a deep breath and began.

"I finished my engagement two days ago and realized I didn't have another booking for nearly two weeks. I thought I'd use that time to learn more about the plans of Wilkes Booth and his companions. I spread the story that some costumes and jewelry had been stolen from my boardinghouse trunk and I planned to remain in Richmond and see if they could be found. I know it wasn't a very good excuse, but it was all I could think of at the time.

"That gave me the opportunity to visit the theatre when it was dark – that's when no shows are scheduled. I managed to hang around the dressing rooms and, just by chance, saw Wilkes and this tall, attractive lady enter his room. I listened at the door and heard them talking about some counterfeit money arriving from Kentucky that would help fund a kidnapping plot. I heard Wilkes complain that '… it didn't work with his wife, but this time I'll get that tyrant Lincoln.'

"Wilkes was really exercised, but the lady was more restrained and tried to calm him. I heard her say they could hold Lincoln for ransom in Richmond. If they did, Wilkes reasoned that the President could be exchanged for the release of Confederate prisoners of war or, possibly, they could force Union recognition of the Confederate government and bring the war to an end.

"Then, Wilkes went into a tirade about Lincoln and began throwing items around the room. Something hit the door and I was so scared I started moving away. I had just taken a few steps toward the stage when Booth came out of the room.

"He screamed at me – 'You, there! What do you think you're doing!' I stopped and explained I had lost something and was crossing the stage to look for it. He immediately accused me of spying on him. I denied it and believe he would have struck me if the woman hadn't interfered. He called her an odd-sounding name … I believe it was 'Antonia.' She got him to calm down and return to the dressing room.

"I left immediately for the boarding house. I packed my things, took a carriage to the railway station and bought a ticket to Cincinnati. As I was waiting on the train, I saw 'Antonia' and a man in a gray suit some distance away. Whenever I'd move, they'd move and they boarded several cars down from me. I haven't seen them since we arrived, but I know they're following me."

Exhausted, Pauline exhaled and swallowed. Mac took a pitcher from a desk and poured her a glass of water, which she drank quickly, then gazed at the ceiling through half-closed eyes.

"There's more," she said. "And **THIS** really scares me."

"I wrote you about the man with the facial scar … they call him 'Major' and, sometimes, 'Zak' … and another who's called 'Powell.'"

Hanged Conspirators

Approximately 1,000 people witnessed the execution of four Lincoln conspirators at Old Arsenal Penitentiary in Washington City on July 7, 1865. Mary Surratt is at far left followed by the bodies of Lewis Powell, David Herold and George Atzerodt. The bodies hanged for some 25 minutes before being cut down. The gallows was constructed with supports under the "drop" portion of the platform. Two soldiers (lower photo) hold supports they would remove to activate the procedure. John Wilkes Booth (at right) was killed and did not hang. – Alexander Gardner photos

Graves of Condemned

Graves for the hanged conspirators were prepared next to the scaffold at Old Arsenal Penitentiary. Pine coffins constructed from arms boxes are stacked in front of the open graves. The bodies were removed in 1867 and released to their families in 1869. Lewis Powell's body was not claimed. – Alexander Gardner photo

Military Commission

The Military Commission that tried the accused conspirators consisted of (from left) Lt. Col. David Clendenin, Col. C.H. Tompkins, Brig. Gen. T.M. Harris, Brig. Gen. Albion Howe, Brig. Gen. James Akin, Gen. Lew Wallace, Gen. David Hunter, Gen. August Kautz, Brig. Gen. Robert Foster, Special Judge Advocates John Bingham and Henry Burnett and Judge Advocate General Joseph Holt. – Library of Congress photo

Those Hanged

The Lincoln conspirators sentenced to hang were (top row) Mary Surratt, George Atzerodt and (bottom row) David Herold (left) and Lewis Powell. – Alexander Gardner photos

Ford's Theatre

Ford's Theatre originally was constructed in 1833 as a house of worship. John T. Ford bought the building in 1861 and renovated it into a theatre. The structure was destroyed by fire in 1862, but was rebuilt the following year. It was the site of the assassination of President Abraham Lincoln on April 14, 1865. After being shot by actor John Wilkes Booth, the President was carried across the street to the Petersen House where he died the following morning. The theatre had a seating capacity of 2,400 and was described as a "magnificent thespian temple." Note guards outside the theatre with black crepe around the windows. – Library of Congress photo

Presidential Box

This photo of the President's Box seat at Ford's Theatre was taken following his assassination. The Lincolns were seated in the area to the right. – Library of Congress photo

Derringer

The .44 calibre derringer (at left) used to assassinate the President was found on the floor of the State Box following his murder. – Library of Congress photo

Surratt Boarding House

*This photo of the boarding house of Mary Surratt (white
structure) was taken in 1900, but the building essentially was
the same as it was in 1865. Mrs. Surratt initially became
connected to the Lincoln Assassination as she rented rooms to
John Wilkes Booth and his fellow conspirators. The house was
the site of conspirator meetings to kidnap and/or assassinate
the U.S. president. The three-and-one-half story structure was
built in 1843.* – Library of Congress photo

Area where
story
takes place

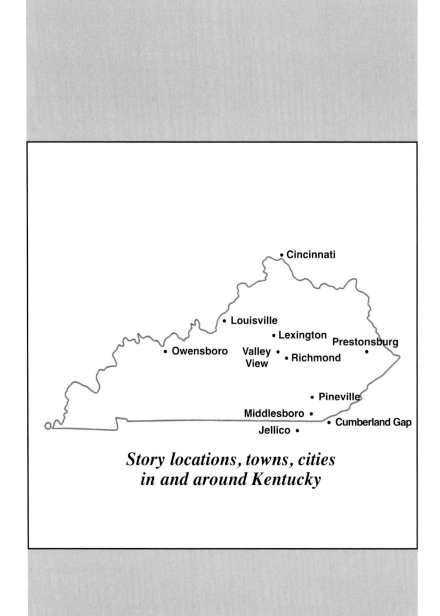

Story locations, towns, cities in and around Kentucky

"I remember," Clay nodded.

"Well, I overheard 'Zak' talking with 'Powell' while they were waiting to see Wilkes. Zak said everything was ready and they'd stop the train after the layover at Morgantown. Powell asked if they were going 'to blow the engine' and Zak said 'yes,' and then they'd attack the freight car where the gold was hidden. The gold apparently is in bars that are being shipped to Washington from Denver. Zak said the bars would be in crates marked 'Mining and Farm Implements.'"

Clay frowned and looked away.

"That doesn't make sense. Why would gold bars be transported to Washington instead of the mint in Philadelphia?" he asked.

"I don't know Marshal," Pauline wearily interrupted, "but that's what he said ... and **YOU'RE MISSING THE POINT!! "THEY'RE GOING TO BLOW UP THE TRAIN THAT YOU'LL BE ON!!"**

She slumped in her seat and covered her face with her hands.

"No! No! No!" Pauline cried. "This is insane ... all of it! How did I get mixed up in this craziness!"

Clay resisted the urge to hold her. He merely sat, expressionless, waiting for Pauline to regain control. He held up a warning finger as she raised her head.

"Stop it, Pauline ... right now! You're tougher than this! What I've asked you to do is no picnic, but it gives us an edge – an upper hand. We couldn't ask for more. With this information, we'll stop this 'craziness,' as you call it.

"And, yes, I'll be on that train they want to destroy. But everyone from the station staff to law enforcement will know about the threat and we'll stop it. We'll win! And you're going to win, too!

"I'll wire the Hamilton County Marshal about the threat on your life and when you get to Cincinnati he'll see to it that 'Antonia' and 'the man in gray' are either disposed of or taken into custody. And, for added insurance, take this."

Clay handed over a small, but deadly derringer.

"This is a .44-calibre weapon that'll make the biggest hole you ever saw. It's loaded and all you have to do is cock it – like this – and pull the trigger."

Mac eased the hammer back down and placed the derringer in Pauline's palm.

"Just be close to your target – not more than ten feet away. One shot is all you'll need. The result will create enough uproar to discourage anyone else from bothering you.

"Hang on to the weapon. If you don't know how to reload it, ask a lawman or a soldier to help you."

Clay then handed her his office card.

"If they have any questions, give them this card and tell them to wire me because you're under my protection. And tell them if you're harmed, I'm coming after them.

"Got it!" the Marshal snapped.

Pauline stood with amazement.

"I've just seen another side of you," she stated with surprise. "I had no idea you were so forceful and I must say I like it. I like it very much!"

"One other thing, Pauline. Put the derringer in your purse so can have easy access to it."

"You mean my reticule?"

"If that's your purse, yes, put it in your reticule. Then, all you have to do is place your hand inside and fire the pistol without having to remove it ... from your reticule."

"Oh, Marshal, I can't do that!"

"Why not?"

"Why it would ruin my reticule and upset my ensembles. That white color goes with just about any spring or summer gown I have."

Clay looked away in disgust.

"Damn it, woman, I'm talking about saving your life! I'll buy you a hundred ... uh-h reticules!"

Pauline placed the derringer in the reticule and smiled sweetly at Clay.

"Marshal," she said, placing her arms around his neck, "you really do love me, don't you? I know you won't say it, and you don't need to. But, we'll work on that after we're married.

"Now kiss me!"

The ticket agent knocked on the door and entered as they embraced.

"Uh-h, pardon me, Marshal," he said. "If you're finished with the interrogation, it's time for the young lady to board her train."

* * *

Antonia Ford sat on a bench, the back of which was against the facade of the Morgantown Depot. The bench was near the end of the building and some distance from the front door. It afforded a good view of who came and went, something she could do with a minimal chance of being seen herself. The "man in gray" stood next to her, leaning against the structure with his arms folded.

As ever, she was the perfect image of a beautiful and refined lady. Her green and white gown was stunning. A broad-brimmed matching hat was pinned on the back of her head and her hand rested atop a folded green parasol. Her dark hair and violet-colored eyes would make any gentleman look twice.

"Here she comes, Roger," Antonia announced, "and she's alone."

The "man in gray" stood upright and watched as Pauline boarded the "new" train bound for Cincinnati. He could see her movement through the passenger car windows as she found a seat and positioned herself so could take-in the outside view. He waited, looking to see if the Marshal would join her. He didn't and when the conductor cried "All Aboard," Roger nodded at Antonia and boarded quickly. He would buy a ticket from the conductor and find a seat where he could keep an eye on Pauline.

Antonia allowed herself a knowing smile. Everything was falling into place. Roger would take care of Pauline, which left her with responsibility for the Marshal. Since he hadn't joined the actress, Antonia would follow the lawman on the trip to Washington. Although not planned, she was used to revising decisions on the spur of the moment, something that was a prerequisite in the craft of secret agentry. JEB Stuart and John Singleton Mosby held her in the highest regard and Stuart had even awarded her a commission as an honorary aide-de-camp. Rose Greenhow, the celebrated Washington mistress of Confederate espionage, had long utilized Antonia as a courier and considered her one of the South's best agents.

Unknowingly, Pauline and Clay now were trapped in a web spun by undercover experts. And, this time, the spies would take no prisoners.

Chapter XVII

Antonia

"Look, we've got a problem here and I need your help!" Mac declared.

The Morgantown station and ticket agents and the conductor of the transfer train to Washington sat with McDowell in the station agent's office. They were veterans, men used to handling crisis situations, whether they occurred before trains arrived or if they were en route.

"What do you need?" Jack Donaldson, the stationmaster, questioned.

"We're used to dealing with headaches," Clayton Pellar, the station assistant, acknowledged. "What's the crisis?"

"There's a group of Southern partisans – I don't know if they're soldiers or civilian volunteers – who are supposed to derail the train to Washington," Clay began. "They believe there's some gold bullion on board in crates labeled 'Mining and Farm Implements.' According to our intelligence sources, they'll attack the train after it leaves Morgantown, blow up the engine and take the crates. I have no idea what they're planning where passengers are concerned, but we've got to assume they'll do whatever is necessary to get the gold. They also may raid the coaches and rob the passengers."

"Forget about the gold, Marshal," Donaldson said. "We had a gold shipment come through here two days ago and it was sent on to Philadelphia. The gold was in bars from Denver. They've had so many thefts and attempted robberies they don't even attempt to make coins in their mint anymore. They're melting everything into bars these days and, mostly, sending it to San Francisco. We had some Treasury agents here who alerted us about the shipment to Philadelphia. We passed it on without problem.

"We've been told there's a Confederate army detachment out of Texas that's been preying on Denver gold. My guess is that this time they got some false information."

"Regardless," Mac stated, "this train is going to be attacked. What can we do to stop it?"

"My guess is that they'll try to torpedo the engine," Matt Flynn, the conductor, said.

"A train torpedo, essentially, is a mine that's placed between the rails and is activated when the engine rolls over it. The explosion is big enough to derail the locomotive and disable the entire train. It's like a ship being dead in the water. After that, they're free to attack the train and take whatever they want."

"Is there any way to prevent that?" Clay asked.

"What we've been doing is to place one or two flatcars ahead of the engine," Donaldson explained. Pellar nodded in agreement and indicated for Jack to continue.

"That way, the flatcars are damaged if they hit a torpedo and we don't lose the engine. The train still is disabled, but at least we don't lose the locomotive."

"That's an expense we need to avoid," Pellar added.

"But, either way, the train still is disabled?" McDowell asked.

"Right," Donaldson acknowledged. "But, at least we save the railroad some time and money."

"Okay, let's concentrate on defending the train after it's stopped," Mac proposed. "We need some firepower … what can we get that's immediately available … artillery or small arms?"

Donaldson and Pellar stared at one another, each waiting for the other to speak. Finally, Donaldson offered a possibility.

"It'll have to be small arms," he said. "It would be great to have a piece of artillery, but we don't have time. In fact, I don't know if we can round up enough men to fight with pistols and muskets. What we need are some Union infantry."

Pellar snapped his fingers.

"Got it!" he cried. "There was a lieutenant who came by this morning with a wagon and some men who were headed into town for provisions. I'll send a runner to find them. The lieutenant can commandeer extra weapons and ammunition if he has to and he has at least a full squad with him that we can place in the freight cars."

Fortunately, it took but a few minutes to locate the soldiers. There were nine men in all, including Lt. Sean Murphy, and, quickly, they were each armed with extra weapons, including revolvers. The plan was to shove open the freight doors when the raiders rode up and open fire.

"Where do you think they'll hit us?" Clay asked.

Donaldson walked over to a wall map and indicated an area that appeared to be about five miles east.

"There's a creek that runs from here over to Reedsville to the south. It's fairly level ground and, once the train is stopped, they could attack from either or both sides."

He tapped the map location several times with a pencil.

"That's where I'd attack," he said.

"I agree," the lieutenant concurred. "We'll be ready when we're stopped. I don't think we can miss hearing or feeling the explosion."

"Lieutenant, why don't you and your men be the last to board," Mac suggested. "I don't know if the opposition has any lookouts or not, but I'd rather have as few people see you as possible."

"Will do, Marshal," Murphy agreed. "We know the value of surprise."

Clay gathered his carpetbag, stripped off his gun belt and placed the weapon inside. He then checked the load of a second revolver already in the satchel. His final act was to slip his badge inside a coat pocket. For this occasion, he needed to blend in.

Mac boarded the passenger coach nearest a freight car where several of the soldiers were located. He found an empty seat about midway down and positioned himself near the window. A newspaper lay on the floor, which he retrieved and began to scan.

His attention was attracted by a feminine voice at the entrance of the car.

"Excuse me!" she uttered several times as she walked along the aisle carrying a large package. The contents were wrapped in brown paper and tied with a string. A carpetbag was clutched in one hand that also was underneath the bundle.

She was a beautiful woman with a winning smile and several men stood, asking if they could assist her.

"No thank you," she responded, "I can manage."

And, she almost did.

As she neared Clay, she tripped and the package fell to the floor. Clay immediately came to her aid. He scooped up the package, which, surprisingly, was very light, and deposited it on the seat. He then offered his hand to the lady and invited her to be seated. Not so ironically, she seated herself next to him.

"Thank you, sir," she smiled. "You're very kind."

She sat on the aisle-side of the bench, took a deep breath and dabbed at her face with a lace handkerchief. She then turned to smile again at Clay.

"You must forgive my clumsy entrance," she said in a soft southern drawl. "You must think me a terrible bother."

"Not at all ma'am," he acknowledged. "You seemed to have your hands full – literally."

"Oh, silly me, I saw this beautiful material and just had to have it," she explained. "When I left Richmond, Sophia – she's my dressmaker – suggested that I purchase some colorful silk for a new ball gown. I'm afraid I got carried away and obtained more than will be needed."

"So you're from Richmond?"

"Yes, my father, Edward, is a merchant there. He's rather prominent … perhaps you've heard of him?"

"And his last name is …?"

"Oh, how stupid of me. I failed to provide his last name. It's Ford … Edward R. Ford.

"I also must apologize as I've failed to introduce myself," Clay said. "My name is Clayton McDowell of Lexington, Kentucky."

"I'm very pleased to meet you, Mr. McDowell. My name is Antonia Ford," she announced, offering her gloved hand and a calling card.

Mac took her hand and bowed his head. He masked his surprise and managed his best smile, realizing that this must be the "Antonia" who was following Pauline.

"I'm charmed to meet such a gracious lady."

"Thank you, sir, but I fear that my instructors at the Buckingham Institute would find my manners and graciousness sadly lacking."

Clay's mind was racing. The Buckingham Female Collegiate Institute was one of the more prominent schools for women in Virginia. Only the very well-to-do and academic elite were invited to attend.

Antonia was putting on an act. She had to be the lady targeting Pauline and the one who was associated with Wilkes Booth. But where was her accomplice – the "man in the gray suit?" Was he on the train or was he on another mission?

What if they had separated and he was stalking Pauline? He chilled at the thought. And, if that were true, why was Antonia with him?

'I'm the one who's stupid,' he thought. 'Antonia must know my identity and plans to eliminate me at the first opportunity.'

Antonia was making mindless chatter and Clay would nod and smile occasionally as if he were listening. Finally, she turned toward Mac.

"And what is your occupation, Mr. McDowell? If you're from Lexington, I'd wager that you must be involved in horses or horse racing."

"Well, yes, Miss Ford, I do have a modest horse farm and have been known to invest in a thoroughbred or two."

He paused and stared intently at Antonia as he said, "I'm also involved in law enforcement."

She had no visible reaction.

"Well, how interesting! You have two livelihoods. Are you also a magistrate or, perhaps, a prosecutor?"

"No, Miss Ford, I'm a U.S. Marshal. I serve the Eastern Kentucky District."

She brandished a broad smile.

"Well, I never! You can meet the most interesting people when you travel by rail."

Conversation was interrupted as the conductor asked for their tickets.

"Are you, by any chance, fond of the theatre?" Clay asked, steering their discourse in another direction.

"Why, yes, I am. Have you ever visited our lovely playhouse – the Richmond Theatre?"

"Unfortunately, I have not," Clay replied, "but I understand one of the favored actors there is John Wilkes Booth. Have you by chance met him?"

"I believe he's the brother of that darling Shakespearean actor, Edwin Booth," she said. "Edwin is one of my favorites."

"I understand that Wilkes Booth can be a very controversial sort on occasion," Mac continued. "I'm told he's a staunch Confederate sympathizer who's not hesitant to express his views."

"Oh, this terrible war!" Antonia complained. "I prefer not to be caught up in it. I'll be so glad when it's over."

"I agree," Clay said. "It's not only the fighting, but all the disruption it causes on the home front. You wouldn't believe all the clandestine activities I have to investigate."

Antonia feigned her surprise and shook her head.

"Imagine that!" she declared.

The thunderous explosion shook the train and brought it to a violent halt. Passengers and baggage were thrown forward against seats and into the aisle with such force that windows were shattered and benches were ripped from floor attachments. Clay's head struck the side of the car, rendering him temporarily addled. As he fought through the waves of darkness, he saw that Antonia had been thrown into the aisle and had collided with another passenger. He pulled her back onto the splintered seat and saw she was bleeding from a nasty gash near the edge of her hairline. He put pressure on the wound with his handkerchief and gently tapped her cheeks as he called her name.

Antonia's eyes finally fluttered open.

"Keep applying pressure with this handkerchief," he ordered.

As she did so, Clay felt the floorboards for his carpetbag. He found it wedged against some stanchions with other baggage under the seat in front of him. Mac had to lie on the floor and fish for the valise with an outstretched hand. His fingers finally closed around a strip of the fabric and he was able to drag it to him.

At that moment, a loud scraping sound signaled attempts to open the entrance to the coach. Antonia struggled to her feet and signaled someone who was leveraging the door with his shoulder. Clay stood and saw a familiar face.

Zak Holston acknowledged Antonia and, with a final heave, opened the door and leveled a revolver at Mac. Clay fell to his knees and fumbled in the bag for his pistol.

Antonia threw herself on top of him and tried to pin Mac to the floor. Clay freed one hand, shoved it in Antonia's face and savagely pushed her into the aisle. Grabbing the weapon, he got his feet under him and was raising up when a shot whined past his ear and buried its missile in the side of the car.

Holston fired twice more, shattering the bench providing Clay's cover. Mac dropped to the floor, but realized in all the chaos he had nowhere to go.

Unmerciful Zak had him at his mercy.

Chapter XVIII

The Attack

The gunfire sent passengers into a panic. Men threw themselves on the floor atop the injured and pulled the women down with them. Clay had to stand to return fire and was hesitant to do so as he presented such a clear target for Holston. He could feel the Major at the ready, waiting for a clear shot.

McDowell desperately needed a break, and the incensed "train captain" was about to give him one.

Conductors often were paranoid about the safety of their trains. Responsibility for their iron transports and passengers was taken seriously, much like a she-bear prepared to defend her cubs to the death. Matt Flynn was no different.

Although he knew the pileup was coming, the devastation was a personal tragedy. Oblivious to the raiders on horseback, he ran through the gunfire examining the damage to each car as he passed. The freight car had snapped the coupling with the adjoining passenger coach and both vehicles had been derailed. Hearing gunfire inside the car, he ran up the steps and peered though the back window. Everything now was quiet except for the occasional cry of a passenger calling for help.

Flynn tried the door and a hard shove threw it open, causing him to stagger inside. An alarmed Holston snapped a shot at the figure and Flynn was hit in the throat. Zak stepped back anticipating returned fire. Mac instinctively bolted for the rear door and, in a stooped-over dash, somehow avoided being hit as he lunged through the opening.

Clay, however, stepped into another bloodbath. Dead and wounded men were scattered along the ground and riderless horses galloped wildly for open spaces. He felt rather than saw something about to strike him and ducked as the butt of a carbine was swung at his head. The Confederate trooper rode past and Clay's shot hit him between the shoulder blades.

A shot struck the passenger car and flew splinters into

McDowell's face. He blinked and saw the shooter kneeling as he reloaded. Clay leveled two quick shots at the bearded soldier and one of the rounds blew a hole in his chest.

Mac fired until his revolver was empty, then jerked open the carpetbag and withdrew his other weapon. He didn't have an opportunity to use it, as a glancing blow from behind knocked him into the ditch alongside the tracks. His hat cushioned the impact, but the one who delivered the clout was on top of him as he rolled. Clay saw Holston swing his pistol to strike him again, but was able to grab his wrist. He ran his other hand behind Zak's forearm and, with both hands, forced the revolver from his hand.

Clay shot an elbow into his assailant's face, knocking him onto his back. As the Marshal struggled to his feet, Holston pulled a blade from his scabbard and slashed at McDowell. Clay kicked the Major in the knee as the Arkansas Toothpick missed its mark. Mac jumped astride Holston as he fell and they struggled for possession of the long dagger.

Zak had both hands on the knife and tried to force it at Clay's face. But being on top, the Marshal had more leverage and slammed the butt of the weapon to the graveled turf. He rotated a forearm onto Holston's throat and began to apply pressure. The toothpick fell from Zak's hands as he grabbed at the arm cutting off his breath.

Clay pushed harder and, with his left hand, felt for the knife. He grasped the handle and thrust the blade into the side of Zak's neck, driving it in nearly halfway. Blood spurted from a severed artery as the wide-eyed victim clawed at his throat.

McDowell rolled off the Major and felt a pistol under his hand. It wasn't his, but he hoped it was loaded. As Union soldiers paused to grab back-up weapons, two riders swung from their horses and into the freight car. Clay thumbed two quick shots and the raiders fell back onto the track.

Another trooper charged his horse at Mac and tried to run him over. The Marshal jumped back, but was sent sprawling from a kick delivered by the rider. He hit the ground and rolled away, keeping his grip on the revolver. As the mounted man turned his horse, Clay squeezed the trigger and the trooper grabbed his chest, but leveled his weapon at Mac. McDowell felt a sharp sting at his shoulder and fell, but his next shot hit the rider chest high and he tumbled from the horse.

Clay continued to fire until the weapon was empty, but suddenly there were no more targets. The silence was surreal.

He heard boots crunching on the gravel and a hand reached down to pull him to his feet.

"It's over, Marshal," Lt. Murphy announced. "We surprised the hell out of 'em. The ones we didn't kill rode off."

"How many did we lose?"

"Don't know yet," Murphy announced. "I've got two men wounded and another who's not going to make it. Some of the railroad men got shot up, but several were armed with shotguns and made a good account of themselves.

"That fireman is a real warrior. He took two men out with a hunk of wood from the tinder."

McDowell found his revolvers and carpetbag. He strapped on his gunbelt, reloaded and shoved the spare pistol into his waistband. The carnage was reminiscent of a major battle. A number of cars were derailed and the freight vehicles were riddled with bullet holes. Dead and wounded men and several horses were scattered over a compacted area of some fifty yards. The lieutenant and some of his men were shooting wounded horses and the uninjured were tending to the wounded.

Removing his coat, Mac checked his wound and discovered it was more of a crease. He placed pressure on it with his bandana. One of the passengers who was helping with the injured, saw the Marshal and wrapped the fabric around the wound and tied it in place.

"Thanks," Mac said. "How are the others?"

"We've got three with broken bones, but mostly bumps and bruises," the woman answered, then returned to assist a passenger who was a physician.

Clay pulled the pistol from his waistband and cautiously peeked into the coach where he had been seated. The car was mostly empty now as passengers had been taken outside into injured and non-injured groupings. Flynn still lay where he'd fallen, but there was no trace of Antonia.

Mac checked for her outside without success. She must have fled with the raiders, he guessed. The thought of such a prim and proper lady riding horseback amused him. She'd have to dispose of her skirt and hoops to manage it, or, she could have driven or ridden away in a wagon – one intended for transporting the sought-after gold. Either way, Antonia would have found a way. He doubted she considered any task without having a backup plan.

The engineer hailed McDowell as he examined the area where the torpedo had exploded.

"We hope to get another train here soon to take everybody back to the Morgantown station," he said. "We caught one of the horses and sent a rider back to make arrangements. It's going to take a while to get the track cleared and repaired, but we'll get on the road to Washington as soon as we can."

"You know the conductor is dead?"

"Yeah," the engineer lamented. "Matt was a good man. I guess if there's any good news, it's that the locomotive is okay. The rails look to be in good shape and when we can get a crew to take care of the derailments, we can back the engine into the station."

"Sounds good," Mac commented.

He walked along the track and stopped as he reached the damaged passenger car. Two men were removing Flynn's body. He waited until they left and entered the coach for a final look. He stood in the doorway and ran his eyes across the devastation. The interior was littered with carpetbags and their contents. He stepped over the bloodstains where the conductor had been killed and ambled to the front.

'I'm wasting my time,' he thought. 'I don't even know what I expect to find.'

He started walking back when something caught his eye. It was the package that Antonia had brought on board. He pulled it from under the seat where it was lodged, removed the string and drew back the paper.

'Well, it's sure not silk,' he grinned to himself. 'She wouldn't want a dress made from this.'

It was a collection of rags of every color and description.

They were clean, but appeared to be destined for shop use. The paper and string appeared also to have come from the Depot.

'Antonia's not a bad actress herself,' he reflected. 'A fake stumble and a dropped package for someone to recover; then, an offer of a seat from your intended victim. Puts you in a good position to assist with his assassination.'

Clay kneeled and began rummaging through other wreckage remains where he'd found the package. The carpetbag was on its side, but still was closed. However, a hurried look at the contents confirmed that it belonged to Antonia. There was an envelope bearing her name, but no address. It had arrived by messenger.

Antonia –

I've sent this by one of the General's messengers, hoping it will arrive before critical information can be obtained by your friend, Frankie Abel. The General has reason to believe that she's a Union counterspy.

She apparently is only posing as a refugee from New Orleans, which is a ruse to enable her to gain your confidence and that of the residents of Fairfax. I understand that you and your father have taken her into your home and are caring for her as if she were a member of your family. Do not show her any documents or have any communication with her that could be detrimental to our cause. Also, be cautious about your contacts with the General and the Colonel. For the time being, it might be better for you to contact them though me.

Also, see if you can obtain any information from Miss Abel that might be helpful to us. When you feel it might be appropriate to remove her, I'll ask the Colonel to handle that task.

Keep me informed concerning the plans of our thespian. We'll continue to gather executive information that might be of assistance to him and his efforts.

Roger will be available to assist you with the problems our thespian is experiencing. He will contact you at the theatre.

Rose

Although names and identities were not disclosed, it was obvious the message concerned information about Confederate espionage activities. Antonia evidently was a spy as was "Rose" and Frankie Abel was spying on Antonia. The "thespian" had to be Wilkes Booth, who was planning a major activity, something that may have to do with President Lincoln. The "General" and the "Colonel" could be any major players in the Confederate army, but, most likely, officers who soldiered out of Virginia.

Clay guessed there was no hesitation to "remove" someone by the most violent means. He and Pauline had been targeted for removal as had Frankie Abel. He was helpless to do anything more for Pauline, but wished he knew the whereabouts of the "man in gray." That must be "Roger." He just hoped Pauline remembered how to use the derringer.

A railroad crewmember saw Mac and called to him through the doorway.

"Hey, Marshal! A work crew is on its way from Morgantown and should be here directly. With any luck, we should have the track cleared and be back at the depot tonight."

"Is the engine operational?" Clay asked.

"Sure is! We can put it in reverse and back into the station."

Mac walked toward the end of the train, noticing that most of the cars still were on track. Four carriages might have to be removed, he observed, but that would go quickly once the maintenance crew arrived.

He hoped the raiders hadn't cut the telegraph line. He needed to wire the marshal in Cincinnati about Pauline.

Surely she could point and shoot.

Chapter XIX

The Meeting

Although he had lost a day's travel due to the raid, McDowell was able to leave Morgantown the next morning. This train was non-stop into Washington City and he'd be at Ward Hill Lamon's office before he could wire him, which he couldn't, as the cut wires wouldn't be repaired until some time in the afternoon.

Mac had taken a window seat and was viewing the countryside when someone said, "Excuse me," and wedged himself and a large carpetbag into the vacant aisle accommodation. He was very average in height and appearance and, apparently, very tired. His eyelids were in a "half-staff" position and he quickly covered a sizeable yawn.

"You've already had a hard day," Clay observed.

The passenger glanced at Mac and nodded.

"I feel like I've been traveling forever," he said. "I finally got from St. Louis to Cincinnati, but had to turn back at Portsmouth because of a train wreck. They said I had to go back to Cincinnati, but, by the time we got there they got the wreck fixed and put me on another train to Morgantown. I was laid over another night until I finally caught this one. I haven't slept but a few hours the last three days.

"I have to change again in Washington, and, after another layover, I'm headed to Manassas."

"You live in Manassas?" Clay asked.

"Used to, but I live now down near Lynchburg. I'll get there in another day or so, that is if I can get through all this in one piece. I'm not a good traveler, but, in my business, travel is a necessity, not an option."

"What type of business are you in?" Clay inquired.

"I used to be in the wholesale and retail grocery business. That was before the war. Now, I'm a sugar broker."

"Must be a tough business, what with the war and all?"

"Well, at least it's a living. I've got a wife and five children to support."

"So, you used to live in Manassas?" Clay inquired. "Did you leave before the war started?"

"Humph! I had to leave because of the war! It started in my backyard."

"You're joking?"

"No, I'm not. A Union cannonball came through my fireplace and nearly killed my children. Gen. Beauregard – he's a Confederate officer – made my house his headquarters and our lives were pure hell from that day on. Finally, we had enough, what with the military running around and through our place all the time. So, I recently pulled stakes and we moved to a little town near Lynchburg that's so small that not even God knows about it, much less the Civil War."

"So, why are you going to Manassas?"

"I still own the house and farm there and need to be sure it's in one piece. Then, it's on home."

The storyteller yawned and rested his head on the seat back. He soon was asleep. McDowell guessed he must have dozed off himself as the next sound he heard was the conductor calling, "All out for Washington City!"

Clay pulled out his carpetbag and nudged his companion.

"We're in Washington," he said.

Still half asleep, the man rubbed his eyes and fumbled for his grip. They remained seated, waiting for the aisle to clear.

"I never did introduce myself," Clay said, extending his hand. "I'm Clay McDowell."

"Wilmer McLean," the man replied. "If you want to get away from it all, come and see me at Appomattox Court House. No one knows it exists."

McDowell and McLean parted ways at the station and Clay hired a carriage to take him to Ward Hill Lamon's office.

Hill Lamon was an imposing figure of a man. He was 6-foot-4 and well over two hundred pounds. He loved good whiskey and a good fight, and could handle himself with aplomb where both were concerned. The Winchester, Virginia, native had been Lincoln's friend and business associate for some twenty years, and when Honest Abe was elected president, he devoted himself to serving and

-127-

protecting the Commander-in-Chief. This was despite the fact that the rest of Lamon's family was loyal to the South.

Eighteen years younger than the President, Lamon first had been introduced to Lincoln in 1848 in Springfield, Illinois, when he was a young practicing lawyer. Although much different in personality and demeanor, they each saw something in the other that resulted in a strong bond. It was said that the President totally trusted and depended upon Lamon and that the latter responded with an unusual devotion and loyalty.

After his election, Lincoln had informed Lamon that he needed him in Washington and that he should be prepared "for a long stay." Hill was appointed U.S. Marshal for the Washington district in 1861 and had devoted himself to the protection of the President as no such person or agency were available for such a task.

In turn, Lamon had sought individuals he could trust to support his efforts for safeguarding the President. Phil Miles of Virginia and Maryland Marshals Roy Barnes and Jack Lewis were among those appointees. And, as Miles had informed Mac, the Kentucky marshal was being included in that close-knit group. That's why, he was told, that he needed to be in Washington for this meeting.

"Gentlemen," Lamon began, "the four of you know the basis of this meeting. I am firmly convinced there is a group or organization solely dedicated to kidnapping or assassinating the President. You also are aware that Mr. Lincoln strongly objects to my constant efforts to protect him. He shrugs off the idea that anyone would use him as a pawn or kill him to change the course of this war. Very honestly, he believes me insane upon the subject of his safety.

"In addition, you know that we have reason to believe we have identified individuals involved in this kidnapping/assassination plot. And, these same individuals are dedicated to destroying the U.S. economy by counterfeiting or any other means to bring the nation to its knees.

"The Washington district, Maryland and Virginia are locations where this plot is most active and centered. But other states also are involved, particularly the Eastern District of Kentucky, which is where Clay McDowell is located. Clay already has uncovered some subplots that tie in with the overall plan, and I'll ask him to report on these activities in a few minutes.

"I know you've heard stories about me having slept outside the President's bedroom armed with pistols and Bowie knife. Well, those stories are true, particularly the one concerning the night of Mr. Lincoln's inauguration. I also have patrolled the White House grounds on a regular basis. And, perhaps you don't know, that on at least one occasion, I have uncovered those who wished to do the President harm.

"One evening, I found a man hiding in the bushes and hit him between the eyes. Unfortunately, the blow killed him, but, in searching him, we found him to be a Southerner in possession of two pistols and two knives.

"But, I digress. Here are some names of individuals we believe to be involved in a Presidential plot, and, please, commit these names to memory: John Wilkes Booth, Mary Surratt, her son – John Surratt Junior, Lewis Powell, George Atzerodt, David Herold and Michael O'Laughlen. There may be others, but we believe these individuals to be ringleaders.

"Mrs. Surratt has a boarding house on High Street that serves as an unofficial headquarters for the plot. We know that Booth stays there during his frequent Washington visits. The others have either visited there or have been boarders.

"We need to keep the boarding house under surveillance, and here's where we need the participation of each of you."

Lamon indicated each of the four marshals.

"We have rented an upstairs room in a house across the street from the Surratt establishment. We want the four of you to conduct around-the-clock surveillance of what goes on, who enters and leaves, and so forth at the Surratt house. We'll do this in two-man, twelve-hour shifts with my brother, John – a deputy marshal, providing support as needed. Gather and write down as much information as you can, including the time and date. This information will be used in obtaining warrants and as possible evidence in court.

"We'll begin surveillance this evening. Your meals will be brought to you and beds will be available. Any questions?"

Miles raised his hand.

"Will we make any arrests?"

"No," Lamon replied. "You would make an arrest only if an outright crime were committed, such as a shooting or stabbing or similar assault on an individual. We don't anticipate that will happen. Basically, you're here to gather evidence."

"Will we have contact with anyone in the Surratt house?" Lewis asked.

"No!" Lamon emphasized. "As I mentioned, unless an outright crime were to be committed, just observe."

"What if we were to accidentally meet or have contact with one of the suspects? What should we do?" Barnes queried.

"Carry it off as if it were an accidental meeting," the head Marshal stated. "Don't engage in an extended conversation. The suspects don't know you. Keep it that way."

Other than queries about meals and incidentals, there were no more questions. Lamon then turned to McDowell for additional comments.

"Some of this you already may know, but let me give you a quick summary. An attempt was made after the Battle of Richmond – that's Richmond, Kentucky, gentlemen – to abduct First Lady Mary Todd Lincoln. We were able to abort that attempt, although one of those involved in the plot, we discovered, was a double agent. Deputy Marshal Mason Sanderson was shot and killed and one other culprit escaped. The man who escaped is Zachary, or Zak, Holston. He's also called 'The Major.' He and I have been combatants on more than one occasion and, in the most recent encounter, I killed him near Morgantown on my way here to Washington.

"Col. John Scott, a Confederate cavalry officer out of Louisiana, has been deeply involved in the counterfeiting activity as has one of his spies, Mary Beth Robinson of Madison County. Mrs. Robinson also is an accomplice of another spy, Antonia Ford of Fairfax, Virginia. I also have had run-ins with each of them.

"Wilkes Booth also has been active in the transport and distribution of counterfeit money. As an actor, he frequently performs in Kentucky and Virginia and has excellent access to Washington for delivery and distribution.

"We have been able to establish a spy of our own, Pauline Cushman, an actress and native of Louisiana, who has been gathering information on clandestine activities in Kentucky and Virginia. Pauline had to leave the Richmond Theatre – Richmond, Virginia, that is – in quite a hurry as Wilkes Booth and Antonia Ford caught her spying on them. Pauline has informed us that a 'Mr. Powell' and a 'John Junior' have met with Booth in Richmond. She also found that Booth has a lady friend, Lucy Hale, who's the daughter of Sen. John Hale.

"In addition, Booth is a friend of John Ford – no relation to Antonia – who owns several theatres in the East and, of course, who has a theatre here in Washington. He allegedly has invited Booth to appear here whenever he wants.

"Now, Booth has no affection for President Lincoln and is believed to have made threatening statements about him. As a friend of John Ford, he has unlimited access to Ford's Theatre. In view of all this, it would seem he might have an opportunity to do the President harm when he attends a production there. And, as we know, the President certainly enjoys and frequents the theatre."

McDowell sat and Lamon nodded his thanks.

"Well, gentlemen, that's it," Hill announced. "We'll have a carriage drop you off a block from High Street and ask that you enter the building separately and at a timely distance apart. We'll have a runner available for delivery of messages between this office and your location.

"Good luck!"

As they left the office, Lamon asked Mac to remain. He grasped his arm and murmured in Clay's ear.

"I understand, Marshal, that you obtained some information from Edwin Booth by plying him with an excellent Kentucky sour mash?"

"That's true, Hill. Why?"

"Just wondered if you might have brought a taste with you?"

McDowell pointed to his carpetbag.

"You might take a look in there, Marshal."

Chapter XX

Surveillance

It was important to keep the room dark and, during daylight hours, be far enough from the windows not to be seen.

Four sets of field glasses – one per lookout – were available to focus on the Surratt Boarding House through the two windows that faced it. McDowell and Miles took the first watch.

Through trial and error, the two lawmen found the most effective reconnaissance technique was for one to watch and the other to record whenever something worthy of note occurred. That, however, was infrequent. Mostly, the effort was downright boring.

Philip Miles sat, binoculars in hand, watching traffic flow past. McDowell sketched an outline of the boarding house and street on a sheet of paper that otherwise was void of information. Roy Barnes was dozing on one of the cots and Jack Lewis was reading a two-day old newspaper. John Lamon, the head Marshal's brother, wasn't due to arrive until nightfall.

"You don't seem to be filling out that piece of paper," Miles observed, stifling a yawn.

"You don't seem to be telling me much," Mac retorted. "I'm not going to note that housekeepers shook out some rugs and bed sheets were hung up to dry."

Phil wiped perspiration from his forehead and made a scan with his field glasses.

"Well, that's interesting," he said.

"What?" Clay asked.

"Two houses down, there's a disagreement brewing," Miles noted. "There's a horse and wagon and two men are talking about the horse. One just lifted its leg and examined a hoof. He's pointing out something and shaking his head, and the other man is throwing up his hands. He's really disgusted."

Phil slid his chair to the left and refocused the glasses.

"The first man is holding up a hand, urging the second man to stop talking. Now, he's reaching into a pocket and pulling out some coins. No greenbacks, just some hard on-the-barrel head dollars. He's counting them out in the other man's hand. He's stopped now and the second man is staring at the money. He's making a fist and shouting. Now, they're both shouting. Uh-oh, he's throwing the money in his face. They're shouting again, waving their arms.

"The first man is removing his coat. Ha-a-a! The second man hit him in the mouth before he could take it off! He's down! The second man is picking up the coins, now he's leaving! The other man is still down! At last, some action!"

A disgusted McDowell sighed and rolled his eyes.

"You want me to write that down?"

"Well, no," Miles shrugged. Then, he brightened.

"Maybe we should be spying down the street," he suggested.

"Or, you could just ask Mary Surratt to liven things up a bit."

"Or, you two could just shut up!" Lewis snarled. "I'm trying to read over here!"

Miles turned to face Lewis.

"You've been at that long enough to have that newspaper memorized."

"And, I'll do it, too! I plan to read every word in this rag. That way, I can say I know everything that happened in this town two days ago."

"It would be easier to memorize what's happening across the street," Barnes suggested. "There's nothing!"

Roy rolled onto his side, returning to his nap.

As daylight began to dwindle, street activity began to go with it. But, in-and-out traffic at the boarding house increased.

"See anybody you know?" Mac asked.

Miles peered through the glasses, then shook his head.

"Must be the usual run of boarders," he said.

Suddenly, Phil straightened.

"Look, that's Mary Surratt!"

Clay grabbed his glasses and focused on the lady standing at the door, talking with a man who was departing. He was surprised at what he saw. She was an attractive woman, not the wicked witch he was expecting.

The dossier that Hill Lamon provided on Mrs. Surratt was very complete. Mac mentally reviewed the highlights as he studied the tall, trim figure that stood looking down at the man on the street.

Mary Jenkins Surratt was a native of Maryland, from the small town of Waterloo. She was in her early forties, had dark hair that was pulled back in a bun, and wore small golden hoop earrings that gave a certain sparkle to her face. Her royal blue dress was tasteful and appropriate for a female engaged in the business world. Her carriage was straight and strong, yet feminine, and she carried herself with the grace of a true lady. She was a woman of character and, although not beautiful, would definitely warrant a second look.

Mary was educated at a Catholic female seminary in Alexandria, Virginia, and had married at the tender age of 17 to John Harrison Surratt, who was 11 years her senior. They had, in quick succession, three children, two boys and a girl, the youngest, a son, John Surratt Junior, who reflected the Southern sympathies of his father.

Her husband had died in 1862 with a number of uncollected debts owed to his tavern. Surratt had developed, on nearly 300 acres of Prince George's County farmland, a tavern, polling place, a post office, and a two-story family house. The area had become known as Surrattsville, and a key facet of the Confederate underground network.

But, after John's death and the mountain of uncollected debts, Mary was forced to rent the complex to a former policeman and move to a townhouse the family owned on High Street in Washington City. She converted the structure into a respectable boarding house. But, thanks to John Junior, it also became the headquarters for surreptitious Confederate meetings.

Even at long distance, there was something special about Mary Surratt. As Hill had told them, "Don't make judgments. We don't make the mess, but it's up to us to clean it up." But, on first glance, Clay wondered if this woman really could be guilty.

"She's going back into the house," Miles announced. "But, wait! This is getting interesting! Look who's coming out!"

"Who is it?" Mac asked.

"Lewis Powell," Phil said. "He's one of the key conspirators!"

McDowell focused his glasses on the broad-shouldered man in the derby hat. Powell adjusted his hat and looked both ways, giving Mac a good look.

"I've seen him in Madison County," he announced. "Pauline Cushman also saw him take a valise into the Richmond Theatre that he and Zak Holston gave to Wilkes Booth."

"Write it down," Miles requested. "Now, we're getting someplace!"

Powell was followed by a "Who's Who" of suspected Confederate agents.

"That's Lewis Weichmann!" Phil declared. "He attended college with John Junior. We're not sure about his involvement, but he's on our list."

After a short pause, several others exited the house.

"Jack, get over here quick!" Miles ordered. "Here, take a look!"

He handed the extra pair of glasses to Lewis who studied the suspects.

"Well, well," he commented. "That's definitely David Herold and George Atzerodt. Looks like we've had a major meeting of the opposition."

"Who's who?" Mac asked, peering through his binoculars.

"That's Herold on the left," Jack said. "He and Atzerodt aren't insiders, but they're definitely what we'd describe as 'soldiers.' They carry out tasks that John Junior has for them."

It was twilight and the day quickly was turning to dark. A knock at the door put everyone on guard, but revealed John Lamon who, with a companion, brought supper to the marshals.

"I'll help reload some things into the buggy and I'll be back," John said. "I'll give you some relief and, at least, another pair of eyes. I don't know how much we're going to see at night, but Hill believes there may be some deliveries – either in or out."

John and his companion left and Miles and McDowell returned to their final hour of surveillance.

"Look, Phil!" Mac stated. "There's a carriage leaving from the rear of the house!"

It was too dark to see who occupied the buggy, but they watched it turn onto High Street toward downtown.

"Can you see who's in it?" Mac asked.

Miles shook his head.

"Let's just the record the time and that two individuals left. I have no idea who they are."

With the darkness, there was little chance of identifying anyone entering or leaving. They continued, however, to keep track of numbers – men and women, by horseback or carriage, and so forth. Another knock at the door stopped everything. It was too late for visitors.

Barnes, who was closest to the entryway, drew his pistol and called, "Who's there?"

"John Lamon."

Roy cracked the door, saw who it was, and let Lamon enter.

"I know you saw that carriage leave, but I doubt you could tell who was in it," he declared. "It was John Junior and Wilkes Booth."

"Are you sure?" Miles asked.

"Absolutely!" Lamon replied. "That's why I'm back so soon. We left from the rear after delivering your supper and pulled our buggy onto High Street from the alley. We hadn't gone very far when I noticed that part of the harness was working loose. We stopped and I got out to fix it when we saw the carriage from the boarding house. It slowed when they reached us and I got a good look at the passengers. John Junior was driving and Wilkes Booth was with him."

"Any idea where they were going?" Clay asked.

John shook his head.

"They were headed downtown and not in too much of a hurry. Did you know they were in the house?"

"No," Miles answered. "We identified Powell, Weichmann, Herold and Atzerodt. They left before the carriage did. We thought there was some kind of meeting, but, now, that seems certain. Surratt and Booth must have called it."

Mac turned to Lamon.

"Do you or Hill know anything about the President's plans? Is he going somewhere in the next few days?"

"He'll be meeting with the Cabinet tomorrow and waiting on a report from Gen. Grant," John explained. "They're closing in on Lee down toward Richmond and Mr. Lincoln is spending a lot of time at the War Department getting telegraph reports first hand. He believes Grant may end it all very soon."

McDowell looked at the others and each man was busy with mental speculation. Finally, Miles broke the silence.

"Well, any ideas about the intentions of the Surratt Group?"

"At this stage, I don't think an abduction is an option," Barnes offered.

"But, what if they could hold the President hostage and force Grant to withdraw?" Lewis questioned.

"Well, they'd have to do it soon," Roy stated. "The best bet would be when he walks over to the War Department building, although it's just across the street from the White House."

"Or, if he should go to the theatre," Jack commented.

John shook his head.

"Hill has convinced the President that he should allow guards to accompany him from the White House to the War Department. Also, Hill is emphasizing that any trips to public places would be foolhardy. I'm not sure Mr. Lincoln agrees, but he doesn't seem inclined to go anywhere but the War Department building since he feels Grant is so close to ending the war."

Lamon paused, recalling another scheme.

"One of the possibilities we heard through our spy network was that the Surratt Group planned to abduct the President by dragging him from a carriage. Now, that is bold, but still remains likely."

Clay stood and looked at the boarding house through the curtains.

"Whichever plan it is, I think we agree that they'll do it soon. The most disappointed men in Washington must be John Surratt and Wilkes Booth. They couldn't be happy about the

President's election to a second term and they must feel their chances to kidnap or harm him are slipping away."

"If Grant whips Lee and the war ends, there really won't be any reason for the group to do anything where the President is concerned," Lewis said.

"You're forgetting one thing," Miles pointed out. "I think Wilkes Booth is obsessed with this plot against Mr. Lincoln. He won't quit even if the war ends."

Mac nodded that he agreed and Lamon offered a chilling comment.

"If you're correct," he said, "abduction is out and that leaves him with one alternative – assassination."

"Come on, John, why would he do that after the fact?" Roy asked. "What's the motive?"

Clay shrugged and looked at his companions.

"One of the strongest emotions common to deranged zealots. Hate."

Chapter XXI

Detection

The marshals had kept the Surratt house under surveillance for nearly a week. In addition to identifying conspirators, they had learned of a conversation that linked the group to a suspected kidnapping attempt at Ford's Theatre. The information resulted thanks to an idea suggested by John Lamon.

Anxious to know what was transpiring inside the boarding house, John had convinced his brother, Hill, that a female spy could be of great value. The plan was to have a young lady obtain lodging and make herself privy to conversations involving the suspects. Agnes Henderson accepted the assignment and rented a room on the second floor, informing Mrs. Surratt that she was awaiting her husband's arrival from Denver. Agnes would have no direct contact with the lawmen across the street, but would provide information to Hill Lamon, who, in turn, would inform the lookouts.

Piecing together bits from several conversations, Agnes learned that Wilkes Booth now wanted to kidnap the President during a performance, knock him unconscious, gag and bind him, and carry him to a waiting carriage at a stage door. They knew Booth had handy access to the theatre and was welcome to enter though an actor's entrance and sit in any unused seats, or just stand backstage. Booth and some accomplices would overcome the President and his party while others would carry the commander-in-chief to an outside door.

It was an intricate plot that involved cutting off the theatre's gaslights and, while in the dark, removing Lincoln from his presidential box and handing him to those waiting below on stage.

However, on the night scheduled for the abduction, the President failed to appear. He was called away on business, but the Surratt Group suspected the plot had been discovered. They left quickly, fearing they may be trapped.

Concerned about discovery, Hill Lamon was prepared to conclude the surveillance. Agnes already had left the boarding house, but John Lamon prevailed upon his brother to give them a few more days. They should have listened to Hill.

Mac suspected they had been discovered as he was working a daylight shift that began at dawn. Lewis Powell left the boarding house during the early morning hours and paused at the street. He scanned the buildings across the way and stopped when he focused on the brick structure where the marshals were located. Clay was sure he could not be seen behind the heavy curtain, but saw that Powell was staring at the window where he was standing. Suddenly, he realized that the oil lamp behind him had not been extinguished. It cast him in a perfect silhouette.

McDowell moved from the window, and Miles, who witnessed Powell's curiosity, quickly turned off the lamp. It was the worst thing Phil could have done. It gave credence to Powell's suspicion that someone was spying on the house and was hoping to avoid detection.

Powell waited as if expecting someone to challenge and arrest him. When nothing happened, he turned and entered the house.

Mac and Phil looked at one another.

"He's on to us," Clay said. "We need to get out of here."

Barnes, Lewis and Lamon did not agree. They argued to remain for one more day. Their reasoning was that a plan of action was imminent and another twenty-four hours might reveal the details. So, they stayed.

Being cooped up in a small room was no picnic. Recently, the marshals had been taking turns and leaving after their shifts to stretch their legs. They were careful to exit by the rear entrance and not to be seen on High Street.

McDowell was tired, but felt that a quick walk would at least relax him mentally. He had eaten supper with the others and told Miles that he would return soon. Twilight was turning to dark as he left through the rear door and paused to stretch. The alley that exited onto High Street was to his right, its opposite side facing an open field. It was a route he did not want to take. But, as he walked in the other direction, he heard a loud noise and the sound of something rolling. It came from the alley and Mac changed direction to investigate.

A large empty barrel was slowly rolling toward him. He lifted a foot to stop the container and saw someone standing near the building at the alley's opposite entrance. The man didn't move. Clay called to him, but received no answer. He loosened the pistol in his holster and walked toward the figure, partly backlighted by lamps from buildings across the street.

Mac was concentrating so intently that he didn't hear the approach behind him. Something slipped over his head and onto his throat. The garroting maneuver cut off his wind as he was pulled backward by his assailant.

Unable to force his fingers through the loop, Clay crashed his boot heel onto his attacker's foot. The man squealed in pain and eased his hold on the garrote, enough that the Marshal could force two fingers through the loop. A backward kick found the assailant's shin and enabled Mac to get one hand through the braided rawhide. He followed by repeatedly slamming an elbow into his opponent's ribs and, finally, jerked free.

McDowell staggered back against the wall, trying to catch his breath. The attacker charged and grabbed Mac's throat, but the Marshal thrust his hands between the man's arms and knocked them aside. He drove a fist into his face and put him in a headlock, pounding the assailant's face with his free hand.

The one who had rolled the barrel ran past Clay as the other dropped to his knees. Mac took a few steps after the runner, but turned as the second man rose to his feet brandishing a knife. It was long and pointed and must be an Arkansas Toothpick, Clay thought.

McDowell drew his pistol and ordered him to drop the knife. Instead, he threw the elongated dagger and ran in the direction of his companion. Clay fired and a returning shot clipped his ear. The Marshal forged ahead, although he couldn't see who he was pursuing. As he ran behind the building and neared its opposite corner, he heard a loud grunt. Someone fell and something was being dragged toward him.

Hearing the shots, the men upstairs ran down to the rear entrance. Someone lit a lantern, casting an eerie glow over the scene. Clay and the other lawmen stood with pistols in hand as Hill Lamon walked toward them dragging someone by the collar. He dropped the body to the ground and looked at McDowell.

"Are you okay, Clay?" Hill asked.

"I'm fine," he answered, "just a slightly damaged ear. Who do you have there?"

Hill rolled the man onto his back and the light was cast onto his face.

"Anybody know him?" the head Marshal asked.

No one did, and, whoever he was, he was dead.

"Who killed him?" someone asked.

"I didn't mean to, but I guess I did," Hill replied.

John Lamon pushed his way to the body and made a quick examination. The man's neck was broken.

"Did you hit him, Hill?"

"Yeah," the big man responded.

John broke into uncontrolled laughter. The others just stared, looking surprised and confused.

"Let's go upstairs and I'll explain," John grinned. "Here, Clay, you're not hurt bad, wrap this around your ear. We need to get our things and get out of here."

Hill had driven to the house in a wagon, having decided that the surveillance should be concluded and all the gear should be loaded and removed. The body was placed in the wagon and they stripped it of identification and the once-fired revolver.

They gathered and loaded everything, then turned to the Lamons. John smiled and nodded at his brother.

"You go first," he said.

Hill scowled at John, then faced the men.

"To begin with, I was bringing the wagon so we could load up and leave," Hill explained. "I parked on the side street just below the house and walked up. It was dark, but I thought I saw McDowell leave and walk up the alley toward High Street. I was working my way toward him when I heard all this commotion and what sounded like a fight. A man ran down the alley and away down the street. Two shots were fired and a second person ran toward me, holding what I presumed to be a pistol. As he drew near, I could see the weapon in his hand. I hit him in the face and knocked him unconscious.

"Then, I saw the lighted lantern and everybody standing with Clay. I dragged the body over and you know the rest.

"Maybe I should have sent word that we were going to leave, but, in the interest of time, I decided to hire a wagon and come straight on over. Agnes already was worried, said she was under suspicion and that the group was getting nervous. She suggested it was time to get out. And, apparently, she was correct.

"In view of what's happened this evening, I'm guessing we've overstayed our welcome and have been discovered," Hill grinned. "Is that about it, Mac?"

McDowell nodded.

"They set up to get one of us, that's for certain. The man you killed, Hill, was on High Street. He must have been signaled when I left and rolled the barrel down the alley. When I investigated, they had me trapped. The one who got away tried to garrote me. I freed myself and they both ran away and I fired. I guess it was the second man who shot at me and clipped my ear.

"I think the man I fought with was Lewis Powell. I found his wallet in the alley and I'm guessing it fell from his pocket when we were wrestling. Miles and I saw Powell staring at our window early this morning and we thought he knew we were spying on them. By now, he's probably gone back to the boarding house and everybody knows."

As one, they turned to John who was chuckling.

"What's so funny about this?" Miles asked.

"As you may have guessed, my big brother doesn't know his own strength," John explained. "This isn't the first time he's hit someone so hard that he's nearly killed them. And, this time he did.

"Hill was with the President about a year ago when a man came up to shake Mr. Lincoln's hand. At the time, neither Hill nor the President knew that the individual was a Confederate sympathizer. He gripped Mr. Lincoln's hand so hard that the President cried out in pain. Well, the man wouldn't let go, and it wasn't the first time someone had done this under the guise of friendship.

"So, Hill hit him in the face and knocked him down. The man wasn't dead, but he wasn't in good shape. Mr. Lincoln looked at the man and said, 'Poor devil. He never knew what hit him.'

"The President then turned to Hill and said, 'For God's sake, Hill, give the man a chance! The next time, hit him with an axe handle!'

"Well, the President wouldn't let it go. When they got back to the White House, he admonished Hill in that dry wit of his. 'Hereafter,' he said, 'when you have occasion to strike a man, don't hit him with your fist. Hit him with a club or crowbar or something that won't kill him!'"

Hill shook his head in disgust

"You won't let it go, will you?" he snapped at his younger brother. "That story gets worse every time you tell it.

"Now," he ordered, "let's get out of here."

"Just a minute," Mac called. "Let me have the lantern."

Clay walked to the alley and searched where he and Powell had been fighting. The light reflected off the blade and Mac retrieved the knife.

He handed the lantern to Barnes and held up the weapon for the group to see.

"This, gentlemen," he explained, "is an Arkansas Toothpick. Don't get in front of it. It has a nasty sting."

All six piled into the wagon, now overloaded with bag and baggage, plus a dead body. Hill turned the horses toward town, and, although the two draft animals labored, they finally got underway.

"I'm glad we're not in a hurry," John deadpanned.

"Shut up, brother!" Hill growled. "I may send you back to Virginia with a one-way ticket."

"Why don't you let me drive?" John asked. "Then, you could get out and talk to the horses. They'll speed up if you threaten them with your fist."

Hill glared and the others smothered a laugh.

Chapter XXII

Surrender

Grant was closing in on Lee as the Easter weekend approached. The talk around Washington was that the Virginia general couldn't hold out for another week, and, when he went down, so would the Confederacy.

Mac sat with the Maryland and Virginia marshals in Hill Lamon's office awaiting the head Marshal's return for a final briefing. They had just begun to meet when Lamon was summoned by the President to make a brief report to the cabinet concerning the just-completed surveillance activity. Some fifteen minutes later, Hill returned with Attorney General Edward Bates, who personally shook hands with the four marshals and deputy John Lamon.

"Gentlemen," Bates said, "Marshal Lamon just made a fascinating report to President Lincoln and the Cabinet concerning your recent espionage activities involving the Surratt boarding house. I asked Hill if I could come by and thank you personally for your work. The information you have obtained substantiates our suspicion of an intricate plot against the President and gives us reason to increase our security efforts where he is concerned.

"As I'm sure Hill has informed you, Mr. Lincoln tends to have little regard for threats against him, but, thanks to your work, he must now face reality. He'll be much more receptive to our attempts to protect him.

"Thank you and be aware that we may need you in the future to testify against the Surratt Group."

Lamon summarized his report to the Cabinet and emphasized that each of the marshals should be prepared to return to the District for testimony. He dismissed them and Mac stopped to return a folder that had fallen to the floor. It was simply marked, "Premonitions."

McDowell stared at the binder and felt Hill watching him.

"Go ahead," Lamon instructed. "Take a look. It's my 'weird' file."

There was a recollection from the President that Hill had recorded. Apparently, Lincoln was speculating if he might die in office from an assassin's bullet. He was reflecting on the occasion when he had ridden his horse to the Old Soldier's Home and a bullet had penetrated his hat. The perpetrator had not been found, but the incident had given the President pause.

"Read on," Hill said. "You know how it's said that some people have 'Second Sight,' the ability to foretell the future? Read that next document. I recorded it recently as closely as I could to the way Mr. Lincoln related it to me."

"About ten days ago, I retired very late. I had been up waiting for important dispatches from the front. I could not have been long in bed when I fell into a slumber, for I was weary. I soon began to dream. There seemed to be a death-like stillness about me. Then I heard subdued sobs, as if a number of people were weeping. I thought I left my bed and wandered downstairs. There the silence was broken by the same pitiful sobbing, but the mourners were invisible. I went from room to room; no living person was in sight, but the same mournful sounds of distress met me as I passed along. I saw light in all the rooms; every object was familiar to me; but where were all the people who were grieving as if their hearts would break? I was puzzled and alarmed. What could be the meaning of all this? Determined to find the cause of a state of things so mysterious and so shocking, I kept on until I arrived at the East Room, which I entered. There I met with a sickening surprise. Before me was a catafalque, on which rested a corpse wrapped in funeral vestments. Around it were stationed soldiers who were acting as guards; and there was a throng of people, gazing mournfully upon the corpse, whose face was covered, others weeping pitifully. 'Who is dead in the White House?' I demanded of one of the soldiers, 'The President,' was his answer; 'he was killed by an assassin.' Then came a loud burst of grief from the crowd, which woke me from my dream. I slept no more that night; and although it was only a dream, I have been strangely annoyed by it ever since."

"The President maintains that no one will harm him, but, he is superstitious, and I think he really believes that he will somehow die in office," Lamon explained. "And, not by natural causes. There are other items in there, but the one you just read gives me chills."

Clay returned the file to the table.

"I'm beginning to understand why you've been so intent about his protection."

Lamon walked Mac to the door.

"Ed Bates could bring charges against the Surratt Group anytime now," he said. "Be ready to return at a moment's notice."

* * *

Good Friday was warm and sunny and Central Kentuckians were basking in all its glory, thoughts of war far from their minds. By mid-afternoon, however, all that changed. But, in a good way.

A young runner from the telegraph office burst in and shouted at Clay and Logan.

"The War's over!! Lee has surrendered to Grant!!"

Stunned, the lawmen sat and tried to grasp the unexpected announcement.

"Let's go see!" Mac cried and he and Perry ran next door.

A throng already was packed around the telegraph office as Fred Thompson was deciphering the code as quickly as he could. Copies were being made of his transpositions and passed through the crowd. Mac gasped as he saw where the surrender had occurred.

'At Wilmer McLean's House!' he reflected. 'It begins and ends with my friend on the train!'

Gen. Lee had arrived at the McLean home shortly before Gen. Grant and the meeting had lasted approximately an hour and a half. The surrender of the Army of Northern Virginia, Clay reasoned, did not officially end the war, but would allow the Federal government to bring increased pressure to bear in other parts of the South. And, that would result in the surrender of the remaining Confederate field armies during the next few months.

Newspapers the next day gave more details as McDowell and Perry, like virtually all citizens, devoured news accounts.

Hang Out Your Banners; Union Victory! Peace!

Surrender of General Lee and His Whole Army.

The Work of Palm Sunday.

Final Triumph of the Army of the Potomac.

The Strategy and Diplomacy of Lieut.- Gen. Grant.

Terms and Conditions of the Surrender.

The Rebel Arms, Artillery, and Public Property Surrendered.

Rebel Officers Retain Their Side Arms, and Private Property.

Officers and Men Paroled and Allowed to Return to Their Homes.

The Correspondence Between Grant and Lee.

OFFICIAL

War Department, Washington, April 9, 1865 – 9 o'clock P.M. This department has received the official report of the SURRENDER, THIS DAY, OF GEN. LEE AND HIS ARMY TO LIEUT. GRANT, on the terms proposed by Gen. Grant. Details will be given as speedily as possible. Edwin M. Stanton, Secretary of War.

Headquarters Armies of the United States, 4:30 P.M., April 9. Hon. Edwin M. Stanton, Secretary of War: GEN. LEE SURRENDERED THE ARMY OF NORTHERN VIRGINIA THIS AFTERNOON, upon the terms proposed by myself. The accompanying additional correspondence will show the conditions fully. (signed) U.S. Grant, Lieut. Gen'l

Sunday April 9, 1865, General – *I received your note of this morning, on the picket line, whither I had come to meet you and ascertain definitely what terms were embraced in your proposition of yesterday with reference to the surrender of this army. I now request an interview in accordance with the offer contained in your letter of yesterday for that purpose. Very respectfully, your obedient servant, R. E. Lee, General*

Sunday, April 9, 1865, Gen. R. E. Lee, Commanding Confederate States Armies. Your note of this date is set this moment, 11:50 A.M., received. In consequence of my having passed from the Richmond and Lynchburgh road to the Farmville and Lynchburgh road, I am at this writing about four miles West of Walter's church, and will push forward to the front for the purpose of meeting you. Notice sent to me, on this road, where you wish the interview to take place, will meet me. Very respectfully, your ob'd't servant, U.S. Grant, Lieutenant-General

Court House, April 9, 1865. General R. E. Lee, Commanding C. S. A.: In accordance with the substance of my letters to you of the 8th inst., I propose to receive the surrender of the Army of Northern Virginia on the following terms, to wit: Rolls of all the officers and men to be made in duplicate, one copy to be given to an officer designated by me, the other to be retained by such officers as you may designate. The officers to give their individual paroles not to take arms against the Government of the United States until properly exchanged, and each company or regimental commander sign a like parole for the men of their commands. The arms, artillery and public property to be packed and stacked and turned over to the officers appointed by me to receive them. This will not embrace the side-arms of the officers, nor their private horses or baggage. This done, each officer and man will be allowed to return to their homes, not to be disturbed by United States authority so long as they observe their parole and the laws in force where they reside. Very respectfully, U.S. Grant, Lieutenant-General.

Headquarters Army of Northern Virginia, April 9, 1865 Lieut. Gen. U.S. Grant, Commanding U.S.A.: General: I have received your letter of this date, containing the terms of surrender of the army of northern Virginia, as proposed by you; As they are substantially the same as those expressed in your letter of the 8th inst., they are accepted. I will proceed to designate the proper officers to carry stipulations late effect. Very Respectfully, Your Obedient Servant, R. E. Lee, General.

The Victory

Thanks to God, the Giver of Victory

Honors to Gen. Grant and His Gallant Army.

A National Salute Ordered.

Two Hundred Guns to be Fired at the Headquarters of Every Army, Department, Post and Arsenal.

OFFICIAL

War Department, Washington, D. C., April 9, 1865 – 9:30 P.M. Lieut.-Gen. Grant: Thanks be to almighty God for the great victory with which he has this day crowned you and the gallant armies under your command. The thanks of this Department and of the Government, and of the People of the United States – their reverence and honor have been deserved – will be rendered to you and the brave and gallant officers and soldiers of your army for all time. Edwin M. Stanton, Secretary of War.

War Department, Washington, D.C., April 9, 1865 – 10 o'clock P.M. Ordered: That a salute of two hundred guns be fired at the headquarters of every army and department, and at every post and arsenal in the United States, and at the Military Academy at West Point on the day of the receipt of this order, in commemoration of the surrender of Gen. Robert E. Lee and the Army of Northern Virginia to Lieut.-Gen. Grant and the army under his command. Report of the receipt and execution of this order to be made to the Adjutant-General at Washington. Edwin M. Stanton, Secretary of War.

* * *

The word that the war had ended spread quickly and celebrations were taking place in major cities across the country. Lexington was no exception. However, following a few moments of elation, Clay began to think about the realities of the conflict and its aftermath:

On this day, April 9, 1865, after four years of Civil War, approximately 630,000 deaths and more than one million casualties, Gen. Robert E. Lee had surrendered the Confederate Army of Northern Virginia to Lt. Gen. Ulysses S. Grant. That was reality one.

The surrender, ironically, had taken place at the home of Wilmer and Virginia McLean in the town of Appomattox Court House, Virginia. Three years, nine months, twelve days and 120 miles ago, the conflict had begun at their home in Manassas. That was reality two.

And the aftermath? A long period of reconstruction, trying to put the nation together again. Massive rebuilding in the South where most of the war was fought. A new industrial class, as planter aristocracy was destroyed. Social and racial upheaval and bitterness between the winning North and the losing South.

The road ahead, McDowell realized, would be no bed of roses. The Marshals service would be busier than ever, attempting to resolve conflicts and maintain peace.

"Well, what do you think, Logan?" McDowell asked as they passed the telegraph duplicates to new arrivals.

"There never was a good war, or a bad peace," he replied.

"Your granddaddy said that?"

"No," the deputy smiled. "Benjamin Franklin beat him to it."

Chapter XXIII

Assassination

For five days during the spring of 1865, the President enjoyed a time of relaxed serenity. The war essentially was over and he and the First Lady were going to celebrate by attending a performance of "Our American Cousin" at Ford's Theatre.

On April 13, the President dispatched Hill Lamon to Union-occupied Richmond. Reluctantly, Lamon agreed to take the assignment, imploring Lincoln to "not go out at night after I'm gone, particularly to the theatre."

However, the next day, the President accepted an invitation to attend the one-thousandth performance of actress Laura Keene in "Our American Cousin." That also was the night Wilkes Booth planned his unexpected appearance.

In a telegram to McDowell and the four marshals in Virginia and Maryland, Lamon, following the President's assassination, lamented his decision to visit Richmond.

"As God is my judge," he informed them, "I believe if I had been in the city, it (the assassination) would not have happened and had it, I know that the assassin would not have escaped the town."

Mac also learned that the Presidential Box that evening was to be guarded by a Washington Metropolitan policeman, John F. Parker, who was a curious choice for a bodyguard in that he had a spotty record as a lawman.

When the play started, Parker left his post outside the President's Box to find a better seat.

During intermission, Parker went to a tavern with the President's footman and coachman and may not have returned. It was evident that Parker was not at his post when Booth arrived.

Several days after the assassination, Clay felt he had the full story after receiving a multitude of telegrams from the attorney general and marshal's offices, plus many newspaper accounts. The *New York Times* story was among those kept in his "Assassination" file:

Awful Event

President Lincoln Shot by an Assassin

The Deed Done at Ford's Theatre Last Night

THE ACT OF A DESPERATE REBEL

The President Still Alive at Last Accounts.

No Hopes Entertained of His Recovery.

Attempted Assassination of Secretary Seward.

DETAILS OF THE DREADFUL TRAGEDY.

OFFICIAL

     War Department, Washington April 15, 1:30 A.M. – Maj. Gen. Dis.: This evening at about 9:30 P.M. at Ford's Theatre, the President, while sitting in his private box with Mrs. Lincoln, Mr. Harris, and Major Rathburn, was shot by an assassin, who suddenly entered the box and appeared behind the President.

     The assassin then leaped upon the stage, brandishing a large dagger or knife, and made his escape in the rear of the theatre.

     The pistol ball entered the back of the President's head and penetrated nearly through the head. The wound is mortal. The President has been insensible ever since it was inflicted, and is now dying.

     About the same hour an assassin, whether the same or not, entered Mr. Sewards' apartments, and under the pretence of having a prescription, was shown to the Secretary's sick chamber. The assassin immediately rushed to the bed, and inflicted two or three stabs on the throat and two on the face. It is hoped the wounds may not be mortal. My apprehension is that they will prove fatal.

The nurse alarmed Mr. Frederick Seward, who was in an adjoining room, and hastened to the door of his father's room, when he met the assassin, who inflicted upon him one or more dangerous wounds. The recovery of Frederick Seward is doubtful.

It is not probable that the President will live throughout the night.

Gen. Grant and wife were advertised to be at the theatre this evening, but he started to Burlington at 6 o'clock this evening.

At a Cabinet meeting at which Gen. Grant was present, the subject of the state of the country and the prospect of a speedy peace was discussed. The President was very cheerful and hopeful, and spoke very kindly of Gen. Lee and others of the Confederacy, and of the establishment of government in Virginia.

All the members of the Cabinet except Mr. Seward are now in attendance upon the President. I have seen Mr. Seward, but he and Frederick were both unconscious.

Edwin M. Stanton, Secretary of War.

Detail of the Occurrence

Washington, Friday, April 14, 12:30 A.M. *– The President was shot in a theatre tonight, and is perhaps mortally wounded. Secretary Seward was also assassinated.*

Second Dispatch. Washington, Friday, April 14 *– President Lincoln and wife, with other friends, this evening visited Ford's Theatre for the purpose of witnessing the performance of the "American Cousin."*

It was announced in the papers that Gen. Grant would also be present, but he took the late train of cars for New-Jersey.

The theatre was densely crowded, and everybody seemed delighted with the scene before them. During the third act, and while there was a temporary pause for one of the actors to enter, a sharp report of a pistol was heard, which merely attracted attention, but suggesting nothing serious, until a man rushed to the front of the President's box, waving a long dagger in his right hand, and exclaiming "Sic semper tyrannis," and immediately leaped from the box, which was in the second tier, to the opposite side, making his escape amid the bewilderment of the audience from the rear of the theatre, and mounting a horse, fled.

The screams of Mrs. Lincoln first disclosed the fact to the audience that the President had been shot, when all present rose to their feet, rushing toward the stage, many exclaiming "Hang him! Hang him!"

The excitement was of the wildest possible description, and of course there was an abrupt termination of the theatrical performance.

There was a rush toward the President's box, when cries were heard: "Stand back and give him air." "Has any one stimulants." On a hasty examination, it was found that the President had been shot through the head, above and back of the temporal bone, and that some of the brain was oozing out. He was removed to a private house opposite to the theatre, and the Surgeon-General of the army and other surgeons sent for to attend to his condition.

On an examination of the private box blood was discovered on the back of the cushioned rocking chair on which the President had been sitting, also on the partition and on the floor. A common single-barreled pocket pistol was found on the carpet.

A military guard was placed in front of the private residence to which the President had been conveyed. An immense crowd was in front of it, all deeply anxious to learn the condition of the President. It had been previously announced that the wound was mortal but all hoped otherwise. The shock to the community was terrible.

The President was in a state of syncope, totally insensible, and breathing slowly. The blood oozed from the wound at the back of his head. The surgeons exhausted every effort of medical skill, but all hope was gone. The parting of his family with the dying President is too sad for description.

At midnight, the Cabinet, with Messrs. Sumner, Colfax and Farnsworth, Judge Curtis, Gov. Oglesby, Gen. Meigs, Col. Hay, and a few personal friends, with Surgeon-General Barnes and his immediate assistants, were around his bedside.

The President and Mrs. Lincoln did not start for the theatre until fifteen minutes after eight o'clock. Speaker Colfax was at the White House at the time, and the President stated to him that he was going, although Mrs. Lincoln had not been well, because, the papers had announced that Gen. Grant and they were to be present, and, as Gen. Grant had gone North, he did not wish the audience to be disappointed.

He went with apparent reluctance and urged Mr. Colfax to go with him; but that gentleman had made other engagements, and with Mr. Ashman, of Massachusetts, bid him goodbye.

When the excitement at the theatre was at its wildest height, reports were circulated that Secretary Seward had also been assassinated.

On reaching this gentleman's residence a crowd and a military guard were found at the door, and on entering it was ascertained that the reports were based on truth.

Everybody there was so excited that scarcely an intelligible word could be gathered, but the facts are substantially as follows:

About 10 o'clock a man rang the bell, and the call having been answered by a colored servant, he said he had come from Dr. Verdi, Secretary Seward's family physician, with a prescription, at the same time holding in his hand a small piece of folded paper, and saying in answer to a refusal that he must see the Secretary, making the same representation which he did to the servant. What further passed in the way of colloquy is not known, but the man struck him on the head with a "billy," severely injuring the skull and felling him almost senseless. The assassin then rushed into the chamber and attacked Major Seward, Paymaster of the United States army and Mr. Hansell, a messenger of the State Department and two male nurses, disabling them all, he then rushed upon the Secretary, who was lying in bed in the same room, and inflicted three stabs in the neck, but severing, it is thought and hoped, no arteries, though he bled profusely.

The assassin then rushed down stairs, mounted his horse at the door, and rode off before an alarm could be sounded, and in the same manner as the assassin of the President.

It is believed that the injuries of the Secretary are not fatal, nor those of either of the others, although the Secretary and the Assistant Secretary are very seriously injured.

Secretaries Stanton and Welles, and other prominent officers of the government, called at Secretary Seward's home to inquire into his condition, and there heard of the assassination of the President.

They then proceeded to the house where he was lying, exhibiting of course intense anxiety and solicitude. An immense crowd was gathered in front of the President's house, and a strong guard was also stationed there, many persons evidently supposing he would be brought to his home.

The entire city to-night presents a scene of wild excitement, accompanied by violent expressions of indignation, and the profoundest sorrow; many shed tears. The military authorities have dispatched mounted patrols in every direction, in order, if possible, to arrest the assassins. The whole metropolitan police are likewise vigilant for the same purpose.

The attacks both at the theatre and at Secretary Seward's house, took place at about the same hour – 10 o'clock – thus showing a preconcerted plan to assassinate those gentlemen. Some evidences of the guilt of the party who attacked the President are in the possession of the police.

Vice-President Johnson is in the city, and his headquarters are guarded by troops.

Through special wires, McDowell learned that Booth had planned well for his assassination attempt. He had carved a notch in the door to the Presidential Box and had a brace jammed in place after entering the box. Being familiar with the play, he timed his entrance to coincide with comedian Harry Hawks' comments that always brought roars of laughter. That laughter covered the sound of Booth's 44-calibre derringer being fired at point-blank range into the back of the President's head. As Booth prepared to leap onto the stage, Major Henry Rathbone grappled with him and threw Booth off-balance, causing the actor to fall and break his leg just above the ankle. However, he hobbled off stage and found his way out back where he mounted a waiting horse and rode away.

As Booth was assaulting the President, Lewis Powell was assigned to murder Secretary of State William Seward, who was recovering at home from injuries suffered in a carriage accident. Powell, however, had only succeeded in stabbing and severely injuring the bedridden Seward. The intruder also had injured Assistant Secretary of State Frederick Seward, son of the secretary, and three others.

Another conspirator, George Atzerodt, was told to shoot and kill Vice President Andrew Johnson, who was staying at a Washington hotel. Atzerodt, however, did not have the courage to carry out the assignment.

Lincoln died the following morning and Booth and fellow conspirator David Herold escaped as did Powell. A massive manhunt was in progress and Clay, along with the Virginia and Maryland lawmen, was ordered to return to Washington to assist in the investigation and subsequent identification of the suspects.

"You're spending more time in Washington these days than you are in Kentucky," Perry observed as McDowell prepared to depart. "Watch yourself and don't corner something you know is meaner than you."

"Long live Granddaddy Perry," Mac wryly replied.

"Words to live by," Logan smiled.

Chapter XXIV

The Capture

The Marshals service remained on the perimeter of the conspirator's manhunt following the assassination of the President.

"Let the military handle it," Attorney General Bates had informed Hill Lamon. "We'll be involved soon enough."

Arresting suspects, rounding up witnesses, providing testimony, and handling other legal matters would keep U.S. Marshals busy through the justice system circus, otherwise known as "The Trial."

McDowell, Barnes, Lewis and John Lamon sat and watched as arrests were made in the Presidential Assassination case and the list was narrowed down to eight conspirators who would stand trial. Implicated were Mary Surratt, Lewis Powell, David Herold, George Atzerodt, Dr. Samuel Mudd, Samuel Arnold, Michael O'Laughlen and Edmund Spangler.

Booth had committed the murder and Herold was charged as an accessory and also as an accessory in the attempted murder of William Seward. Powell had attempted to assassinate Secretary of State Seward and Atzerodt and Mary Surratt had conspired with Booth and were charged with various other crimes.

Mudd had set Booth's broken leg and was charged as a Booth conspirator and Arnold and O'Laughlen were charged with conspiracy to kidnap the President. Spangler was found guilty for aiding the escape of Booth from Ford's Theatre.

As McDowell watched and waited, Booth was killed and Herold surrendered on April twenty-sixth in a tobacco barn near Port Royal, Virginia. The President's assassin was viewed in the North as a madman and monster, while, in the South, Booth was cursed for inflicting the revenge of an incensed North, rather than the reconciliation promised by the President.

Clay arrived in Washington several days after Booth's death. He and the marshals who had conducted surveillance of the Surratt Boarding House were to be taken to the Old Capitol

Prison to view and identify suspects. At the earliest, it would be at least another day before the trip was to occur, as the district was reflective of the grief, outrage, and, even prejudice, felt throughout the North and South. In just a short time, Clay discovered the cry for blood was louder than the cry for justice, and politics outweighed it all.

Mac took the opportunity to walk around the nation's capital, and found himself just a few blocks east of the White House at one of Washington's most impressive non-government landmarks. The Willard Hotel had housed a Peace Congress early in 1861, a last-ditch attempt to avert the Civil War. Julia Ward Howe had written the "Battle Hymn of the Republic" there later the same year. And, the President had spent several weeks at the Willard prior to his 1861 inauguration, conducting meetings in the lobby and business from his room.

McDowell ordered a bourbon from the bar and took a seat in the lobby to watch the "Who's Who" of Washington mingle, deliberate, and debate the fate of the nation. Initially, he sat by himself, but soon was joined by a Union officer who took a chair adjacent to the small table they were sharing.

"It's quite a scene, isn't it?" the Lieutenant commented, gesturing toward the lobby gathering.

"I imagine a lot of things are decided here," Mac replied. "Maybe even some things concerning the assassination."

The Lieutenant took a sip of his drink and nodded.

"I've never ceased to marvel at it," he said. "I suspect that decisions really are made here then formalized at meetings and hearings."

Clay reached across the table to introduce himself to the officer.

"I'm U.S. Marshal Clay McDowell," he said. "I represent the Eastern District of Kentucky."

"First Lieutenant Edward Doherty, Sixteenth New York Cavalry," the officer replied. "What brings you to Washington?"

"I've been involved in resolving the plot against the President for some time," Mac replied. "I'm here to sew up any loose ends against those involved."

"I'm here for something similar," Doherty commented. "I'm scheduled to meet with the Attorney General."

Clay thought for a moment, then recalled the name.

"Doherty ... Doherty ... Right! You're the officer who tracked down Wilkes Booth!"

Somewhat embarrassed, the Lieutenant nodded.

"Yeah, that's me. The story has been in the newspapers, but Secretary Bates wants to hear it from me firsthand."

"Well, you caught Booth, which is better than what we did in the Marshals service. I, personally, always seemed to be at least one step behind him and the conspirator's group."

"Well, we had enough men, a good lead as to where Booth had gone, and orders to stay on his trail until we found him," Doherty explained. "And, it took about sixty hours non-stop to do it. Also, everyone involved was dedicated to the pursuit and capture."

"I understand you caught Booth and his friend at a house in Virginia?" Mac asked.

"Yeah, it was a farmhouse at Port Royal near Bowling Green. A Mr. Garrett owned it and he and his sons were hiding Booth and David Herold."

"I know you're must be weary of telling the story, but I would like to hear it from the man who made it happen," Clay said. "Particularly since I've tracked Booth and his companions across two states and Washington City and had no success in preventing the end result."

Doherty smiled.

"Okay, Marshal. I'll give you the capsulized version, but let's get a refill."

"I'll buy," Clay replied.

With glasses in hand, they obtained refills, then returned to their seats and the Lieutenant began.

"We did a lot of travel by boat and in the saddle and awakened and questioned a number of people before we narrowed the search down to the Garrett farm. Now, the Garretts fed and housed Booth and Herold, but claimed they did not know their identities nor knew that the President had been assassinated.

"Keep in mind that we had plenty of men in our party. We had twenty-six enlisted personnel and myself, plus Lt. Col.

Everton Conger and Luther Baker, intelligence officers assigned by a special agent from the War Department. In all, we had twenty-nine men.

"We surrounded the house and I sent six men to station themselves back of the barn and outbuildings. Mr. Garrett said Booth and Herold were in the woods, but one of Garrett's sons advised his father to tell us where they were. I grabbed Garrett by the collar, pulled him into the yard, and placed my pistol to his head and demanded that he tell me where Booth and Herold were. He said they were in the barn and I jerked him around and told him to take me to it. We got there on the run and I left Garrett with some of my men and posted the others around the building. When I returned, Garrett was coming out of the barn and, apparently, had encouraged Booth to surrender.

"Booth wouldn't do it. Conger and Baker wanted to fire the barn, but I opposed it. I wanted to wait until daylight and send men in to overcome Booth and Herold. Conger, Baker and I argued about Booth surrendering, but he refused to do it. One of my men, Sgt. Boston Corbett, asked permission to enter the barn alone, but I refused.

"Finally, we threatened to burn the building if Booth didn't surrender, and, gave him ten minutes to make up his mind. Up to that point, Booth denied that anyone else was in the barn. But, he finally said there was someone there 'who wants to surrender awful bad.'

"I told Herold to put one hand at a time outside the door and, I took hold of both his wrists and jerked him out of the barn. Conger then ignited the hay in the rear. Through a crack between boards, Sgt. Corbett saw Booth raising a carbine and fired, hitting Booth in the neck. I dragged Herold with me back into the barn and we found Booth lying on his back. We found a rope and secured him and removed him from the building, which, by now, was burning pretty well.

"As he was dying, Booth said, 'Tell my mother I died for my country.' He died in about two hours. I sewed up the body myself in a blanket and placed it in a wagon. We then left for Port Royal and crossed the river in a scow. That was on the morning of April 26. We placed the body on board a steamer and I delivered it to Washington early on the twenty-seventh."

Doherty sighed and took another sip from his drink.

"That, in a nutshell, is how it happened."

They sat quietly for a moment, then the Lieutenant turned toward McDowell.

"You were after him for some time," he said. "Any thoughts about what drove him to the assassination?"

"I think he really believed Lincoln was the source of all the South's troubles," Clay declared. "Some of our people are going through Booth's diary and personal papers and I was told he had been recording information for six months – the same time the conspirators had worked to capture the President. But, when they realized their cause was lost, it was decided that something decisive and 'great' had to be done.

"Booth wrote – and I'm quoting him directly – that he 'struck boldly, and not as the papers say. I can never repent it, though we hated to kill.'"

Clay placed his glass on the table and wiped his mouth with a napkin.

"Never underestimate a zealot," he concluded.

As the dinner hour neared, lobby traffic increased. Familiar faces from Congress and the government passed by, and, then, one individual who immediately attracted McDowell's attention. She was tall, dark-headed and beautifully gowned and walked past him with the grace of a lady attending court. She stopped a short distance from Mac, and walked back to where he was seated.

"Marshal McDowell?" she asked.

Clay stood, then stared in alarm as he recognized her.

"Antonia Ford!" he cried. "What are you doing here?"

"I thought I recognized you!" she smiled, extending her gloved hand.

Mac automatically took her hand, then straightened and gave her a cold look.

"I don't know whether to arrest or shoot you," he stated. "The last time we met, you and the Major were trying to kill me!"

Antonia laughed and seductively cocked her head.

"The war's over, Marshal. We're on the same side now."

Caught off guard, Mac groped for a response, then turned to the Lieutenant who was standing.

"Miss Ford, this is Lt. Doherty. Lieutenant, Miss Ford, a former adversary."

"Good afternoon, Lieutenant," she smiled. "But, actually, it's Mrs. Willard now."

Doherty bowed and clicked his heels.

"A pleasure, Mrs. Willard. Are you by chance related to Mr. Willard, the hotel proprietor?"

"I'm the wife of his son, Lieutenant. It's a pleasure also to meet you. And, are you by chance the officer who captured Mr. Wilkes Booth?"

"Yes, I am, Mrs. Willard. I see my reputation has preceded me."

"As mine has with Marshal McDowell," she smiled, then winked at Clay.

Mac blushed and again was at a loss for words

"But how ... and why ...????" he stammered.

Doherty pulled up another chair and invited Antonia to be seated.

"Thank you, Lieutenant," she said. "I can only stay a minute as my husband and I have a dinner appointment with some friends."

"Miss Ford, er, rather, Mrs. Willard, I believe you owe me an explanation," the Marshal declared.

"Indeed I do," she replied. "And, Lieutenant, permit me to explain that the Marshal and I were on opposite sides when we last met and, as he stated, it was my intention to 'do him in,' as the British cockney would say.

"You see, I was a spy for the Confederacy, and, along with my father, was arrested. We were exchanged, but I was arrested again – this time by my future husband, Major Joseph Willard – and placed in the Old Capitol Prison here in Washington. Major Willard and I fell in love and he succeeded in getting me released after I took an Oath of Allegiance to the Union. We were married a little more than a year ago.

"As a spy, I worked with Wilkes and a group headquartered in Richmond."

She paused, smiled at Clay, and said, "That's Richmond, Virginia, Lieutenant, not Richmond, Kentucky."

"But, pardon me, I digress," Antonia apologized. "Wilkes and our group were working throughout Kentucky, Virginia and Washington distributing counterfeit money and devising a way to kidnap President Lincoln. Marshal McDowell and his actress lady friend ..."

"I never said that Pauline was my lady friend!" Mac interrupted.

"As I said, the Marshal and his lady friend, Pauline Cushman, caught on to us and it was decided that we had to remove them. The plan was to eliminate them when they were traveling by rail, but the Marshal and Pauline outwitted us and escaped. I returned to my home in Virginia, but soon was captured by the Union army and you know the rest."

Clay returned his glass to the table with a little more force than he intended.

"She and a compatriot tried to kill me, Lieutenant!" Mac snapped. "I killed The Major – a renegade named Zachary Holston – and Mrs. Willard escaped after they blew up and wrecked the train.

"Incidentally, Mrs. Willard," he scowled. "How did you escape?"

"Well, not in the most ladylike fashion," Antonia replied. "But, remember, Southern girls are very adaptive and I was able to procure a horse and ride away. You may not realize it, Marshal, but I can ride as well as any man."

Antonia stood and extended her hand to Clay and the Lieutenant. Doherty kissed it and Clay merely held it, staring coldly at Mrs. Willard.

"As my Daddy says, 'All's fair in love and war,'" Antonia related. "I hope there are no hard feelings, Marshal. We were just doing our duty. And, I'm very happy that both of us have survived. Good day, gentlemen."

Doherty watched her departure with great esteem.

"What a charming lady," he said.

"Yeah," Clay replied. " She almost charmed me to death."

Chapter XXV

Back to Washington

"Hill, I don't understand?" Clay asked. "Why are we here? What are we supposed to do?"

Hill Lamon slammed a sheaf of papers on the table then banged his fist on its surface.

"Dammit, don't ask me that!" he roared, glaring at the four marshals and his brother, John. "I've got a new attorney general and a War Department secretary breathing down my neck who are as lost in this case as I am, and all they can tell me is to 'get my house in order' because the biggest trial in the history of this country is about to begin!

"Nobody knows what's going on! We're plowing new ground here! We didn't make this mess, but, for damn sure, it'll be up to us to clean it up!"

John Lamon stood and held up his hands.

"Easy, Hill!" he called. "Let's calm down.

"Look, men," he said to Mac and Marshals Barnes, Lewis and Miles, "The Washington bureaucracy is after blood here. I doubt that reason, the letter of the law or justice will have anything to do with what is about to happen. But, let's don't let the Marshals service be the whipping boy if anything goes wrong. Hill is trying to protect our asses, although he doesn't act like it."

John scowled at his brother. Hill responded in turn, but, in fact, did take a deep breath and changed his demeanor.

"Look," he said. "I've been hounded, questioned, propositioned and threatened. When politicians smell blood, they take advantage to promote themselves. Now, they're **ALL** long-time friends of the President – even those who are his long-time enemies. They're shocked and appalled by his assassination and demanding that someone pay. And, I don't just mean those involved in the plot. Someone in the government also will be blamed, and it's sure as hell not going to be us!

"Why are we here? We're here to make ourselves look good.

The Metropolitan Police are being blamed for Mr. Lincoln's death, not us. We're going to continue investigating, doing anything that will be of assistance and supportive for the Attorney General and the War Department.

"What are we supposed to do? Anything that will be of help. Be sure of all our facts and provide solid testimony that will support the prosecution's case. Get to really know those who have been charged.

"One thing we're going to do is visit the cells of each of the eight conspirators. I want you to see them up close, look into their eyes, examine their souls, and relate that to what you saw under surveillance."

Miles cleared his throat.

"I'm not second-guessing you, Hill, but is this really necessary?"

"Hell, I don't know!" the head Marshal snapped. "But if the defense asks how thorough our investigation was or how well we know the conspirators, we'll be prepared. We'll interrogate each other, we'll go over our testimony, and there will be no question that we did our job and we did it well.

"If you have any more questions, let's hear them now!"

There were none.

"Okay," Hill said. "Now here's what we're going to do. We're going to Old Arsenal Prison in teams. Clay, you and Phil will go with me, and Roy and Jack will go with John. Each of the conspirators is in a private cell and separated from each other. Precautions have been taken to prevent any communication or collaboration with other possible witnesses. Mary Surratt and David Herold are on the third floor. Lewis Powell and George Atzerodt are on the second and the others are scattered throughout the prison.

"We're not there to interrogate them. The guards have been instructed not to communicate with the prisoners, and that goes for us.

"The male prisoners, except for Dr. Mudd, wear cotton hoods at all times. Their eyes and ears are covered with only a small opening for the nose and mouth. We'll have the guards remove their hoods so that we can see them. Also, the men are shackled with leg irons and handcuffs. And, Powell's hood is padded to keep him from injuring himself. He keeps banging his head against the walls.

"Mrs. Surratt, as I said, is not wearing a hood, nor is she shackled. However, she's refusing to eat, and, if that continues, she'll have to be force fed.

"And, the cells are small. About three and one-half by seven feet and about seven feet in height.

"There's also a courtroom that's been constructed on the third floor. We'll also take a look at it."

Lamon took a deep breath and shoved his hands in his waistband.

"Okay. That's it. We'll begin our rounds this afternoon."

Mac and Phil began the afternoon with some trepidation. They weren't sure what to expect, nor, really, what Hill Lamon was expecting from them. They'd seen condemned prisoners before. So what? What was the difference now?

Then, realization set in.

"Remember what John said about Hill protecting our asses?" Phil asked.

"Yeah, you must be thinking the same thing I am," Clay replied.

"I know. It just dawned on me," Miles commented. "This is a long shot, but he doesn't want the bureaucrats to find any chinks in our armor."

Phil smiled.

"Why, we could even get medals for going above and beyond our duty."

"Don't hold your breath," Mac said.

McDowell, Miles and Hill Lamon started at the cell of Lewis Powell on the second floor. They stood outside the small enclosure as the guard removed Powell's hood. The prisoner blinked several times as his eyes became accustomed to the light. He then saw the three marshals outside his cell. He smiled as he studied them one at a time, then scowled as he focused on Clay.

"I know you!" he snarled. "Come in here and let's finish it! I'll kill you with my bare hands! Not even these shackles can stop me!"

The guard shoved Powell back onto the bench.

"Shut up!" he ordered, "or I'll put the hood back on you!"

If someone ever had the eyes of a killer, Mac thought this man possessed them. But, more than that, he appeared unbalanced, deranged. Clay studied Powell's bio, noting that the son of a Baptist minister had been born in Alabama and joined the Confederate Army at age 17 in Florida. He'd been wounded at Gettysburg, had escaped from a military hospital in Baltimore and had joined a Confederate Cavalry unit known as Mosby's Rangers.

Powell had assaulted and threatened to kill a black maid in Baltimore who, he judged, had not properly cleaned his boarding house room. He was recruited by Wilkes Booth to participate in the kidnapping of the President, and, when that failed, had been given the assignment of killing Secretary of State Seward.

Also known to Federal authorities as "Payne" or "Paine," Powell had been arrested when he showed up at the Surratt Boarding House while Mary Surratt was being questioned by military investigators.

"I'll kill you! I'll kill you!" Powell shouted as McDowell walked away from the cell. He and the others could hear Powell's rants as they walked to George Atzerodt's enclosure.

A German immigrant, George Atzerodt had operated a carriage business in Maryland, and had helped Confederate agents, including John Surratt, cross the Potomac River. He was a heavy drinker and decided to drink at a hotel bar before carrying out an assignment to kill the vice president. He failed to follow through, but willingly admitted his participation in the kidnapping conspiracy.

Clay and Phil carefully checked the profiles as they viewed each of the prisoners.

Dr. Samuel Mudd, who had treated Booth and set his leg, was a country doctor, who, many said, was at the wrong place at the wrong time. He denied he recognized Booth when he treated him, but prosecutors claimed he had helped Booth and Herold escape, and witnesses said the physician had welcomed conspirators into his home "dozens of times" prior to the assassination.

Michael O'Laughlen, who was to extinguish the gas lights at a proposed Ford's Theatre kidnapping, was a discharged Confederate soldier who Booth recruited for the kidnapping plot. O'Laughlen was in Washington shortly before the assassination, but his role in the plot was not clear.

Edman Spangler, described as a "heavy drinker," was employed at Ford's Theatre as a carpenter. He had met Booth there and often tended to the actor's horse upon his arrival. Booth had asked him to keep his horse during the assassination activities, a chore Spangler may have turned over to another theatre employee, Joseph (Peanuts) Burroughs. Spangler was charged with being Booth's accomplice.

Samuel Arnold was arrested in Virginia after a letter to Booth was found, in which Arnold expressed his overwhelming agreement with the kidnapping plot. However, his role in the conspiracy was not clear.

David Herold, who was apprehended with Booth, was considered the mastermind of a conspiracy to destabilize the U.S. government. Herold also had admitted to a witness that he and Booth were "the assassinators of the President." He also had accompanied Powell to the home of Secretary Seward.

The marshals stopped to exchange their thoughts before proceeding to the last stop, a visit to the cell of Mary Surratt.

"That Powell fellow is crazy as hell," Miles observed. "And, he sure doesn't like you," he grinned at McDowell.

"You think they'd hang a crazy man?" Mac asked.

"There's no doubt in my mind," Hill replied, and Miles shook his head in agreement. "They're after blood and Powell even looks like a criminal."

They leafed through the profiles and agreed that Herold and Spangler were death penalty candidates, but opinion was divided on the fates of Atzerodt and Mudd, O'Laughlen and Arnold were thought to receive life sentences.

"Which ones did you see at the Surratt House?" Hill asked.

"Booth, Herold, Powell, Atzerodt and, of course, Mary Surratt," Mac responded. "You agree, Phil?"

"I do," he said, "but I'm just not sure about the others."

"They may have been on Roy and Jack's watch," Hill commented. "And, John may be able to identify some of them."

"What about Mudd, O'Laughlen and Spangler?" Miles questioned. "They may not have visited the house, or, for that matter, Arnold may never have been there."

"We probably saw more than half," Lamon guessed. "Our testimony can place most of the key conspirators at the Surratt house.

"Now, let's go see Mary."

When they arrived at cell number 200, Mary Surratt was praying.

She was kneeling and holding a rosary before a bench on which a Bible was placed. She was thinner and had a pale complexion, compared to the way Clay had viewed her at the boarding house. They stood with the guard outside her cell and waited as she mouthed words they could not hear.

Mac examined her bio as he watched and wondered if she really knew of Booth's involvement in the assassination plot, or if she was merely running errands for a man with whom she and her daughter had become infatuated. There was a notation concerning information about Mary that had been obtained from Powell. He claimed that Mrs. Surratt was innocent. The most damning evidence against her came from John Lloyd, proprietor of the Surrattsville tavern that she owned. He claimed that Mrs. Surratt had dropped off two carbines, ammunition, about twenty feet of rope, and a monkey wrench and had asked him to conceal them at the tavern. Three days before the assassination, Lloyd said Mrs. Surratt told him the "shooting irons" would be needed soon and, on the day the President was killed, told him some parties would call for the weapons that evening.

Clay halted his review as Mrs. Surratt crossed herself and rose to her feet. She looked at the men outside the bars, nodded and smiled. Despite her loss of weight and prison pallor, McDowell could not help but to be impressed. She had most unusual gray eyes and a face that radiated compassion and goodwill. She was a handsome woman.

'Hold it, Mac!' he said to himself. 'Don't be taken in. Remember that in war, truth is the first casualty.'

"Excuse me, Sir," she said to McDowell. "You look very familiar to me. Have we met?"

Clay shook his head, gave a sideway glance to the guard, and said quietly, "No, ma'am. I don't believe we have."

Mary shook her head, looked down, then back at McDowell and smiled.

"You have a very kind face," she said.

They left to view the courtroom further down the floor.

"Don't forget what I said, Clay," Lamon reminded the Marshal. "'We didn't make the mess, but it's up to us to clean it up.' Don't get involved."

Chapter XXVI

Trial

The rectangular courtroom was of pragmatic construction with little or no attention to style. The Prisoners Dock was at one end with a door that led from the cellblocks directly to the raised area where the eight conspirators were seated with a guard stationed between each prisoner.

Two small tables for the prisoners' counsel were in front of the dock while a long table for the nine-member military commission was to one side. A table for reporters was opposite it and a witness stand and two smaller tables were in the center of the room facing the Military Commissioners. Boxes containing what was described as "assassins' implements" were located adjacent to the room entrance. Three supporting posts in the center of the room would, on occasion, hinder the view of witnesses.

Lamon, his brother and the four marshals looked around the empty room, void of any positive emotion.

"Yeah, but it fits the mood of the trial," McDowell observed. "Grave, unfriendly and controlled.

"When will court convene, Hill?"

"Oh, I'm sure there'll be the usual objections and posturing," Lamon said. "There's already been some. But there's a push to get to business as soon as possible. There were a lot of objections to having a military trial versus one in a civilian court, but the new Attorney General was ordered by President Johnson to prepare an opinion on the legality of a military commission. It was no surprise that James Speed reasoned that a military court would be proper."

Hill paused to provide an aside to McDowell.

"He's one of the Louisville Speeds, Clay, but I'm sure you know that. Also, Gen. Lewis Wallace is one of the voting members of the commission. You remember him from the Battle of Richmond. And, another Kentuckian – Judge Advocate General Joseph Holt – is in charge of the prosecution.

"Anyway, Speed wrote that an attack on the commander-in-chief before the full cessation of the Civil War constituted an act of War against the United States. Consequently, the War Department would become the body to control the proceedings.

"President Johnson then ordered the conspirators to be tried before a military commission with some very specific rules: that conviction could result from a simple majority vote and a majority of two-thirds could impose the death penalty."

"Did the President order the prisoners confined the way we witnessed them?" Barnes asked.

"No, Secretary Stanton did that," Hill explained. "I don't know the reason for the hoods, but he sure didn't want them to be comfortable. I can understand them being shackled to balls and chains, and maybe even having their hands confined by iron straps, but the hoods I don't understand.

"Now, the War Department probably will try to do more with the trial than just prosecute the eight charged conspirators. I hear they'll also pull Booth into their arguments, plus Jeff Davis and the Confederate Secret Service."

As much as he tried, McDowell couldn't keep Mary Surratt out of his mind.

"As an attorney, Hill, do you think all eight will be convicted?" he asked.

"I'd say, yes, without a doubt," he responded. "There's a lot of evidence against them, including what we've uncovered. But, I'll grant you, some of it is circumstantial. But, I'll also bet you that some of that evidence will be ruled admissible and used against them."

"If you were going to bet," Clay continued, "how many would you say will receive the death penalty?"

Hill sat at the commission table and smiled.

"I'll throw that back in your laps," he said, glancing at the marshals. "What's your guess?"

"They'll all be judged guilty," Clay replied, "and Powell, Herold and Spangler will be condemned to death."

"Add Atzerodt to the death penalty," Miles added. "I agree on the others."

Barnes and Lewis thought Arnold and O'Laughlen would receive light prison sentences. John Lamon agreed.

"Okay, but what about Mary Surratt?" Hill asked. "What will happen with her?"

"Ten to fifteen years," John suggested.

McDowell, Barnes and Lewis agreed.

"I'd say twenty," Miles stated.

Hill rubbed his chin and grinned.

"Interesting," he said. "No one thinks she'll receive the death penalty?"

"Hang a woman?" Miles questioned. "That won't happen."

"Never," John added.

"There's not enough evidence to warrant that," Barnes declared.

"Most of the evidence against her is circumstantial," Lewis commented.

"I agree," Clay said. "What do you say, Hill?"

The head Marshal leaned forward, resting his arms on his knees.

"Don't forget what I said earlier. Someone's really going to pay. Who better than Mary Surratt? Hang her and you really underscore the seriousness of the crime."

On May 8, seven days after President Johnson ordered the trial conducted before a military commission, the group convened for the first time. The following evening, the charges were read to the prisoners in their cells. Hoods were removed and each defendant was allowed to read the document and, if requested, have the copy read to them. Testimony began May 12.

Mac sat at the rear of the room near the prisoners dock listening to the on-going drone of testimony. It was hot and uncomfortable and the same questions seemingly were asked time after time. It was after the noon hour when a recess was called and, gratefully, all stood and prepared to leave. Mary Surratt, seated on the raised dock near Clay, stood and a Bible fell from her lap, through the spindled railing and onto the floor. Instinctively, McDowell stood and retrieved it, but paused when he saw the guard stand in front of Mary.

Recognizing Mac, the guard nodded and stood aside and the Marshal offered the worn volume to the prisoner. Mrs. Surratt peered at the guard through her veil, and, upon receiving a nod of approval, reached for the book. She took it in both hands and recall led to a smile as she remembered McDowell as the man at her cell. She placed one hand over his.

"May God bless you," she whispered.

The trial continued for seven weeks, and, during its course, the Commission heard testimony from 371 witnesses. Clay and the other marshals told their stories as the three-member prosecution team presented a mountain of evidence. Judge Advocate General Holt, a native of Breckinridge County, served in dual roles as chief prosecutor and legal advisor to the Commission and had overall responsibility for prosecution of the conspirators. John A. Bingham served as Special Judge Advocate and handled examination of witnesses and gave the government's summation. Judge Advocate Major Henry L. Burnett was the third member of the prosecution team.

Mac patiently gave evidence against Powell as the man who had attacked him and how he had found his dropped wallet. The defense asked and rephrased its questions as it attempted to find loopholes in the testimony. Finally, defense attorneys sought to plead their client as "having a fanaticism that bordered on insanity."

Attorney W.E. Doster argued that "slavery made him (Powell) immoral, that war made him a murderer, and that necessity, revenge and delusion made him an assassin." It was a beautiful summation.

Powell, Clay noticed, seemed indifferent to the proceedings and would frequently smile as though he feared nothing. The commission found him guilty and sentenced him to death.

David Herold was considered guilty before testimony even began. As a result, the defense sought to focus on his lack of mental capacity. A physician said he considered Herold to be a mental dwarf, someone with the capacity of an eleven-year-old. It was argued that the defendant was "only wax in the hands of a man like Booth."

The ploy didn't work. Herold was given the death penalty.

Michael O'Laughlen fared better. Nine witnesses were produced who supported his alibi that he had strolled the streets of Washington and spent much of his time drinking while the plot was in progress. Nevertheless, the Commission believed he was linked to the abandoned plan to abduct President Lincoln. The verdict – life in prison.

The graveled-faced Edman Spangler, who failed to maintain Booth's horse at the theatre, was judged to be aware of Booth's guilty purposes in requesting his assistance. As an accomplice, he was sentenced to six years in prison.

Although it was argued that Samuel Arnold "backed out" of the plot to capture the President, the letter he wrote to Booth proclaiming that no one was more in favor of the plot than he was, decided his fate. Arnold was sentenced to life in prison.

George Atzerodt, who had admitted his willingness to join the kidnapping conspiracy, was pictured as being a non-participant in the assassination plot. Atzerodt claimed he first learned of the plan to assassinate the President less than two hours before the shooting. However, prosecution witnesses allowed that Atzerodt had met often with Booth at the Pennsylvania House in Washington. A livery stable employee also said that Atzerodt and Herold had brought a dark bay mare to the stable with them, presumably the mount that Booth used for his getaway.

The Commission gave Atzerodt the death penalty.

Dr. Mudd's defense fell apart when it was found that he had lied to investigators about not recognizing Booth when he treated his broken leg. Mudd had spent hours with Booth the previous November, something, "on reflection," he finally remembered.

It also was found that the physician, early in 1865, had said that "the President, Cabinet and other Union men" would "be killed in six or seven weeks." In addition, the prosecution contended that Mudd had pointed out to Herold the escape route that he and Booth should take upon leaving his farm.

The verdict was life in prison, his life being spared by a single vote.

That brought the process down to Mary Surratt. McDowell, after hearing the after-hours "shop talk," felt the consensus would be guilty, but that a token prison sentence would be levied.

The most damning evidence against Mary was that of John Lloyd, the Surrattsville tavern keeper who linked her to the weapons that John Surratt Junior, David Herold and George Atzerodt had left there. By telling him when the weapons would be needed, Lloyd claimed that Mrs. Surratt was part of the assassination plot. The Commission believed his testimony and found her guilty of conspiracy and sentenced her to death.

The public was aghast with the verdict and those involved with the trial were surprised and, even shocked, as was McDowell.

"What will happen next concerning the Surratt verdict?" Mac asked Hill Lamon.

"Well, it could be overturned by President Johnson," Hill explained. "And, I've heard that some of the Commission members may recommend to the President that her punishment be reduced to life in prison."

That, in fact, was what five of the Commission members did. In the record transmitted to the President, the life-in-prison decision was their suggestion in view of "her sex and age." Judge Holt presented the petition to the President.

President Johnson, however, refused. He declared that he would not change the sentence as Mrs. Surratt had "kept the nest that hatched the egg."

Ironically, even Lewis Powell had insisted throughout the trial that Mary was innocent.

'Well,' Mac thought, 'Hill was right. Someone has to pay.'

A last-ditch effort to delay Mary's prosecution was attempted through a writ of habeas corpus, an order requiring a prisoner's court appearance in view of illegal detention or imprisonment. President Johnson, to popular dismay, declared the writ suspended for the case.

"That will do it, Clay," Lamon explained. "You and many others won't agree, but Mary Surratt will become the first woman executed by the United States."

As the month of June ended, the nation readied itself for the final act of the assassination plot – the execution. McDowell was walking back to Old Arsenal in the late morning when a horseman he recognized as Gen. Winfield Scott Hancock was exiting the prison. He was walking his horse as if in a trance, grimed-faced and staring straight ahead. Mac's greeting was not acknowledged. The General was in another world.

The guard who provided Clay's entrance was unusually quiet.

"What's going on?" Mac asked. "Why is everyone so solemn?"

"Gen. Hancock just made a delivery from the War Department," the guard explained. "He brought four sealed documents and there's no need to ask what they contain."

McDowell failed to understand.

"Then, I guess I'll ask," he said. "What do they contain?"

"Death warrants," the guard responded. "We'll know officially when word gets out that the Commandant and Gen. Hancock have delivered them. I don't envy John Hartranft or Gen. Hancock. They'll have to deliver them personally to the four prisoners in solitary confinement."

"I guess they do that for each individual," the Marshal surmised.

The guard nodded.

"They have to go cell by cell, let each prisoner open the envelope, and read the warrant. Or, the prisoner can let Gen. Hartranft open and read it.

"There's only one job that's tougher than this," the custodian continued. "And that's the execution itself. I'd never want be the one to drop the trapdoor."

Clay thought for a moment, then asked, "Do you get to know those who'll be executed?"

"Yeah, if you work the cellblocks, and I have. The guards have been told not to communicate with any of the conspirators in the assassination case unless absolutely necessary. But, the prisoners will talk to you. And, in some cases, spill their guts."

"Does it bother you?" Mac asked.

"Yeah. Especially when it's someone like Mrs. Surratt. When I see her, I think of my mother. I guess I'm not permitted, but I have a genuine compassion for Mrs. Surratt. She's told me she's innocent."

"Do you believe her?"

"Yeah."

Mac exhaled and clapped the guard's shoulder.

"So do I," he said.

Chapter XXVII

Execution

The end was near and Lamon said they should follow the activity to conclusion.

His reference concerned the final phase of the Lincoln Assassination affair – the execution.

Each of the marshals had witnessed and been a part of executions, so the process was not unfamiliar. But this one was historic and was subject to change. So the six lawmen who had been associated with the Lincoln plot for so long, stood in the broiling sun at the Old Arsenal Prison Courtyard waiting for the final chapter to unfold.

The Washington rumor mill was in high gear on this miserably hot day of July 7. Would Mary Surratt become the first woman in U.S. history to be hanged by the government, or would President Johnson have second thoughts and commute her sentence to life imprisonment? As of noontime, the odds favored a reprieve for Mrs. Surratt.

McDowell, Barnes, Lewis, Miles and the Lamon brothers stood at the front of the gallows platform as the hour of the execution drew near.

Shortly after 1 p.m., the doors of Old Arsenal were opened and the prisoners, led by Mary Surratt, were taken into the courtyard where the gallows platform stood some fifty feet away. The platform was twenty feet in height and thirty feet across and contained two large hinged drops, one for two each of the condemned. The width was sufficient to provide space for spiritual advisors, soldiers standing guard and the hangman. Mrs. Surratt and Lewis Powell were to be hanged at the first drop, but simultaneously executed with David Herold and George Atzerodt.

Capt. Christian Rath, who had been assigned to supervise construction of the gallows, had prepared four nooses. Three were tied with seven knots each, but the one for Mary was tied with five knots and set aside. The consensus was that

Mrs. Surratt's execution would be commuted, and Rath did not believe he would need to finish the noose.

Testing of the drops was critical, and Rath was experiencing his share of problems. One-hundred-and-forty-pound weights were used for testing, and one of the drops repeatedly failed to meet expectations. That meant tests were repeated time-after-time until the drops performed evenly and simultaneously.

McDowell had supervised executions and knew how unnerving the tests were for the intended victims. Since a gallows always was constructed near the cells where they were held, those to be executed could clearly hear the thud of the falling drops. Mac could only guess how frightening the sound must be.

At one point, he saw Atzerodt appear suddenly at his barred window, drawn by the heavy pronouncement of death.

Four graves were dug next to the gallows and the victims were to be buried there immediately after being declared dead. Four ammunition containers were converted to coffins and placed near the graves, and four soldiers were stationed beneath the platform to knock down the posts supporting the trap doors.

Gen. Hancock, still aware that President Johnson might grant Mrs. Surratt a reprieve, ordered troopers to guard and clear points along the roadway from the White House to the penitentiary. It was a precaution to ensure that a message could be quickly received.

At twelve thirty, Hancock asked Rath to proceed. The surprised Captain asked if that also included Mrs. Surratt, and the General affirmed that she could not be saved.

Mary was taken from the prison first, still clad in a black, long-sleeved dress, veil and bonnet. It was the same clothing she had worn throughout her trial. Two guards helped support her as sedatives she'd been given made her unsteady. They virtually carried her up the fifteen steps to the gallows platform.

The hands and arms of the accused were bound, as were their legs and ankles. Mary complained that the wrist constraints were too tight, but she was told, "It won't hurt long."

When her veil and bonnet were removed, the noose was placed around her neck and she stared vacantly into space.

Mac watched as a priest offered his final prayer and Mary could be heard asking if she should say anything. McDowell couldn't hear the priest's response, but all the marshals clearly heard her final declaration.

"I'm innocent," she said, "but God's holy will be done."

Miles looked at Mac and shook his head.

White hoods were placed over the prisoners' heads and they were moved forward onto the trap doors. Mary stood unsteadily and asked that she not be allowed to fall.

Rath gave the signal and the support beams were removed. Mrs. Surratt died instantly and Herold and Atzerodt soon followed. Powell, however, struggled for several minutes, his thick neck apparently not broken.

McDowell felt as if a cold wind had passed over the scene. It was as if a dark page in the nation's history had been turned and nothing would ever again be the same. Hate had overcome justice and Lincoln's affirmation that "A nation divided against itself cannot stand," rang with more truth now than ever before.

Saddled with four bloody years of malevolence and mistrust, the Marshal wondered if America could ever be brought together again. Typically, winners would take all and the losers would be left with the dregs. The man who might have been able to bring the country together was gone, and so were the hopes and dreams of the South.

Clay left the courtyard remembering the words of Cassius Clay as the Civil War began.

"This entire war is a stupid mistake!" he'd said. "Some greedy bastards in the North are forcing it because they want to line their own pockets. Greed! Somebody wants something somebody else has and they're willing to sacrifice the lives of others to get it."

The South had become tired of being told what to do, the General had said. So Booth and his group decided to take matters into their own hands, but, in the process, had gone too far-too late and now had backed a Northern bulldog into a corner. And, as the South had done, the bulldog came out fighting, and had fought to the death. And the death in this instance was the demise of a group that started with only the intentions of winning.

The result, as Cassius had predicted, was a conflict that had torn the nation apart, killed off its best people and, making it necessary to rebuild the nation nearly from scratch.

'The war didn't determine who was right,' Clay thought. 'Only who is left.'

Suddenly, McDowell was sick of it all. And, as Hill Lamon had said, the Marshals service would be up to its elbows in cleaning up the mess. Their work really was just beginning.

Lamon had a final meeting scheduled for tomorrow. All hoped it would be brief as they were looking forward to a return home.

"Let's get out of here," Lewis growled, as the wait continued for the official pronouncement of the conspirators' death.

"Let's go to the Willard," Barnes suggested. "The first round is on me."

The Willard Hotel lobby was packed with politicians, government officials and the general public. And the central topic was about one thing – the hanging of Mary Surratt.

Barnes and Lewis forced their way into the Round Robin Bar while Clay and the others secured a table and some chairs. Mac remembered that Sen. Henry Clay, among other historic luminaries, had come here. In fact, it was the Great Compromiser from Kentucky who had introduced the mint julep to the Round Robin.

But, mint juleps were far from anyone's mind.

"This is a sad day and you're a sad-looking bunch," Hill Lamon said. "But, here's to each of you for a job well done. Let's hope we don't have to do this again."

They drank to Hill's toast and listened to the conversations that seemed to spring up all around them.

"Gentlemen," one man cried, "what we saw today was murder! Mrs. Surratt never had a chance!"

"Frankly, I'm disgusted and outraged!" another stated. "President Johnson should be horsewhipped! He should have had the decency to spare her. A prison term would have been sufficient."

"I see this as a vengeful and vindictive act by the Northern political machine," a Southern politician declared. "This is the wrong way to treat a fine lady and heal our Southern wounds."

"I don't care about any Southern wounds!" another stated. "The South got what it deserved! If I had my way, I'd execute every damn Rebel I could find!"

John Lamon had gone to get another round of drinks and Hill suggested that it should be their last.

"Things are getting out of hand," he observed. "Let's drink up and leave before they get us involved."

They finished and prepared to depart when a well-dressed man staggered into their party.

"Don't leave, Gentlemen," he said. "I'm buying a round for anyone who'll join me in a toast to the Union. You are for the Union aren't you?"

"Of course, we are," Barnes said. "But duty calls and we have to leave. Maybe next time."

"Hold on!" the drunk ordered. "Very politely, I've asked you to join me in a toast to the USA. Only fools and Rebels would refuse such an invitation. Which one of those are you?"

"Neither, friend," Roy replied. "Why don't you just relax and let it go?"

"You're a damn Rebel!" the drunk snarled. "You helped kill our President and you think that Surratt woman is a saint. Well, she got what she deserved. She should have been strung up to a high oak tree and left for the buzzards! What do you think of that?"

The drunk was big, rough and was used to getting his way, by intimidation or through physical force.

McDowell stepped in, guided the man to a chair and pushed him into its seat.

"Look, friend," he said, "don't mess with us. We're U.S. Marshals and if you give us any more trouble, we'll throw you in jail. You just sit there and sober up. We have other business and we don't have time for you. Now shut up! We're leaving."

They started walking away, but the drunk wouldn't let things go.

"You gutless SOB! You're like all Johnny Rebs! Your women are whores and your men are cowards! We hung one of your harlots today and we'll rape and hang the rest of them when we take over the South!"

McDowell stopped and took a long breath. It had been a grueling day. He was tired, angry and frustrated. He turned, walked back and grabbed the man by his hair. Mac drove a knee into his face, rotated his arm into a hammerlock and pushed the drunk toward the door. Hill Lamon and the others followed.

"He's your prisoner, Clay," Hill said. "Want to take him to jail?"

"Yeah!" the drunk taunted. "Take me to jail! You're not man enough to take me on right here and now! Are you yellow belly?"

Mac tightened his hold and pushed the drunk into an alley back of the hotel. He stripped off his coat and tie and tossed them to Lewis. Rolling up his sleeves, he turned to face Lamon.

"Hill, if you want to fire me for this, that's okay. And, if you want to take both of us to jail when I've finished, that's also okay. But, I'm going to whip this asshole if it's the last thing I do."

The drunk was taller than McDowell and outweighed him by twenty pounds. But the Marshal never hesitated. He walked directly toward him and shot a right to his mouth. A left caught the side of his head and Clay drove another right into his stomach.

The drunk went down, but Mac jerked him up by his hair and swung another right to his nose, breaking it. He continued to hold his adversary by the hair and pound punches to his face. The drunk dropped to his knees, spitting blood and waving for Clay to stop.

"No more! No more!" he coughed, and fell to the dirt roadway.

Clay kicked him twice in the ribs and reached to pull his victim to his feet. Hill placed a hand on McDowell's shoulder.

"That's enough, Marshal," he suggested. "For God's sake, give the man a chance. Next time, hit him with an axe handle."

Chapter XXVIII

Going Home

Clay was exhausted. The last few days had been draining, both mentally and physically. He slumped in his seat and rested his head against the side of the passenger car. Pulling his hat over his eyes, he folded his arms and hoped to get some sleep.

The train pitched forward, then maintained a steady rhythm as it gained speed. The swaying motion was rocking him to sleep.

"Hi, Marshal. Could you offer a girl a seat?"

Half asleep, Clay thought the voice sounded familiar. It wasn't until he caught a whiff of her perfume that recognition jolted him awake. He raised the brim of his hat and glanced to the right. There she stood, beautiful as ever, wearing that bewitching smile.

"Pauline!" Clay jumped to his feet and crushed her in an enduring embrace.

"My word!" the lady in the seat behind exclaimed. "Hr-rumph!" the man beside her disapproved.

They quickly sat as Pauline blinked and tried to catch her breath.

"You seem glad to see me!" she declared.

"Where have you been?" Clay demanded. "I lost track of you after Morgantown. Logan said you broke jail in Cincinnati and no one had heard from you since!"

"Oh, not really," she said, straightening her hat. "That nice marshal didn't arrest me, he placed me in protective custody after I showed him your card and explained the situation. He helped me get away the next day and even showed me how to load the derringer. Clay, it's really not that difficult. Bill gave me some ammunition and showed me how to clean the gun, and he suggested that I conceal it in my shoes or boot instead of ..."

"Who's Bill?" he interrupted.

"Bill Taylor, the marshal for Southern Ohio," Pauline explained. "You know him. He's got a nice office in downtown

Cincinnati and knows all the best dining establishments. We ate at a nice restaurant just off Fifth Street …"

"You ate at a restaurant?"

"Well, yes. Bill thought I'd enjoy eating in a restaurant rather than having a meal at the jail. He also took me to breakfast the next morning before I left."

"I was worried sick about you, Pauline! But now, I wonder why! It sounds like you've been having nothing but a good time!"

"Well, not so good, really," she said "I had sort of a bad time with that man in the gray suit. He followed me onto the train."

"We figured he would follow you. But did he try to harm you?"

"Well, actually, he did. He followed me into a passenger car and sat several seats away. After a while, I decided to change cars, but he caught up with me and tried to push me off the train. That's when I shot him."

"He pushed you and you shot him! How did that happen!" Clay demanded.

"Well, I did what you told me. I cocked the derringer and shoved it into his stomach and pulled the trigger. He fell off the train."

"Oh, before I forget it, you'll have to buy me a new white reticule. Maybe more than one, because I remember you saying…"

"Then what happened!" Mac interrupted.

"Well, this lady screamed that I'd shot a man and shoved him off the train. She was at the doorway waiting to change cars and I guess all she saw was me shooting him. The conductor and some other men came running, took the derringer and said I was going to be arrested for murder. I tried to explain what had happened, but they wouldn't believe me. When we got off the train, they said they were taking me to jail when Bill Taylor showed up. He had the wire you'd sent and said he'd keep me in protective custody pending official charges. Bill took me to his office and when he found out you weren't coming, said he was going to release me as there was no corpus delicti and that

I shouldn't say anything … something about the lady's word versus mine and the judge was out of town. He brought in a Union colonel who said he was involved in the spy network and wanted me to infiltrate the Confederate army in Tennessee. I was to use my New Orleans background as a pretense and explain that I was looking for my brother who left home to join up at the start of the war.

"Bill said I'd have to stay in jail overnight, but instead put me in his room and he slept in a jail cell. He was awfully sweet about everything."

"Then what happened?"

"After breakfast, I caught a train south and kept going until I reached Knoxville. I eventually worked my way into Nashville and Chattanooga and followed the Confederate army wherever it went. I got to know a lot of Southern soldiers and gathered quite a bit of information that I passed on to Union contacts. Then, I ran into trouble.

"I had some confidential papers from Gen. Rosecrans – Bill's a Union general – that someone found and turned over to Gen. Bragg – that's Braxton Bragg who commanded the Confederate Army of Tennessee. Well, I've never seen anyone as mad as Gen. Bragg. I was arrested and sentenced to be hanged. And, I would have been if a Col. Scott hadn't interfered.

"Now, I got to know John really well and we became good friends, mostly because he also was from Louisiana. In fact, he knew a lot of people in New Orleans who were friends of my family. And, one day when he visited me in jail, he found out that I knew you. Oh, and before I forget it, he said to give you his regards if I ever saw you again and tell you that Mary Beth is doing fine. He said you'd know what he meant."

"Yeah, yeah, I know the Colonel!" Clay snarled. "And, I know Mary Beth! But what about this other garbage! It sounds like you were real cozy with all the officers!"

"Forget that! What about Mary Beth?" she asked.

"Mary Beth Robinson," Clay declared. "She's also a spy and also real friendly with the Colonel. I'm beginning to wonder if any woman isn't.

"But, back to the subject. What about John Scott?"

"Well, the Colonel talked with Gen. Bragg and told him it would be wrong to hang a Southern woman, especially since no one in the war had ever hanged a woman; of course, that was before Mary Surratt. John urged the General to exchange me or have me give an oath of allegiance to the Confederacy. But the General said I'd done too much harm to the Confederate cause and he was going to hang me if it were the last thing he did.

"I declare, Marshal, that general is the most stubborn and disagreeable human being ..."

"Pauline!! Get back to your story! Why didn't he hang you?"

"Well, Col. Scott said I should pretend I had fallen ill and that would delay the sentence. We were near Shelbyville, Tennessee, at that point and the Federal forces hit that area so quick and hard that General Bragg had to turn tail and run. He forgot all about me.

"When I told my story to the Union command, they sent me back north and said I was now too well known to serve again as a spy. So, I got back into acting and was performing wherever I could find a job when I learned that President Lincoln wanted to honor me for all that I had done.

"Look at this," she announced, removing a roll of parchment from her carpetbag. "It's an honorary major's commission! When I received this, they asked me to tour the country dressed in uniform and lecture about all my espionage adventures. I'm still doing that, but now that the war is over I don't know how much longer it'll last."

Clay shook his head in awe.

"Unbelievable! You always seem to land on your feet. But, what in the world are you doing here?"

"Well, I was booked into Lexington and went over to your office hoping that I could see you. Logan was totally surprised and said neither of you knew if I were dead or alive."

"Well, it has been almost two years," Logan pointed out with a scowl.

"I know, but there was no way I could contact you. I've been a little busy. And, I found out, so have you.

"Logan told me everything that had happened with you since Morgantown, including the assignment in Washington and the Mary Surratt trial. He said you were finished in Washington and would be returning through Cincinnati. I found out the train would be stopping in Cumberland and I arrived here last night."

Pauline dropped her chin and shyly smiled.

"He even told me how worried you were when you couldn't contact me in Cincinnati after the wires were cut," she said softly. "Logan said you were really sweet on me."

Clay reddened and cleared his throat.

"Logan talks too much! After all, it was important that we stop that Richmond group before it went any farther.

"Oh, and before I forget it, I bought you something in Washington. It's a 'thank-you' gift for all that you've done."

Mac reached into his carpetbag and removed an object in badly wrinkled tissue paper.

"I had this with me when I saw you in Morgantown, but with all the excitement I forgot to give it to you. It's banged around in this bag since Donald Strathmore delivered me your letter about the goings on at the Richmond Theatre."

Pauline pulled away the paper covering a silver music box.

"Oh, Marshal, it's beautiful!"

She then fingered a large dent on the top.

"Please don't mind that," McDowell said. "It got hit by a glancing minie ball. Don't ask any details, just let me wind it, then open it!"

Pauline raised the top and activated the familiar strains of "Aura Lea."

She sat mesmerized by her favorite melody, then placed her hand on top of Clay's. Tears formed in her eyes.

"This is the most beautiful and wonderful gift anyone has ever given me!" She smiled. "I think it's time for me to retire from the theatre and become a full-time wife."

McDowell looked out the window.

"Hold on a minute. I, uh, haven't said anything about marriage. If I got married again, I'd have to find the right woman."

"Oh, we're going to be married alright, and, I am the right

woman!" she announced. "That is, unless you've married someone else in the meantime. You haven't have you?"

Clay shook his head.

"That's good," Pauline said. "If you had, my daddy would have to shoot you. Or, maybe I could do it myself. I've still got your derringer and I learned how to load it."

McDowell turned his head to say something, but Pauline put both hands around his face and kissed him solidly on the mouth. It ended up in a passionate embrace.

"Well!" the lady behind them cried. "I'm shocked! I've never seen such an embarrassing public display of affection in my life! Young lady you should be ashamed of yourself! Didn't your mother teach you proper behavior?"

She emphasized her point by smacking Pauline's shoulder with her parasol.

Pauline stood and walked back to where the lady was seated. She took her hand and, with tears in her eyes, knelt and offered her apologies.

"Madame, I'm so sorry and I beg your forgiveness. I have acted inappropriately and, you're correct, there can be no excuse for such shocking behavior. You see, I haven't seen my husband for years because we've been separated by this terrible war. I don't even know if the children still remember him. I truly thought he was dead.

"And, then, just by chance, I happened to take this train and who should I see but the man I love and cherish. This is the happiest day of my life!"

Pauline sobbed and lay her forehead on the lady's hand.

"There, there, dear!" she said, patting Pauline's head. "This war has been devastating for us all!"

Her husband, leaning forward, added, "We are the ones who should be asking for forgiveness. You have endured more than any human spirit should have to bear."

Pauline hugged them both.

"You are the most kind and understanding people on earth! May God bless you!"

She wiped her eyes and returned to her seat, burying her

face in her hands. A puzzled Clay reluctantly patted her shoulder.

"Parkersburg! All out for Parkersburg!" the conductor called.

The elderly couple made their departure, squeezing Pauline's shoulder as they passed.

The conductor walked by checking tickets.

"You two are headed for Cincinnati, right?" he asked.

"Then on to Lexington," Clay added.

He looked at Pauline with a questioning expression.

"Husband? And children?"

Pauline exhaled, dried her eyes and smiled.

" I told you I was a good actress. That crying scene was one of my best."

The train lurched forward and began to gain speed.

"I can't wait to see your farm, Clay," Pauline beamed. "I just love horses. Did I tell you I was a good rider? I'm going to like being a farmer's wife!"

McDowell stared with surprise.

"Do you realize that's the first time you've ever called me Clay?"

Pauline slipped her hands around his arm.

"Better get used to it, Marshal. That's what married couples do – call each other by their first names."

Mac sat in silence, overcome by the events of the last few minutes.

"You understand that I'm not going to quit marshalling, don't you?"

"It doesn't matter. The children and I will be there for you on the farm. You'll have a home to come to instead of an office."

Pauline looked up at her intended.

"You do want more children don't you? I think four or five might be just right. And, we can build a new house right there on the farm. We'll be close to Tom, Maddie, Sarah Anne and Claude and you can see them every day. I can't wait to meet them! "

Mac looked at her and shook his head.

"Pauline, I don't think I've ever known anyone quite like you. You're really impossible, you know?"

She smiled and kissed him on the cheek.

"Oh, Clay! We're going to be so happy!"

Somewhat stunned, Mac looked out the window.

'Oh, well,' he thought, 'maybe she is the right woman.'

* * *

As the train left Parkersburg, Pauline tightened her embrace around Mac's arm and rested her head on his shoulder. The train lurched forward and began to gain speed. Pauline closed her eyes and drifted into a restful sleep.

Clay placed his hand over that of Pauline and gazed at the passing countryside. He was relaxed and felt free and easy. It was a great feeling, something he hadn't experienced in a long time. With the war over and Pauline beside him, the world definitely had a brighter look.

Mac began to doze as the rhythm of the ride had a hypnotic effect. Suddenly, that changed.

Passengers and baggage fell forward as brakes were applied and the car shook violently. Clay felt the car fishtail and passengers were thrown aside. For a moment, the vehicle seemed to balance on one side's wheels. Then, it fell and began to skid. The sides and top of the coach were torn away and its contents – including passengers – were thrown down a slope, finally stopping after striking the side of a hill.

The derailment was massive with debris scattered for hundreds of yards. The sounds of the crash were thunderous and seemed to last an eternity. But, suddenly, there was silence and no indication that survival was possible.

Some time later, consciousness returned for McDowell. He was lying on his side with one arm extended toward the tracks. He was numb and found he could make no movement, other than the fingers of the extended arm and hand. Some yards away, he saw Pauline. She was lying on her back in a pile of rubble. As he watched, she opened her eyes and focused on the

Marshal. Painfully, she reached as if to touch him, not realizing she was too far away. She tried to smile, then mouthed the words, "Help me!"

Instinctively, Clay tried to reach out for Pauline, but he could only open his hand, his fingers beckoning for her to come. Then, things began to grow dark and her vision faded away.

Then, there was nothing.

* * *

"No! No!" Clay shouted as he bolted from the cot.

He reached desperately for the image burned into his mind's eye. His hand struck the wall and slowly reality set in. She wasn't there; it was The Dream.

McDowell found a pad of paper and a pencil, sat on the edge of his bed and made his usual notations on what had transpired in his flight of fantasy. Somehow, he knew the experience was finished. The Dream now had a beginning and an end. It had been an unbelievable journey, a complex tale mixed with real events, real people and an improbable storyline beyond comprehension. And, he wouldn't dream it again.

'Well, for better or worse, it's finished,' Mac thought. 'Now, it's time to deal with reality.'

But, reality would have a few surprises for the Marshal. Dreams and reality would become more intertwined and the line between them would become more smudged than definitive.

Chapter XXIX

The Chase

The deer, blinded by the headlights, was unsure what to do. So, he just stood, stock-still.

In the early morning darkness, the driver of the prison bus was not fully awake and didn't see the animal until he was nearly on top of him. He hit the brakes and spun the wheels hard to the right, but it was too late. The vehicle struck the big buck with a thud and careened down the roadway. The bus skidded for some twenty yards as the deputy fought to gain control. The twenty-six prisoners chained behind the screen were thrown forward as were the four armed guards.

The bus went into a slow one-hundred-and-eighty-degree spin and, just when it appeared that it may right itself, the rear wheels struck the shoulder and went over the embankment. The rear of the bus momentarily was suspended above the culvert, then it fell, pulling the rest of the vehicle after it.

The occupants were thrown to one side, the side that landed with a crushing impact. The momentum sent the bus into a roll and it somersaulted over rocks and brush as prisoners and guards were propelled through broken windows and rips in the vehicle's flesh. It finally came to an upside-down stop against some huge oak trees and was so sufficiently hidden by the foliage that those in passing vehicles might not even see it.

There were no sounds except for the trickling noise of a liquid. If the gasoline reached the engine block, flames would engulf the carnage. Then, the accident certainly would attract attention.

Tyrell Holston came out of his fog, unsure where he was or what had happened. Groans from the injured jolted him back to reality. He moved his arms, but a heavy weight lay across his legs. Pushing up to a sitting position, he saw an unconscious guard lying across the lower half of his body. Grasping the guard by his shirt collar, he pulled the body away, but found it difficult to stand because of the pain in his left leg. Using both hands, he explored the area just below his knee. Nothing appeared broken, but something either was torn or badly sprained.

Using a broken tree limb for support, Holston stood and surveyed the wreckage. There was sufficient moonlight to view the accident's aftermath. The body of the bus and its passengers were scattered from the drainage ditch to the wooded hillside where he was standing. No one was moving and the groans he had heard earlier had faded away.

Holston lowered himself beside the guard. He extracted a key ring from the officer's belt and began trying keys until he found the ones that unlocked his cuffs and leg irons. He sat, enjoying his freedom.

The sky in the East was beginning to soften and sunrise probably was no more than an hour away. Northbound traffic was moving at a steady clip, but drivers still were unaware of the accident involving the twenty-six passengers, twenty of whom were federal prisoners who had been temporarily lodged at the Atlanta Penitentiary pending transfer to other locations.

After weighing his options, Holston began removing the uniform from a guard, who was about his size. He put on the blue shirt, and, after wrapping his knee with strips torn from his prison shirt, pulled on the dark blue trousers. With the guard's gun belt and cap, the transformation was complete. He checked the 9mm pistol and found it undamaged. Also, the guard had several additional rounds of ammunition and an ID that revealed Clyde S. DuPree was a federal security officer. Now, for the getaway.

Holston found he could maneuver sufficiently by using the tree limb for support. He made his way across the drainage ditch and painfully worked his way up to the highway. Using the flashlight that had been attached to the gun belt, he began flagging cars, signaling for help. Most vehicles slowed, but refused to stop. Finally, one did.

Hobbling to the driver's side, Holston explained his situation to an attractive brunette.

"Thanks for stopping, ma'am," Holston said, flashing his ID. "There's been a bad traffic accident and I need to get to a phone to call 911. Can you take me to a location where I can get help?"

Mary Margaret Thatcher reached into her purse and removed a cell phone.

"No problem, Officer," she said, "I can make the call from here."

"Uh, better let me call," Holston replied, snatching the phone from her hand and settling himself in the back seat. "I can give them the details."

Hitting three random numbers, Holston listened for several seconds before delivering his message.

"This is Sgt. Clyde DuPree, security officer at the federal pen in Atlanta," he reported. "We've had an accident involving the transportation of federal prisoners. Our bus overturned on I-75 about five miles north of Atlanta. All on board have been injured or are dead and we need immediate medical and law enforcement assistance."

Holston paused as if listening to the other party.

"That's right," he continued. "I'm with a motorist who has lent me her cell phone. Call me at this number and I'll guide you in."

Holston removed the phone from his ear, asked for its number and relayed it to his phantom source.

"Thanks, ma'am," he said, "you've been a big help. I'll just hang on to the phone until we get some help, if that's alright?"

Mary Margaret nodded while looking in the rear view mirror.

"I think help already has arrived," she said.

A patrol car with flashing lights stopped behind the Thatcher vehicle. A Georgia highway patrol trooper approached and tapped on the driver-side window.

Mary Margaret lowered the window and offered her driver's license as the trooper flashed a light inside, illuminating the driver and Holston.

"I saw you parked and your flasher and figured you needed

some assistance," the trooper smiled, "but I see that another officer beat me to it."

Holston's pistol barked twice as he shot the trooper in the chest. Mary Margaret stared in shock, but had no chance to respond as Holston grabbed a handful of hair, jerked back her head and shoved the pistol against her neck.

"Move it, Lady!" he ordered, "or I'll do the same to you!"

"But, what have you done! I don't understand ..."

"Shut up and drive!" Holston snarled. "Go! Now!"

Mary Margaret floored the accelerator and moved onto the pavement as the cars behind her hit their brakes and skidded into a pile of bent fenders and twisted metal. She was up to eighty-five before Holston told her to slow down and observe the speed limit.

"Do what I tell you and I'll let you live," he said. "I'm a convicted felon and I have no hesitation about taking you out. Stay at the speed limit and keep driving until we reach Kentucky. When we get to Middlesboro, I'll give you more directions."

Mary Margaret nodded, but could not respond. Her mouth was too dry.

* * *

Clay, still half asleep, fumbled to turn off the alarm clock. But, it wasn't there.

The ringing continued and finally the Marshal was aware he was in his office, not at his farm. Exhausted after awakening from The Dream, Mac had fallen into a troubled sleep. He sat for a moment on the edge of the cot, then reached for the telephone.

"Marshal's Office, McDowell speaking."

"Mac, this is Logan. Where the hell have you been!"

"Right here," Clay yawned. "What time is it?"

"It's five a.m.," his deputy replied, "I've been trying to reach you for an hour. I got nothing but voice messages when I called your home and cell phone. Have you been at the office all this time?"

"Yeah, I had a late night with the Porters and decided to sleep here. What's up?"

"We've got to join a manhunt," Logan Perry answered. "I got a call from Atlanta when they couldn't reach you. It seems a Federal prisoner escaped when a prison bus overturned on I-75 just north of Atlanta. He abducted a car and driver headed north. We arrested him several years ago and they think he may be heading back into an area around Middlesboro where we caught him."

"Who's the escapee?"

"His name's Tyrell Holston and he's a mean one. You and I picked him up after he hijacked a truck in Bell County and killed the driver. We had a shootout with him and tracked him for several days before we caught him hiding at a mountainside farm."

Mac stood as he recalled the chase.

"He's the guy we caught in the outhouse?"

Perry chuckled.

"Yeah, he's the one you jerked off the pot. Remember, the state police said you caught him with his pants down?"

"Where are you now?"

"I'm at home, but I can be there in 15 minutes."

"That'll give me enough time to pull some things together," Mac said. "You can fill me in with the details once we're on the road."

Mac made a quick trip to the restroom, then began gathering up weapons and ammunition. Holston wasn't one to give up easily, the Marshal recalled. He remembered that it took both Logan and himself to subdue Holston, who vowed that he would kill them should he ever get the opportunity.

When Logan arrived, Mac helped him load their vehicle with the firepower and they quickly headed south toward Middlesboro. Perry gave Mac an abbreviated report.

"The Marshals service was taking twenty Federal prisoners from Atlanta early this morning for relocation," Logan began, "when the bus overturned on I-75 just north of the city. The driver apparently tried to keep from hitting a deer, lost control and the bus fell into a drainage ditch, overturned and rolled over several times. Five people were killed and all the rest sustained injuries – some of them pretty serious. The only person not accounted for was Tyrell Holston, who, apparently, changed clothes with a dead officer and hijacked and kidnapped a car and driver. A Georgia state trooper who had stopped to help was shot by Holston and later died. But, he was able to tell what happened and had the billfold and identification of the kidnapped driver. He said the car continued north and our agency believes that Holston is headed to Middlesboro where he has accomplices who'll help and hide him."

"Who's the kidnapped driver?" Mac asked.

Perry shook his head.

"You're not going to believe this," he said. "Mary Margaret Thatcher."

"You're kidding?"

"Nope," Logan replied. "I had a hard time believing it myself. But it's that Civil War author you think is so great."

Clay sighed in disbelief.

"Of all the people," he said, "what are the odds that it would be a Civil War writer?"

"Don't worry about it, Mac," Logan responded. "All we have to do is save her."

"Got a description on her vehicle?"

"Yeah, it's a red four-door Ford Taurus. And, get this, the license is one of those vanity plates – 1861 CW."

"Yeah, I get it," the Marshal replied. "The year the Civil War began."

"Thought you would."

McDowell leafed through some paperwork he'd pulled from the files. A color photo of Holston showed a thin, light blue line that ran down the left side of his face. It was either a birthmark or an old wound. Mac immediately placed it with the knife-scarred face of the Holston in his dream. 'Weird, really weird,' he thought. But, back to reality.

"I wouldn't give odds that Ms. Thatcher will get out of this alive," he said, stuffing the paperwork back in his briefcase.

Chapter XXX

The Escape

"We're getting low on gas," Mary Margaret announced.

Holston shoved the pistol barrel harder against the driver's neck, squinted at the gauge and noted that the indicator was nearing the empty mark.

"Give me your purse," he commanded.

Emptying the contents on the back seat, Holston pawed one-handed through the items.

"Where's your billfold?" he growled.

"The trooper had it when you shot him," Mary Margaret replied. "It's back there where we left him."

Holston smacked her head, hard.

"You stupid bitch! You'd better have some money or a credit card somewhere!"

"Sorry, everything was in the billfold."

Mary Margaret had recovered from her initial fear, and terror now was tempered with cool reason. If she were to escape, she had to think logically and clearly. Forcefully, she filed her panic on the back burner.

Holston cursed her and the ill turn of events, then rifled through his pockets. DuPree's wallet contained ninety-three dollars in cash plus a number of credit cards.

"Take the next exit," he commanded.

Holston saw what he wanted ahead and to the left, a huge multi-pump truck stop with lots of activity. He told Mary Margaret to pull up at a vacant self-serve pump. Stuffing the pistol in its holster and the car keys in his pocket, he began pumping the fuel, cautioning Mary Margaret to "sit still and keep quiet."

Pulling the cuffs from his belt, he walked to the driver's side and ordered his hostage to get out and place the cuffs around her wrists. He then took her arm and led her inside to the cash register. The female attendant stood wide-eyed as she saw the handcuffs.

"Don't worry, Miss," Holston assured her. "She's under control. Don't do anything to call attention or create any alarm for your customers. I'll just pay the bill and we'll be out of your way."

By paying with cash, Holston reasoned that he'd leave no trail.

Mary Margaret looked directly into the eyes of the register attendant.

"Look, Miss," she said in a steady, conversationalist tone. "This isn't what it seems. This man is not a police officer. He kidnapped me in Atlanta and is an escaped federal prisoner. My name is Mary Margaret Thatcher and I'm a professor at East Tennessee State University. Please notify the police."

Holston forced a laugh and shook his head.

"Don't believe her, Miss. This woman is well-known for her confidence schemes. She's sweet-talked and swindled thousands of dollars from unsuspecting people."

"Wow!" the register girl exclaimed. "She really is convincing."

Mary Margaret shook her head.

"Remember what I said," she reminded the girl.

"Let's go," Holston ordered, taking Mary Margaret's arm.

"I need to go to the restroom," she protested.

Holston walked her outside and knocked on the restroom door. Receiving no response, he opened the door and shoved Mary Margaret inside.

"I need my purse," she said. "I can't freshen up without it."

"Shut up! Get in that stall and hurry up. You've got sixty seconds and keep that door open."

Embarrassed and frustrated, Mary Margaret relieved herself, but had no time to leave a message or develop an escape plan. Holston removed the cuffs when they returned to the car and gave her the ignition keys, this time after sliding into the front passenger seat.

They continued north through Tennessee and soon were nearing the Kentucky border.

"Take the exit at Jellico and drive east toward Middlesboro," he ordered.

Mary Margaret did as she was told. She continued to look for an opportunity to escape, but there was none. Holston sat close beside her with the weapon held against her ribs. It was then she noticed the car in the rear view mirror. It had been following since they entered Kentucky. If help was on the way, she needed to keep her captor's mind occupied.

"You must know someone around here," she stated. "Mind telling me where we're going?"

"Shut up and drive!" Holston ordered. "You'll know when we get there."

"Look," she said, pointing. "Isn't that a hawk over there? I'm fascinated by predators."

"So what? It's just a bird!"

Holston then smiled.

"If you really like predators, then you're going to love me. We'll have some fun before I take you out."

"You mean to kill me?" Mary Margaret asked. "What in the world for? I'm helping you escape and you're really going to owe me big time. Not many women would do what I'm doing for you."

"As if you had any choice!" the convict snarled.

"Look at it this way," she said. "I was going north anyway, I just expected to do it alone. I didn't expect to have a charming companion."

"Yeah, I'm going to charm the hell out of you, Lady. Just wait until we stop."

"You never did tell me where we're going," Mary Margaret continued. "You haven't forgotten the way, have you?"

"Just shut up, Lady! My leg's killing me and I don't need your infernal yapping!"

"Oh, I didn't know about your leg. What happened?"

"I must have sprained it when the bus crashed … DAMMIT! WHAT'S GOING ON HERE! You're a nut case! I've never heard anybody talk as much as you do. Just shut up and drive!"

Mary Margaret shrugged. A glance in the mirror confirmed the car still was following.

"Talking makes the time go faster. I thought a little conversation might help."

"If you want to help, SHUT UP!"

"Okay," she replied. "But you don't have to be so disagreeable. I know we'll never be friends, but …"

Holston shoved the pistol against her temple.

"If you don't shut up and just drive, I'll blow you away right now!"

"Not a good idea," she said. "Shoot me now and we'll wreck. Then you'll never get to where we're going ... wherever that is."

Holston threw up his hands in frustration.

"I don't believe this! Of all the people who could have stopped, it had to be you! Lady, you need to be locked away in a padded cell! I'm going to take a chance and pop you now!"

He again placed the weapon against her temple.

"Okay, okay, I get the point," she said. "I'll stop talking."

Holston pulled the pistol away and glared through the windshield.

"But, if you change your mind ..."

"Boy, are you asking for it!" he murmured, scooting closer.

"Uh, sorry about that. Just never mind. I'm finished."

Holston nodded.

"You're right about that. And, it'll be soon."

They drove past Middlesboro and Holston ordered her to go north to Pineville. After several miles, she was directed to take a gravel road that led to a neat frame house. Whoever lived there kept the place in good condition, she thought, noting that the exterior recently had received a fresh coat of white paint. They proceeded to a garage at the rear of the house where a man was tinkering with the engine of a tan Ford coupe. Two other similar vehicles were close by and all three appeared well cared for and in excellent condition. Plus, they seemed to be built for speed. Moonshiner cars, she thought.

Holston took the car keys, placed Mary Margaret's hands through the steering wheel and cuffed her. He exited the car and was greeted by the "mechanic," who seemed glad to see him. They talked for several minutes before the "mechanic" stooped and peered into the vehicle. He walked a few steps closer and gazed intently at Mary Margaret.

"Hi, there!" she waved. "Good to see you. Sorry we can't stay, we're just passing through."

The man shook his head and returned to talk again with Holston. Their conversation became louder and more animated and she heard one of them say something about "dead hostages." That wasn't something she wanted to hear.

The "mechanic" went into the garage and returned with a set of keys that he gave to Holston. He then pointed down the road and indicated that something was off to the right. They shook hands and Holston returned to the car.

"Are we on the road again?" she smiled.

"Shut up and get back on the road. Turn right when I tell you. We're looking for an old logging road that leads into the forest."

"What then?" Mary Margaret asked. "Are we taking the scenic route to Grandma's house?"

"Shut up, bitch! We're looking for a cabin where we can hole up for awhile."

The logging road was littered with rocks and holes and the going was slow. After some three miles, Holston directed her to pull over and drive into a copse of trees. He took the keys from the ignition, pulled Mary Margaret after him and out the passenger side. He cuffed her around a small sapling on the opposite side of the trail and began swinging a leafy branch across the tire tracks. The back-and-forth motion helped upright the spare grass that had been flattened by the vehicle.

When satisfied that the path had a more normal appearance, Holston returned to Mary Margaret and removed one cuffed hand, attaching the other cuff to his left wrist.

"Are we going to look for Smokey the Bear?"

Holston slapped her across the mouth. It hurt and brought blood.

"I guess not," she mumbled.

Choosing a rocky terrain, Holston pulled her after him as they entered the deep woods. Thorns tore at her pants suit and she nearly fell several times as her footwear was unsuited to the route they were taking.

They came on to the cabin suddenly. It was hidden in dense foliage and not likely to be found unless you stumbled onto it. Holston opened the padlock on the door and they walked into a surprise. Bunk beds were built into the far wall, a fireplace was to the right and a sink, cabinets and a wood-burning stove covered most of the left wall. A fuel-fired generator and several kerosene heaters were stashed in a corner. A hand-pump was at one end of the sink and evidently provided well water. The cabinets were well-stocked with non-perishable foods and ready-to-eat meals. A table and four chairs were in the center of the room. It was a great hideout.

"Don't bother carrying me across the threshold," Mary Margaret said. "I can make it on my own."

Holston moved her to one of the bunk beds and cuffed her around one of the supports.

"You'll stay here until I rustle up something for us to eat," he said.

"Where's the bathroom?" she asked.

"It's an outhouse," Holston said. "It's behind the cabin and I'll take you there when you need to go. And, I guess you need to go."

"You're a mind reader," Mary Margaret nodded. "I need to go."

Holston uncuffed his hostage and led her out the rear door.

"Don't try to get away, City Girl. You're safer with me than you would be in the woods. There are plenty of poisonous snakes and wild animals out there. You wouldn't stand a chance."

"I didn't know I had a choice," she responded. "Tell me, just how safe am I here with you?"

"Don't try my patience!" he warned. "You've served your purpose and just look on any time you have left as a bonus."

"So, you're going to kill me?"

"Not just yet, but don't push it!"

Mary Margaret was surprised to find the outhouse was a two-holer complete with toilet paper. She guessed she must wash her hands in the cabin.

"Nice place you have here," she said as Holston led her back to the dwelling. "One room and a path with all the comforts of home."

"Shut up!" Holston snarled, "or I'll push you down the shit pit."

"In that case, I'll choose quiet," she replied.

Mary Margaret wasn't ready to give up, but her prospects were getting dim. Hopefully, there still was a car following them and the cavalry was on its way.

Chapter XXXI

Closing In

"That's it!" Perry shouted.

Clay McDowell and Logan Perry were waiting for the traffic light to change when the red Taurus passed before them.

"The license plate checks out," Mac said. "Follow, but don't get too close. This is a real break!"

Logan turned left with the change of the light. If he could stay about a block behind they had a good chance of not being detected.

"A woman was driving," Perry noted. "It must have been the Thatcher woman."

"Could be, but it was her car for sure," McDowell replied. "And, there was someone with her."

Traffic was light in Middlesboro and Perry was hard-pressed to keep a vehicle between him and the Taurus. For the most part, he was successful, but there always was the worry that Holston might have spotted the tail. But, so far, so good.

Logan dropped back even more as the surveillance continued on the road to Pineville. The two-lane highway passed through a continuing series of rural venues filled with hills and valleys and a multitude of curves. More than once, Perry would lose sight of the Taurus, only to pick it up again when they reached a straight stretch. That continued until he was forced to slow down for a series of serpentine curves. When he reached a straight area atop a hill, the lead car was nowhere in sight.

They continued for several miles until it was obvious they had lost their prey.

"They must have taken a side road," Logan said, stopping at a turnoff to a nearby farmhouse.

"Well, let's retrace," McDowell ordered. "They may have taken that side road several miles back."

Perry turned around and they backtracked slowly. When

they reached the graveled side road, Logan turned cautiously and stopped.

"If they turned here, I don't want to blunder into them," he said. "How do you think we should play it?"

"Let's proceed like we know where we're going," Mac said. "Chances are, this is where they turned. We're in an unmarked vehicle and, if they are up ahead, it's not likely that Holston would recognize us. If we see them, don't stop. We'll have to do another backtrack and hope for the best."

They passed by the white house, seeing no one, and Perry soon ran into the road's rough section. Their car lurched around holes and rocks and the deputy observed that "no one in his right mind" would follow such a route.

"Forget about being undetected," he said, downshifting. "Holston will have made us before we can get into second gear."

"I still think he's somewhere up ahead," Mac observed. "Let's just play it by ear and see what happens. If he's on this road, he sure can't outrun us."

"He could if he's on foot," Logan replied, as the car bottomed out. "Let's find a place to pull off. We need four-wheel drive to keep going."

They found a spot and Perry lumbered to a stop.

"Look off to the right there," Mac pointed. "Either someone has tried to hide their tracks, or some kind of vehicle passed this way a short time ago."

Pulling their weapons, the lawmen exited their car and followed the trail leading into a wooded area. Proceeding with caution, they found the Taurus hidden in the copse of trees.

"Well, they won't have any transportation out of here," Logan said, pointing to the oil-soaked ground. "They've ruptured a line or something and lost all their engine oil."

"Call for some backup," Mac said. "They can't be too far."

Perry called for assistance and suggested officers come in four-wheeled drive transportation.

"What now?" he asked.

"Let's see if we can track them," the Marshal said. "I'd like to find their location before help arrives."

After several unsuccessful attempts, the lawmen found the trail leading to the cabin. They could have stumbled onto the structure or missed it entirely except for a light that was shining through a window. They pulled back into the brush and watched intently, but no one was in sight. They each had an M16 in addition to their pistols. It was decided to wait and see what developed.

"Glad you brought the assault rifles," Perry said, continuing to look for movement inside the cabin. "How many clips did you bring?"

"I didn't count," Mac replied. "But there are some 40-rounders mixed in with some 10s. Just hope we don't have to use them."

"You know Holston won't give up, Mac," Logan noted. "We can't take him alive."

"Yeah, but we don't want to jeopardize the hostage. We can't shoot unless we have a clean target."

"If he doesn't need her, he'll kill her himself. Odds are that neither one will get out of this in one piece.

"And maybe we won't either."

Both turned as they heard a noise behind them. A camouflaged lawman held a finger to his lips. Crawling forward, he positioned himself between McDowell and Perry.

"McPherson," he announced. "I'm with the state police. I brought a SWAT team with me and they're fanning out around the cabin. Anything happen?"

"Not yet," Clay said. "We believe Holston is inside with the hostage, but we haven't seen any movement."

Even as he spoke, a man appeared at the window and surveyed the scene. Logan had glasses focused on the image. The deputy didn't speak until the man moved away.

"It's Holston!" he stated.

"Are you sure?" Mac asked.

"I'm sure. I even saw that scar down the side of his face."

The state trooper looked at McDowell.

"It's your show," he said. "How do you want to handle this?"

"Did you bring a bullhorn?"

The trooper nodded.

"Radio your team and be sure they're in position. Then, I'll call him out."

With everything set, Mac raised the bullhorn to his mouth.

"Tyrell Holston, this is the police. We have the cabin surrounded and we're giving you a chance to surrender. Send your hostage out first, then throw out your weapons and walk out with your hands behind your head. We don't want anyone to get hurt."

There was no response.

Mac repeated his message, but, again, there was no reply.

He waited a few minutes then repeated his call for surrender. This time, there was the sound of breaking glass as Holston smashed his pistol against the window.

"Who's out there?" he called.

"The U.S. Marshals Service and the state police," Mac responded. "Give it up, Holston. We don't want to kill you."

"Go to Hell!" Holston shouted. "I've got a hostage and I'll shoot her."

"We don't want anyone to get hurt," Mac replied. "You don't have a chance. Just give it up and we'll end this without anyone getting injured."

There was no response. After several minutes, McDowell repeated his message.

"Who's out there?" Holston demanded. "Is that you McDowell?"

"I'm here," Mac said. "Give it up!"

A lengthy silence followed, then Holston replied.

"Tell you what, McDowell. You put down your weapons and walk up to the cabin and I'll bring out the hostage. We'll negotiate from there."

"Don't do it, Clay! That SOB will shoot you sure as hell!" Logan said.

Mac laid down his rifle and handed his pistol to Perry.

"You and McPherson cover me," he said. "Tell the SWAT team to get into position and take out Holston if he aims at me. The team can nail Holston as soon as he moves his weapon off the hostage. This is a chance we've got to take. We could end it right now."

"I'm coming out, Holston!" Mac called.

He raised his hands and walked slowly toward the cabin. As Clay walked, Holston pushed open the door and stepped out with his left arm around Mary Margaret's throat and a pistol in his other hand. The fugitive glanced around and ordered the Marshal to stop, but with his hands raised.

"Now, the rest of you," Holston said. "I know they're eight of you out there. I saw your entire team from the cabin. First, the deputy marshal and the state police officer – step out where I can see you and drop your weapons."

They did.

"Now, you six with the SWAT team. Move out where I can see you and drop your weapons. All of you! Keep your hands up where I can see them."

"Do it," McPherson ordered. "Don't anybody think about being a hero."

When everyone was in front of the cabin, Holston ordered McDowell to walk slowly toward him.

"Keep coming!" he commanded. "I want you so close, Marshal, that I can touch you."

Mac stopped when he was within three feet of Holston.

"Now, take your left hand and drop that ankle gun. You do the same deputy, and you too, state police."

"I guess you won't believe we're not armed," Mac offered.

"Shut up, asshole! All of you! Drop those guns, now! Then, kick 'em over here!"

Slowly, each lawman removed his weapon and kicked it toward Holston.

"Now, let the woman go," Clay said. "You're in control."

"You're damn right I am," Holston growled. "Now, Marshal, unbutton your shirt with your left hand all the way down to the waist."

Mac did as he was told.

"Pull the shirt open."

Clay did.

"Well, well, no flak jacket or body armor," Holston said, his pistol shoved under Mary Margaret's jaw. "You may remember, Marshal, that I said I was going to kill you when you arrested me before. Think about that. I'm still going to do it, but not now. No, not now, because I have to get away.

"You, state police, fish out the keys to your vehicle and throw them over here where I can see them ... ah, ah ... easy now. Don't try anything fancy."

Holston kept the pistol under Mary Margaret's jaw as he turned his gaze upon McDowell.

"When do think I should kill you, Marshal? Tomorrow? Next week?

"Or, how about now!"

Quicker than the blink of an eye, Holston flashed his weapon toward Mac and shot twice before again forcing the barrel under Mary Margaret's jaw. It happened so quickly that no one had time to react.

Clay fell back as both rounds entered his chest. He lay on his side, unable to move. There was no feeling of pain, just numbness.

"Well, gentlemen, I have to leave you now," Holston said. "I don't think you have any doubt that I'll take out anyone who's in my way."

"You'll never make it," Perry said.

"Sure I will, deputy. Nobody here is going to shoot me, because I have the upper hand. If I were to take a bullet, my reflexes would cause me to pull the trigger and I couldn't miss my hostage at this range. That is, unless someone wants to try me. How about it? Any takers?"

Holston smiled as he glanced around the circle of lawmen. No one moved.

"I thought not," he said.

As Holston talked, McDowell fought to remain conscious, angled his head toward Mary Margaret and caught her attention. He flicked his eyes from her to his ankle weapon that now lay just in front of her. He did that several times before the hostage caught his meaning and made a slight nod that she understood.

Holston took a step away from the cabin, his attention focused on the lawmen, pulling his hostage with him. Mary Margaret groaned and went limp, falling in a heap at Holston's feet. At the same time, McDowell called out for help and painfully rolled over on his back.

Mary Margaret's hand grasped the snub-nosed .38 as she fell upon it. Holston's attention was diverted momentarily to Mac, just enough time for the hostage to point and empty the weapon into Holston's body.

The surprised fugitive staggered back and fell, firing his pistol wildly into the cabin.

Everything happened so fast that, for several seconds, no one moved. McPherson then wrenched the pistol from Holston's dead hand and Logan found his weapon and, just for sure, trained it on the fallen outlaw.

Mary Margaret crawled to Clay's side and stuffed his shirttail into his chest wounds.

"Don't die on me, Marshal!" she pleaded. "You just saved my life!"

Chapter XXXII

The Wrap Up

Mary Margaret tapped on the door and cracked it open.

She recognized the tall figure blocking her view as that of Logan Perry. The deputy marshal turned and, when he recognized who it was, motioned for her to enter.

"I was just leaving, Professor," he grinned. "Our patient is now among the living. I was explaining how you saved his life."

"See you later, Clay," Logan waved, pulling up a chair for Mary Margaret.

However, instead of sitting, she walked to the bedside and took Mac's hand.

"I've stopped by several times," she said, "but this is the first time I've found you awake."

"I'm still in a fog," Mac said. "They're pumping so much medication into me that I feel like I'm on a cheap Saturday night drunk."

"I'm not going to stay long. They told me at the desk I could only see you for a few minutes. They said you really need all the rest you can get. You must be hurting, but this is a good sign you're getting better."

Clay nodded and tried to smile. The two shots he had taken missed his lung, but broke his left collarbone before exiting his upper back. It would take a while, but he'd recover.

"It's not fun ... but sure better than the alternative."

"You bet it is," Mary Margaret grinned, squeezing his hand. "Thank you, Marshal, for saving my life. I don't think ..."

"Like Logan said ... I should be thanking you," Mac interrupted. "You handled that gun like a real pro. You saved all our lives. How about signing on as a deputy?"

Mary Margaret laughed.

"I've shot weapons all my life," she explained. "When I caught on to what you wanted, I noticed the .38 was double-action. All I had to do was grab it and pull the trigger."

"Ever shot a man before?" Mac asked.

"No, and I've had some sleepless nights about it. It's a terrible thing to realize you've killed somebody."

"Holston was a killer," Clay said. "He meant to kill you and would have killed anyone else who got in his way. Don't second-guess yourself. You did what had to be done. It took real courage to do it. You did all of us a favor."

Mac squeezed Mary Margaret's hand.

"I'm a big fan of yours," he said. "I've read just about all your books. It's a real pleasure to see you in person."

"You must be a real Civil War buff," she smiled.

Clay nodded.

"You'll never guess how much I've enjoyed your work," he said. "I've got to tell you …"

A nurse pushed open the door and checked one of the Marshal's IVs.

"I need to do some work here, Marshal. Sorry, ma'am, but he needs to rest now."

Mac was tired, but he wished Mary Margaret would stay.

"I'll be back, Marshal," she said.

"Good," he whispered. "Let's talk about … Civil War … and …"

He closed his eyes and drifted off as the sedative began taking effect.

Mary Margaret withdrew her hand, smiled and left.

The campus at East Tennessee State still was all abuzz when Mary Margaret, after having been debriefed by the state police and Marshals service, arrived in Johnson City. Media reps – national as well as regional – were on hand to do follow-up stories and everyone wanted to see and hear the local heroine who had shot her way out of a kidnapping and certain death. Teaching, research and a return to normalcy was impossible and, after a final news conference, the administration gave her a temporary leave of absence. It had been a hectic week.

Packing some essentials in a new car provided enthusiastically by a local dealer, she headed northwest. She was unsure of her destination; it was just good to get away by her lonesome. As she entered Virginia, some instinct led her back toward Cumberland Gap. Once there, Middlesboro wasn't that far away.

Mary Margaret accepted the fact that she was drawn to the historic Bell County city not by geography, but by the man she again wanted to see. She made her way to the hospital and was told at the desk that Henry Clay McDowell was well on his way to recovery.

"Go visit him," a nurse said. "He's a lot better and he'll be glad for some company."

Tucking a manuscript under her arm, Mary Margaret tapped on the door, then peered inside. Clay was sitting up sipping a soft drink.

"Hi, Marshal. Could you offer a girl a seat?"

Clay was startled, realizing where he'd heard that before. The final train ride with Pauline was a highlight of The Dream. He smiled and waved Mary Margaret to his bedside. She gripped his right hand, leaned forward and kissed him on the forehead.

"How's my favorite lawman?" she grinned.

"Great!" Mac replied, "Now that you're here."

"You passed out on me last time," she said. "Think you can stay awake for a few minutes?"

They exchanged pleasantries and soon fell into conversation about their ordeal with Tyrell Holston. Mary Margaret then lay her manuscript on the bed.

"I wanted to show you what I was working on before your friend Holston kidnapped me."

Clay smiled in surprise.

"Is that the book about the Lincoln plot and Mary Surratt?"

"You know about it!" Mary Margaret exclaimed.

"I told you I was a fan," Mac replied. "Fill me in; when will it be published?"

"I'm still in rewrite," she explained. "My publisher is pushing to have it ready in another month and I hope I can make it. I hate deadlines, but sometimes I work better under pressure."

"I saw a television interview where you suggested that Mary Surratt was innocent," Clay said.

"Well, I believe she was innocent as far as the assassination plot was concerned. But, there is evidence she supported the kidnapping plan."

"I agree," Clay noted, "but I can't believe that woman would support assassination of anyone. She had beautiful and unusual gray eyes and a soul that radiated nothing but compassion and goodwill."

Mary Margaret sat upright in surprise.

"How do you know that? You talk like you knew her!"

"Well, uh … I feel like I do," Mac fumbled. "I've done some research on her. I was warned not to be taken in by first impressions. But, maybe I was."

Mary Margaret frowned.

"First impressions? What else do you know about her?"

"Well, I think President Johnson used her as a scapegoat. God bless Gen. Hancock. He did everything he could to save her. He stood there in that broiling sun at Old Arsenal soaked in perspiration and ordered the army to clear the road to the White House. He really believed that Johnson would send someone with a reprieve. I've never seen a man with a sadder expression than the General when he finally told Capt. Rath that Mrs. Surratt couldn't be saved."

"Wow! Maybe I should have done my research with you! You sound like someone who actually witnessed the execution!"

"Well, I did … I mean … I've studied it a lot … I feel like I was there."

"Really, Marshal?"

They stared at one another in silence. She was unsure she had heard him correctly. Maybe the medication was affecting him.

"Mary Margaret, I feel like I really know you," Mac said. "You'll probably think I'm crazy – and maybe I am – but I want to tell you something that's beyond comprehension. Are you willing to listen with an open mind?"

The startled author blinked.

"Well, yes … I guess I could."

"Please, just listen to what I'm going to tell you."

Mac told her about his dream, sparing no detail. He explained about the Marshals service, the kidnapping of Mary

Todd Lincoln, his involvement in opposing the spy ring, the assassination of the President, the execution of Mary Surratt and how he and Pauline Cushman had fallen in love.

He finished the story, paused and looked steadily into the eyes of his visitor.

"I know you, Mary Margaret, because I knew you when," Clay said softly. "You were or are Pauline Cushman. You have her personality, her smile and her beauty.

"You said once that I wouldn't admit that I loved you. But, after all these years, I'm saying it now."

The silence was deafening, embarrassing and uncomfortable. Her mind was reeling after what she had heard.

"You've had a terrible ordeal, Marshal. I don't know if you realize what you're saying. You're telling me you were alive during the Civil War, and so was I. And we knew each other. That's not possible."

Clay looked down and slowly shook his head.

"Why would you say that?"

"Well, how could it be?"

"I can't answer that. But, I know it's true."

"Don't do this, Marshal," she finally cautioned. "The medication is making you irrational. Sometimes I've felt as though I was there during the war, but that comes from being too close to the story and the history."

Mary Margaret was stunned. Other thoughts and recollections were troubling her, things she couldn't share with anyone. She finally stood on wobbly legs, retrieved her manuscript and swallowed with difficulty several times.

"I have to go," she said. "You're not over the shock of being wounded. You need some rest. I have to go. Sorry, but I have to go … now."

Her voice quivered and her expression was a mixture of fear and disbelief. She was pale and on the verge of losing control.

"Why are you reacting this way?" Clay asked. "Please, you have to believe me!"

Mary Margaret stumbled toward the door and, upon reaching it, turned and stared at McDowell.

"Good luck, Marshal," she whispered, "I have to go."
She walked away.

* * *

Several months had passed and Clay was back at the office
part-time. He was limited to office work until his healing was
complete and, at this point, he was bored to death. He and the
office secretary had updated the files, completed all reports and
paperwork and had even worked some on next year's budget.

He again picked up the morning newspaper and did another
scan. Turning to the business page, he began to re-read some of
the news, including a piece about a publishing house merger and
expansion. He skipped over most of it until seeing an item he
had missed. It was buried in the middle of the story mentioning
some of the firm's prominent authors. Mary Margaret
Thatcher's name jumped out at him. It also noted she was
completing her newest Civil War book.

He hadn't heard from Mary Margaret since her last visit at
the hospital. That session went so badly that Mac doubted he'd
ever hear from her again.

After returning from lunch, Clay was briefed by Logan on
some upcoming investigations. All were routine and mostly
concerned old and continuing cases. They were interrupted by
the intercom.

"What's up, Marlene?" Mac answered.

The office manager chuckled before responding.

"Ordinarily, I wouldn't put through a call like this, but this
woman is persistent.

"She's called for you several times, but refuses to provide a
name or a subject. Just says that you'll know her and what it's
about. Should I tell her you're not available?"

"Put her through," Mac said, welcoming a break from his
routine. He answered, and after a long pause, the other party
spoke.

"Marshal," she said quietly, "this is Mary Margaret
Thatcher. You may not want to talk with me after our last

encounter, but I really would like to meet with you. I'm at the Campbell House. Can you see me?"

Startled, Clay could only ask, "When?"

"Now."

"This sounds urgent."

"No, but it is important."

Mac looked at his watch.

"I could be there in about thirty minutes."

"I'll meet you in the lobby."

With that, she broke the connection.

Clay sat on the edge of the desk and exhaled. A myriad of questions raced through his mind.

"Well!" he said aloud. "Surprise, surprise!"

* * *

Mary Margaret stood to greet him as Mac entered the lobby. She was beautifully dressed, but the dark circles beneath her eyes indicated a lack of sleep. She managed a weak smile and suggested they adjourn to the coffee shop. They were served and she quickly downed a substantial mouthful of the strong black liquid.

"Sorry," she apologized. "That wasn't very ladylike, but I really needed that."

Clay managed a thin smile, but said nothing.

"I've been in New York the past few days conferring with my agent and publisher about the Surratt book," she explained. "I've thought a lot about our last meeting and decided to fly to Lexington to see you. Last time, you talked and I listened. This time, I want you to listen. I've got a lot to say.

"I'm forty years old, was born in Metairie, Louisiana, was graduated summa cum laude as a history major at Tulane and have a master's degree and doctorate from Louisiana State. I was married at twenty-five, but my husband died a year later after suffering a heart attack on the tennis court. I've taught history on the high school and college level and have a reputation as a Civil War scholar. Two years ago,

East Tennessee State offered me the directorship of its Center for Civil War Study and a full professorship in its department of history. I've written six books about the Civil War, three of them bestsellers, and have, as you know, another coming out this fall about the trial and execution of Mary Surratt.

"My family still resides in Louisiana and my brother and his family live in a house I own in Baton Rouge. I also own and live in a townhouse in Johnson City. I travel, lecture, do research and publish extensively in addition to carrying my teaching load.

"My father was a high school social studies teacher and a Civil War re-enactor in the Confederate cavalry. My brother and I attended events with him and learned to ride and shoot and became particularly efficient in loading and firing black powder weapons.

"We had relatives who fought for the North and the South and we honor them all and their willingness to stand up for what they believed.

"As a young girl, I would occasionally have dreams about the Civil War and, more than once, was aware of being in the midst of military men preparing for battle. Other times I was standing at a station waiting for a train or viewing lavishly dressed ladies and gentlemen in a theater audience. As time passed, I realized I was seeing the audience from a stage. In other words, I was a performer, an actress.

"As time passed and the dream kept reoccurring, I reasoned that I had an overactive subconscious. My great-great aunt had been an actress during the Civil War and, in my dreams, I was role-playing – I had taken her persona. She was my heroine. She was bold, beautiful, imaginative and unafraid. I even had a dream that she was a spy and had escaped death through her skill and cunning."

Clay leaned forward and started to speak, but Mary Margaret raised her hand and stopped him.

"At one point, I dreamed she fell in love and was determined to marry a courageous champion of justice. That man was a law enforcer, a national policeman."

This time, Clay did interrupt.

"By any chance, was that woman Pauline Cushman?"

"She was. So, now you see why I was so shocked by the story of your dream. It was uncanny how it matched mine about Pauline. But, it had to be an incredible coincidence. If not, is it possible that two people really could be aware of and share something they experienced in a past life? I couldn't accept that. I don't belief in reincarnation or a previous existence.

"Long ago, I concluded that my dream was based on what I knew about my aunt. Her story was full of color, glory and passion and, subconsciously, I drew on that to form a dream, a fantasy.

"I like to think I'm a realist, someone who's pragmatic and who deals with fact, not fantasy. But, after the account of your dream, several things disturbed me. First, I was aware – from my dream – of how much Pauline loved this man. I felt this love myself when – in a dream – I assumed her identity. Then, after you sacrificed yourself to rescue me and I thought you were dying, I was overwhelmed by this same emotion. I was desperate to stop the bleeding because I couldn't bear the thought of losing you again. How could that be? How could I love a man that I didn't even know? And why did I remember something about a train wreck, an event that separated us forever."

"So, do you still believe our dreams are just a coincidence?" Mac questioned. "We didn't know one another in a prior life?"

"Let me finish, Marshal," Mary Margaret continued. "Your story uncovered something I couldn't explain. It was about a gift, a gift Pauline received before she died. When you spoke of it, I was dumbfounded. It made chills run up my spine. When I left the hospital, I drove directly to Baton Rouge. I went through articles and family archives stored at my house. And, in the attic, I found this."

She placed a box on the table.

"Please open it, Marshal," she said.

Clay glanced uncertainly at Mary Margaret, then carefully removed the lid. He lifted an object wrapped in a flannel cloth and hesitated.

"Please, go ahead," she requested.

The ancient music box, although faded in color, was in good condition, except for a large dent on the top. He rubbed a finger over it … the scar from a minie ball.

Mac glanced at Mary Margaret, who smiled and pointed to a key inserted in the front.

"Wind it, then lift the cover," she instructed. "I paid a lot of money to have this restored."

The strains of "Aura Lea" wafted over them.

Too stunned to speak, Clay stared at the music box. He touched it with both hands, maintaining contact with it – and her – until the music stopped.

"That was her favorite song," he said quietly.

"I know," Mary Margaret replied. "It's mine, too."

"I gave this to her the last time I saw her."

"It was on the train," she smiled. "I remember."

"You do?"

"Marshal, I can't explain any of this and I'm guessing you can't either. I loved my husband and I'm sure you loved your wife. And, we'll probably always miss them. But, for me, I've felt that something was missing in my life. I couldn't put my finger on it, I didn't know what it was. Until I met you.

"Let's just take things slowly – a day at a time. There was an accident that pulled us apart, but that's in the past."

She leaned forward and pulled Mac's hands to her breast.

"But now, you've come back to me," she whispered.

Mac's kiss confirmed it.

Epilogue

Although this book is historical fiction, much of it is based on what actually happened in Central Kentucky during the Civil War conflict of brother against brother, which certainly was the situation in the Commonwealth. The state was very much divided as to its sympathies for the Union and the Confederacy.

Many of the characters in this story were real participants in the Civil War.

Cassius Clay, a friend of Abraham Lincoln who aided his election to the presidency, was a staunch supporter of the Union, but one who was steadfastly against slavery. He was a realist about war and the rights of all Americans, but not an individual you wanted as an enemy.

The victory at the Battle of Richmond – Kentucky that is – was a major Southern achievement of the 1862 Confederate invasion of the Commonwealth. Confederate Col. John Scott, a Louisiana cavalry commander and a key figure in that battle, was one who very much believed in the cause of the South. He also was someone who both men and women truly liked, and, in all probability, he had the charm and charisma that made many women fall in love with him.

Mary Todd Lincoln is an individual who may have been abused by American history. She evidently was considered a "real catch" by Kentucky admirers, who were smitten by her young beauty and membership in a prominent and aristocratic Lexington family. Cassius Clay was among her suitors and might have become her future husband had it not been for the gangly rail splitter from Hodgenville. Mary, however, was truly devoted to Abraham Lincoln, a Kentuckian who was doomed to die as he sought to keep the Union intact.

Pauline Cushman was an attractive actress and Union spy who fared much better in her fictional role than she did in real life. Pauline actually was married three times and had two children. The New Orleans-born thespian died in poverty at age

60 in a San Francisco boarding house following an intentional opium overdose.

The Booth family of actors were major players in the nineteenth-century theatre. Edwin Booth was well known, but his prominence was surpassed by his younger brother, Wilkes, who was an outstanding performer, but best known for his assassination of President Lincoln.

Antonia Ford, a member of a well-to-do Virginia family, was a highly successful Confederate spy who probably would have died in prison had it not been for the man who arrested her. Union Major Joseph Willard of Willard Hotel fame really did fall in love with Miss Ford, fought successfully for her parole, and married her.

Ward Hill Lamon, who headed the U.S. Marshals Service in Washington City, was a devoted friend of President Lincoln and one who assigned himself as the President's personal bodyguard. However, his association with Clay McDowell and the other fictional marshals from Virginia and Maryland was just that – fiction. And, as for Marshal McDowell, he was drawn from several characters who were Federal lawmen for the Eastern District of Kentucky.

The convicted conspirators and others mentioned in the assassination plot were, of course, real people. And, as for Mary Surratt, many consider the jury still out as to her guilt or innocence.

A number of minor characters also were actual persons, such as the Breck family in Richmond, Kentucky. Gen. William "Bull" Nelson was the ill-fated Union commander in the Battle of Richmond and Brig. Gen. Mahlon Manson was the Federal leader who tried to defend Madison County in spite of Nelson and his absence.

Major Gen. E. Kirby Smith, commander of the Confederate Army of Kentucky, and Brigadier Gen. Patrick Cleburne were key figures in the overwhelming Southern victory at Richmond. And, U.S. District Attorney Thomas Bramlette went on to become governor of Kentucky.

Union Col. James Garfield, winner of the Battle of Middle Creek, became America's twentieth president, and, unfortunately, became the second commander-in-chief to be assassinated. He defeated the Confederate army commanded by Gen. Humphrey Marshall, a native of Frankfort, who served four terms as a Kentucky Congressman and was Minister to China.

John Ford owned several theatres during the war and was a well-known friend of the Booth family. And, of course, Capt. Robert Lincoln was the son of the President and one of the Union officers who was present at the surrender at Appomattox Court House.

The story of Wilmer McLean and his family is one of the war's genuine ironies. His home in Manassas really was victim to the Civil War's first major land battle. And, his home at Appomattox Court House essentially was the site where it ended with Lee's surrender to Grant.

The actual members of President Lincoln's cabinet are mentioned, as are officials associated with the assassination trial. Union Lt. Edward Doherty really was the officer who tracked down John Wilkes Booth and his account of the capture is taken from the official report he submitted to Lt. Col. J.H. Taylor, chief of staff for the Department of Washington.

Kentucky's involvement with the plot against President Lincoln is fiction. However, other plot details, such as the printing of counterfeit money, are based on fact. And, the described locations and other Civil War events in Kentucky are real and really happened.

Time has erased many memories and sites. But not all.

The ferry at Valley View, founded in 1785, is still there and remains in operation as the oldest continuous business in Kentucky. Today, the ferry transports, on average, 250 cars a day as a free service from the Kentucky Transportation Cabinet.

About the author

An award-winning corporate editor and public relations specialist with Ford Motor and The Goodyear Tire & Rubber Companies, Ed Ford has edited newsletters, newspapers and magazines in addition to producing brochures, booklets and other promotion pieces for public relations campaigns and fund-raising programs.

He is the author of *The Draw*, a historical fiction book based on the Civil War Battle of Richmond, Ky., and *Silent Witness*, a booklet and play about the Surrender at Appomattox.

He has media experience as a reporter and editor with weekly and daily newspapers and has written and produced

– George Terrizzi photo

radio and television advertising and scripted and produced film and video promos and documentaries.

An early member of the Battle of Richmond Association, the Berea, Ky., native has served as president and a director of that Civil War organization. He also is a member of the Kentucky Civil War Sites Association, the Richmond Chamber of Commerce, the Society of Professional Journalists and is editor of *The Kentucky Civil War Bugle*, an online publication.

The University of Kentucky journalism graduate operates his own public relations firm in Richmond, Ky., and has served as public relations director for Berea College and as a staff writer for *The Lane Report* business magazine.